T0269774

PERILOUS WATERS

PERILOUS WATERS

Terry Shames

SEVERN HOUSE

First world edition published in Great Britain and the USA in 2024
by Severn House, an imprint of Canongate Books Ltd,
14 High Street, Edinburgh EH1 1TE.

severnhouse.com

British Library Cataloguing-in-Publication Data
A CIP catalogue record for this title is available from the British Library.

ISBN-13: 978-1-4483-1180-4 (cased)
ISBN-13: 978-1-4483-1181-1 (e-book)

All Severn House titles are printed on acid-free paper.

Typeset by Palimpsest Book Production Ltd.,
Falkirk, Stirlingshire, Scotland.
Printed and bound in Great Britain by TJ Books,
Padstow, Cornwall.

Praise for Terry Shames

"Razor-sharp, propulsive, and filled with heart-thumping action"
John Lansing, author of the Jack Bertolino series

"An irresistible, full-throttle thriller"
Reece Hirsch, author of *Dark Tomorrow*

"May be the best regional crime series around today"
Library Journal Starred Review of *Guilt Strikes at Granger's Store*

"Readers . . . will expect, and get, shocking revelations"
Booklist on *Guilt Strikes at Granger's Store*

"Should win Shames new fans"
Publishers Weekly on *Murder at the Jubilee Rally*

"A neat character-intensive combo of clever police work and family angst"
Kirkus Reviews on *Murder at the Jubilee Rally*

"A surprise ending makes this entry one of Shames' best"
Kirkus Reviews on *A Risky Undertaking for Loretta Singletary*

"A careening powerboat of a thrill ride! Jessie Madison is adventurous, capable and a bit reckless. A compelling heroine you can't help but root for"
Matt Coyle, bestselling author of the *Rick Cahill crime series*

About the author

An avid sailor for many years, **Terry Shames** has had adventures sailing on the US east and west coast, Mexico, the Bahamas, the Caribbean and the Mediterranean. She is a member of Sisters in Crime, the Mystery Writers of America, and the Texas Institute of Letters. Originally from Texas, she now lives in Marina del Rey, California.

www.terryshames.com

To my dear friend Susan Shea, partner in crime.

ONE

As my 'goodbye to the Bahamas,' the weekend excursion to the opening of Trophy Cay Resort promised to be a winner. The brochure gushed about the luxurious rooms, the sumptuous meals, and the island-style entertainment. Having worked in the Bahamas as a dive instructor for three months, I knew to take the photos and the promises with a grain of salt. But it hardly mattered, because the weekend was free, courtesy of my roommate, Shelley. Or rather, a gift from a regular at the bar where she worked as a cocktail waitress.

The trip to Trophy Cay on the high-speed ferry from Nassau took four hours, so it was dusk when the island came into sight.

I had almost missed the ferry because of an incident with an inexperienced diver who had panicked with a balky regulator. I'd had to stay late to fill out an incident report. My boss, Jeremy, knew I was trying to catch the ferry, though, and had speeded up the process to help me. I felt guilty that he was being so kind. He didn't know that as soon as I got back from the weekend, I was quitting. It was time for me to get home to Virginia to pick up the pieces of my shattered life. Surely, by now it was safe to go back.

'Jessie, look! It's gorgeous!' At my elbow, Shelley was practically bouncing up and down with excitement.

I murmured my agreement. Palm trees lined the pristine beach that glittered in the last rays of the late-afternoon sun. The ferry's wealthy patrons chattered their approval as they pushed their way to the boat's off-ramp. Once we were on the dock, we were directed toward the hotel, a magnificent white wooden island-architecture structure with lanais and patios, adjacent to a huge, inviting swimming pool.

We were met by white-jacketed men and sarong-wrapped women, bearing trays of mai tais and pina coladas.

'Let's get this party started!' Shelley exclaimed as she grabbed a mai tai.

Upstairs, in our elegant, airy room, we changed into bathing suits and headed down to the pool, where guests were already settling into chaises and sipping drinks. We spotted a fake grass hut bar at the far end of the pool and I went for drinks while Shelley grabbed chairs.

We had come to party, but it didn't take long for reality to set in. Most everyone here was in couples – older couples. Shelley was disappointed by the lack of eligible men. I was OK either way. I just wanted to relax and contemplate my future. Meeting an interesting man would have complicated my situation. We swam, drank rum, and relaxed until midnight.

Maybe because I knew I was nearing the end of my enforced vacation, I didn't sleep well. For three months, I'd firmly banished memories of my humiliation back in the States out of my mind. Now, the thoughts crowded in, and I'd fall asleep only to jerk awake several times a night dreaming disturbing images: finding Diego Boland's body surrounded by my sister's bloody footprints, or my trainer, John Farrell, scolding me for my bad choices.

The next morning, we slept late and then had brunch poolside. We had just ordered when my gaze feel on two men walking onto the patio. I jumped up. 'Johnny!' I called out and waved. He waved back and said something to the man he was with before they headed over to us.

Jean Durand was a boat captain I'd flirted with at a party a few weeks back. Around thirty, he was lanky and tanned, with longish, sandy-colored hair that flopped endearingly over his forehead. He was dressed in baggy cargo pants and a scruffy white T-shirt, looking as if he'd just gotten off the boat.

As the two men neared, I realized his friend was a man I'd seen on the boat yesterday afternoon.

'What are you doing here?' Johnny said, kissing me on both cheeks.

'You mean, how can I afford this? My rich roommate got us tickets.' I poked Shelley. 'Shelley, meet Johnny Durand. He's French and his real name is Jean, but he likes to be called Johnny.' I remembered being surprised to find out he was French. He had no accent.

Shelley giggled, but if Shelley was anything, she was honest. 'I'm not really rich,' she said. 'Somebody I know gave me the tickets.'

Johnny winked at me. 'However you got here, I'm glad to see you. This is Nick Garnier.' His friend stepped forward, nodding to us. Shorter than Johnny, he was more muscular, and his movements reminded me of a panther: a supple body, ready to spring. His eyes were dark pools, and his black hair close-cropped. A sexy shadow of beard didn't completely hide a light scar along his left jawline. Wearing khaki pants and a black T-shirt, he was overdressed and looked out of place. I noticed that he seemed restless, even hyperalert. His eyes flicked around us as if he was on the lookout for something.

'I didn't see you on the ferry,' I said to Johnny.

'I sailed here. I told you I was a boat captain.'

I remembered that he said it was a gem of a job, with wealthy owners who weren't around often. 'Nice that you could be here.'

'I'm on my way back to Nassau and decided to stop in and see what the party was like.' He looked down at his rumpled clothing. 'I should probably go get changed before they chase me out of here.'

Shelley said, 'I'm so glad you guys came. Everybody here is, like, old.'

'You don't like old people?' Johnny teased.

Shelley fluffed her hair. 'I was hoping to find a rich playboy here, preferably young.'

'Don't look at us,' Johnny said. 'I'm just the hired help. And Nick is . . .' He shrugged as Nick frowned at him.

'Go get your bathing suits,' Shelley said, 'and let's go for a swim.'

We nabbed two more chaises on the poolside deck while the guys went to change. Johnny was staying on his boat, but Nick said he had a room at the resort. I wondered what kind of business he was in to afford this blowout. Johnny had said the decision to stop here had been last-minute. So how had he and Nick arranged to meet? Or had it been some kind of weird coincidence?

The four of us spent the rest of the day swimming, walking on the beach, and lying on the chaises, dozing. Or at least three of us dozed. Nick Garnier sat upright, reading something on his phone or staring off into space. At some point, Shelley and Johnny went for a swim, so Nick and I were alone. My never-ending curiosity got the best of me. 'You don't seem very relaxed. Why are you here?'

Nick looked surprised. 'Sorry, I've got a lot on my mind.' He had a slight accent that I hadn't noticed before. He hadn't answered my question.

'How do you know Johnny?' I asked.

'Jean and I are old friends. I've known him for a while. What about you and Shelley? You two don't seem much alike.' It was such an obvious question to divert me that I almost laughed.

I explained that when I came down to Nassau, Shelley happened to be advertising for a roommate. 'You're right, we aren't alike. She's barely out of her teens and I'm twenty-three, plus she's really happy-go-lucky, and me, not so much. But we get along well. I'll miss her when I go back.'

Nick swung his legs over the side so he could sit facing me. I was aware of his muscular, hairy legs that hadn't seen the sun in a while. 'Are you going back soon?' he asked.

I shrugged. 'Probably.'

'Don't you like it here?' I was aware of his intense gaze and wondered if he ever really relaxed.

'I do. It's beautiful.'

'What kind of work do you do?'

'I'm a dive instructor.' At least until I could get back and re-channel myself from the career I'd wrecked. From FBI trainee to what? Who knew?

He glanced at my body. 'Yeah, that fits.'

Before I could turn the conversation back to questioning him, Shelley and Johnny showed up to tell us that waiters were setting up a lavish buffet and that a steel band was soon going to start playing out on the beach. 'I'm starving,' Shelley said.

No one else seemed to be dressed for dinner, so we rinsed off at the outdoor shower and got in line for food. I was famished, not having had time for lunch. We were almost at the food table when a portly man, who introduced himself as Alan Christy, the resort manager, announced that there would be a limbo contest at nine o'clock.

Eyes sparkling, Shelley said to me, 'Are you going to do it?'

'When have you ever known me to turn down a limbo contest?' I asked, laughing.

Johnny put his arm around my shoulders, casually. 'This I've got to see,' he said.

The four of us went to sign me up. There were five other contestants – only one other woman, and I heard her say she was doing it on a dare. One man, a muscular island guy, looked like a real threat.

'Should we bet on you?' Johnny said before I went to join the emcee.

'Yes!' Shelley said. 'She'll kick butt.' Her eyes were shining. She gave me a hug for luck. I noticed Nick rolling his eyes. He might be surprised.

TWO

S weaty and thirsty after the limbo contest, I swigged a bottle of water and looked around for Shelley and the two guys. It was fully dark, and fairy lights had come on all over the patio. It looked magical.

I found Johnny and Nick in the billiard room, deep in conversation. Their heads jerked in my direction, and Nick frowned.

'Hi, guys,' I said. Something in the atmosphere made me feel awkward. 'I was wondering where you were. This could be fun.' I nodded to the table. 'Let's play some pool later.' My eyes fell on a backpack lying open on the table. Next to it was a package wrapped in brown paper.

'Sounds good,' Nick said, but his voice was clipped, as if he was impatient.

'Yeah, let's play.' Johnny's voice had an edge to it.

'I think I interrupted something,' I said.

'Not a problem,' Johnny said, glancing at Nick. 'By the way, you were awesome. Where did you learn to limbo?'

I shrugged. 'It not something you learn, really. Just takes practice.' I couldn't help shooting a triumphant look at Nick, but he wasn't looking my way. 'I'll go look for Shelley,' I said. 'You guys can find us when you're ready.'

As I closed the door, I heard Johnny say, 'Are we OK?'

Back on the patio, Shelley came rushing up, a drink in her hand. 'Jessie, oh my God! You won! That was so amazing! I kept telling people I know you!'

I brandished my prize, a bottle of champagne. 'Champagne breakfast tomorrow morning!'

'I don't know where the guys are,' she said, looking around, and then her face brightened. 'Here they are.'

I turned to see Johnny grinning at me. Nick still looked strained, but he forced a smile.

'Where did you learn to do that?' Johnny asked.

'Long story.' I wiped my brow with the back of my hand.

Nick glanced between Johnny and me with a frown. I wondered what his problem was. Was it because I had barged in on them in the billiard room? Were they engaged in some criminal activity? Whatever, I figured it wasn't personal. He caught me staring, and his expression slipped into neutral.

'We're going to the pool,' Shelley said. 'Want to come?'

'Sure,' Nick said. He was being polite.

Johnny ran his fingers lightly up and down my back. He slipped his hand around my waist and whispered. 'Let's go down to the beach.'

I hesitated. Did I want to leave Shelley with Nick? Something about him didn't sit well with me. He was too tense for a casual vacation.

Johnny pre-empted my caution by saying to Nick, 'You guys don't mind if we skip out for a while, do you?'

Shelley grinned at me and raised her eyebrows suggestively. Too bad she wasn't the one with Johnny. I thought they would like each other. But three months in the islands had taught me to be more spontaneous. I snuggled in and put my arm around Johnny.

'Don't forget we need to finish our talk,' Nick said to Johnny. He was scowling.

'We've got all day tomorrow,' Johnny said. 'We'll catch up with you later.'

We left the bottle of champagne at the front desk and headed out to the sand. The air caressed my skin, typical of an evening in the islands. Close to the water, we watched tiny waves lap at the shore, phosphorous in the waves sparkling.

Johnny turned to face me, drew me close, and kissed me. In spite of my reservations, my body responded, and I shivered.

'Let's go to my boat,' he said. 'I'd like you to see it.'

'Is this where you show me your etchings?' I said.

He grinned. 'Something like that. We can stay here if you'd rather.'

Oh, what the hell! Johnny was appealing in a roguish way – someone I could have some fun with as a last fling before I left the islands. 'Let's go,' I said.

We walked to the marina, several hundred yards away. The dock was well lighted. There were slips for a lot more boats than the handful that were occupied. But the ones docked here were impressive – big yachts that were probably worth millions.

Several people were strolling on the dock admiring the boats. Johnny led me to his catamaran, called *Island Ice*. It was a boxy, squared-off style, not particularly attractive, but it looked like it was big enough to live on comfortably.

'This is the boat you brought here?' I asked. 'It's huge. How big is it?'

'Forty-five feet stem to stern, twenty-five across the beam. There are bigger cats, but this one is really comfortable.'

'How many bedrooms?'

'Ahem. You mean, staterooms.' He used a la-di-dah voice. 'Three. One big one on the starboard side and two smaller ones on the port side. Each with its own head.'

'Wow. A floating condo.'

We stepped off the dock onto the deck of the boat and then three steps down into the rear cockpit. There was a big table surrounded by cushioned seating.

'Did you sail here with the owners?' I asked.

'No. I'm taking the boat to Nassau. I'll meet them there.'

'Where did you come from?' I sat down on the cushioned banquette.

'Chicken Town.'

I laughed. Chicken Town was the nickname for Georgetown. The story was that a lot of people thought they would sail from the Bahamas, south to the Caribbean. Georgetown was the last substantial port of call on the way. The problem was you got to Georgetown by sailing onto the Atlantic side, a lot rougher sailing than the gentle Bahamian bank, which was usually like sailing on a big lake. By the time they got to Georgetown, many pleasure sailors were frazzled by the turbulent water, and they chickened out. Thus, Chicken Town. Whether the story was true or not, it entertained tourists.

'You sailed it here by yourself?'

Johnny plopped down beside me, his legs sprawled out in front of him. 'No big deal. This cat handles really well. The owners were supposed to make the trip with me, but at the last minute they had to fly to New York.'

I vaguely remembered the owners from the party where I'd met Johnny. He had pointed them out to me – a couple in their fifties. The man was tall and thin; the woman short, busty and with a loud mouth. 'Still, it's a long haul. What were you doing in Georgetown?' I knew I was being nosy, but the trip sounded suspicious to me. A lot of drugs came into the islands from Georgetown, and I wondered if Johnny was involved with that. Even the owners could be.

He grinned at me and reached out to run his fingers along my cheek. 'I was there because the owners told me to go there. Do you always ask so many questions?'

I laughed. 'I'm naturally curious.' And naturally wary. I'd heard too many stories of drug deals in the Bahamas.

'When I see the Turpins, I'll tell them you had your suspicions.'

'Are you getting along better with them? You told me they were hard to take.'

'He's OK. She's a little obnoxious, but they pay well and they spend most of their time in New York.'

I started to say more, but he put his hand up. 'No more questions about them. I try to forget them when they aren't around.' He leaned over and gave me a long, lingering kiss. Still keyed up from the limbo contest, my earlier reluctance gave way. I leaned back against the banquette. He cupped my breast and kissed me again, deeper.

'Come on. Let's go below,' he whispered. He stood up and put out his hand, and I took it and stood up.

He pushed me against the sliding doors to the salon and pulled me to him, kissing me harder. When he reached behind and undid my halter top and his hands cupped my breasts, I gasped, instantly aroused. I ran my hands along his smooth chest and down to the top of his shorts. I was fumbling with the button when some people walked by, talking, sounding as if they were only steps away.

Suddenly, he stopped and pulled away. 'Shit!'

'What?'

'God, I can't believe this. I left my backpack in the lobby.'

'Text your friend Nick and ask him to get it for you.' I didn't want to stop.

'No. Can't do that.' His voice was sharp. 'I'll be right back.' He bounded up the steps, jumped off onto the dock and sprinted away.

Startled by his abruptness, I hooked my top and stepped onto the dock and watched him until he was out of sight. When I turned to step back onto the boat, I noticed a large man standing at the end of the dock, gazing in Johnny's direction. He was wearing shorts and a dark T-shirt that strained over his muscular torso. When Johnny was out of sight, the man lit a cigarette and then climbed back into a cabin cruiser.

I got back aboard the catamaran and tried the sliding glass door to see if it was unlocked. It slid open easily and I stepped into a large open saloon. I didn't know how to turn on the lights, but in the glow of lighting from the dock, I could see the interior well enough.

To the right, there was a galley almost as big as the kitchen in my apartment, with a double sink, teak cabinets and a four-burner stove.

In front of me was a large teak dining table with banquette seating on two sides and a padded bench on the side nearest me.

The furnishings inside the boat made up for its plain exterior. There were Oriental rugs on the floor, and the padded seating was covered with rich, blue suede. I picked up one of the throw pillows and rubbed it along my cheek. Pure luxury. I was used to dive boats. They were the opposite of luxurious.

I wandered over to the navigation station, forward of the galley. The nav lights were turned on, and in the dim, green glow, I saw a bank of radios and radar screens, and a bewildering array of toggle switches. I often had to drive dive boats, but they were simple crafts. I wouldn't begin to know what to do with all this equipment.

I ventured down the steps and stuck my head into the stateroom in the starboard pontoon. Aft, there was a huge bed, a desk, and storage areas on one end. You could lie in bed and look out the big, square portholes. The forward end had a luxurious shower – at least luxurious for a boat.

When I heard Johnny come back aboard, I trotted back up to the saloon. 'This is amazing!'

He had his backpack with him. 'I'll stow this in the cabin. Come down with me.'

I had lost the mood. 'I'd rather hang out up here for a while.'

'That's good. We can go up on the bridge. You'll like the view.' He stowed the backpack, then came back and grabbed a bottle of wine from the refrigerator along with a couple of glasses. We took the ladder up to the top.

'Wow, you can see everything from up here,' I said.

'The flying bridge is the best feature of the Lagoon 440,' he said. 'You can steer from up here and you have a total view of your surroundings. If the weather's bad, you can steer from inside, but it's nicer up here.'

We sat down on the padded cushion behind the wheel and sipped wine and gossiped about the party. He kissed me a few times, and I began to get into it.

'I have an idea,' Johnny said. 'Let's take the boat to one of the small cays close by.'

'I don't know, Johnny. It's dangerous to move the boat at night.' Also, if I accepted, it was a given that we'd have sex. I was no prude, but I was having second thoughts about jumping into bed with a guy I barely knew.

'It can be dangerous if you don't know the waters. But I know this area well. We'll only go to the next island over. It isn't far from here and has a nice, protected cove. I want to wake up with just the two of us tomorrow morning. We can swim and have breakfast . . .' His French accent was stronger when he was being persuasive.

I hesitated. It sounded nice, but I felt bad leaving Shelley alone. Sometimes, when she drank too much, she got anxious and needed a pal. Nick didn't seem like the type to be soothing. Still, I reminded myself that before long I'd be going back to the mainland to who-knew-what kind of life. Certainly not the joy of being on a boat in the islands. This weekend was meant to be my farewell to the Bahamas. I might as well do it right.

'OK, let's do it.'

We went back down to the main level. Johnny jumped onto the dock, unplugged the power cords and got the lines ready for quick release. Then he went back up to the bridge to turn on the engines.

When the boat moved away from the dock, I drew the last line off the dock cleat and hauled in the fenders before I joined Johnny back up on the bridge. He put his arm around me and steered the boat out into open water, due south.

Soon the lights from the resort faded. The sky was luminous with stars, and a half-moon lit a shining path on the water, but out of that path, the water was murky and mysterious. I knew the water wasn't as deep as it appeared to be. The average depth on the Bahamian Shelf was only twenty feet. Average. Which meant some of it was a lot shallower. That's why it was risky to move a boat in the dark in the Bahamas, because even though the depth could go deeper than twenty feet, some places were so shallow that you could easily run aground or damage your keel. But Johnny said he knew the area well, and anyone who could single-handedly bring this boat from Georgetown had to know what he was doing.

A half-hour later, we dropped anchor. In the waning light from the moon, I saw that ours was the only boat in the cove. Now that we were truly alone, I felt more relaxed. We drank another glass of wine.

'How do you know Nick?' I asked. 'He seems a little tense.'

'Oh, Nick's OK. I do some work with him.' He leaned in and kissed me, but his vague answer increased my curiosity.

'He's into boating?'

'Not exactly.'

What were they up to? Drugs, most likely, which was troubling. If he had drugs aboard, and for some reason, we got caught with them, the penalties were steep. I wondered if I should press him on the subject.

But he pulled me onto his lap and began undressing me.

At some point, I heard an engine noise off to one side. I looked over and saw that a boat had slipped into the lagoon. 'We've got company,' I said.

Johnny glanced over to the boat. 'A powerboat,' he said. He sounded annoyed.

'Is that a problem?'

He shrugged. 'I don't like powerboats. They're noisy, and a lot of the people around here who run them are party people. We could be in for rowdy neighbors. I was hoping we'd have this cove to ourselves.'

Johnny's worry that it was a party boat was ill-founded. The crew anchored the boat efficiently, and as soon as the anchor was set, they went inside and soon the lights went off.

'Let's go below,' Johnny said.

When we climbed onto the big bed, Johnny whispered that he was going to take his time. He began teasing me, kissing me lightly and running his fingers along my torso. I was getting more and more turned on, and I was glad I'd said yes to this adventure. We shed our clothes, and his caresses became more urgent. When he kissed my breasts, it was like an electric charge went through me. I whimpered and wrapped my legs around him. He grabbed my hair and pulled my head back and kissed my throat. I felt like I was on fire. His breathing was quick and raspy.

Suddenly, I thought I heard a shout and a bang. 'What was that?' I sat up, alert.

Johnny sat up with a groan. 'Damn it, I thought they'd gone to bed. Come here.' He tried to pull me back down, but the sound we'd heard bothered me.

'That sounded like a gunshot,' I said.

He grew still. 'A gunshot?' He turned onto his side. I could barely make out the glint of his eyes in the dim light. 'Jessie, how would you know what a gunshot sounds like?'

I kept quiet. I hadn't told him I'd been in the FBI training program and I didn't plan to. But I'd heard plenty of gunshots and that's what it had sounded like.

'Maybe somebody dropped something,' he said. He was running a finger down my breast. 'Or a door slammed. You know, sound carries in these coves.'

He was right – sound did carry, and working on dive boats, I'd heard plenty of random 'bangs' when someone dropped an air tank.

I lay back down.

'Now, where were we?'

I was still unsettled, but trying to relax, Johnny kissing and teasing me, when suddenly he stopped abruptly and put his hand over my mouth. I didn't like it and tried to jerk away, but he pressed harder and said, 'Shh!' in my ear.

I tensed as I felt a jerky movement of the boat and heard a scuffing sound. *It sounded like someone had come aboard.*

My gut clenched. Had I been right? Were there drugs on this boat and somehow the authorities had found out? Or maybe I was overreacting. Maybe it was petty thieves, taking advantage of the resort opening. A few remote islands in the Caribbean had reported problems with pirates, and boaters were warned to stay away from those islands. But this close to Government Island, pirates wouldn't risk trying to hijack a boat, would they? And then I thought of another possibility. It froze my blood.

'This could be trouble,' Johnny whispered. 'I'm sorry.'

'No, it might be my fault.' After many weeks of no sign that I was being pursued, I had let my guard down. I should have warned Johnny that there might be people after me.

THREE

When we had anchored, there had been a silvery half-moon low in the sky, but it was gone now and the cabin was so dark that I could barely make out Johnny's form. He slid away from me, and I heard him putting his shorts on. He leaned over me, his mouth at my ear. 'I have a gun in the nav station. I'll try to get to it.'

He crept toward the steps leading up to the saloon.

I groped around frantically and found my bathing suit on the floor and slipped it on. My brain was in high gear. If these were Diego Boland's friends from the mainland, how had they found me? What a ridiculous irony it would be if they had found me now, just as I was planning to go back.

I heard footsteps striding across the saloon – more than one person. Whoever they were, they clearly felt no need for stealth.

There was no clearance next to the bed for me to hide, so I crouched down in the shadows on the floor at the bottom of the bed. If Johnny didn't get to the gun, maybe I could surprise them. We had come down into the stateroom in the dark, so I didn't know if there was anything I could use as a weapon.

The silhouette of a burly man appeared at the top of the gangway leading down to the cabin, haloed by the dim backlight from the main deck. Johnny had hunkered down next to the steps. As the man started down them, Johnny lunged at him. The man raised his arm and I saw the glint of a weapon. He brought it down onto Johnny's head. Johnny grunted and slumped into the wall.

I stayed quiet, ready to spring if the man came close to me.

The cabin light flashed on. In its glare, I saw that Johnny's assailant was a beefy, hairy, bald-headed man in his mid-thirties, in jeans and a sleeveless T-shirt. He smelled strongly of sweat and something like motor oil. He was looking down at Johnny, his face twisted in a snarl. He turned his head and saw me, and his expression changed to alarm. I leaped to my feet and charged him, grabbing the hand that held the weapon, and twisting. He slammed my shoulder and threw me off my feet. I landed with my head banging against the wall. He lunged for me.

'Get away from me!' I shouted.

'Louis, bring her up here.' There was another, larger, man, standing in the doorway.

I didn't like being dressed in only a skimpy bathing suit in front of these men. 'I'm going to put some clothes on,' I said.

'Hurry up!' Louis said. He had what sounded like a French accent, but it was different from Johnny's – more guttural. French. Not Spanish. I'd been wrong. These were not Diego's friends.

I had left my shirt up on the bridge, but Johnny's was on the floor, and I slipped it on. I moved slowly, stalling, to give myself time to think. There had to be a way out of this. I was strong, and if Johnny could shake off the blow to his head, we might be able to fend off these men.

'Go!' Louis snarled and prodded me toward the steps.

The boat listed as a third person boarded. Despite the warmth of the air, I shivered. Maybe we could overpower two men. Three would be harder.

Johnny stirred, moaning. I went to his side and dropped to my knees, shaking him. 'Johnny, get up,' I whispered.

Louis seized me by the hair and pulled me to my feet. 'Leave him,' he growled.

'Oww!' I twisted around and punched him in the stomach. It was like punching a wall. He grabbed me by the arm and shoved me toward the steps. 'Cut it out!' I yelled.

'Upstairs,' he said. There was that odd accent again.

I stumbled up the steps, and the man standing at the top pushed me farther into the saloon. It was so dark that I couldn't see details, only shadows. I could make out the third man standing in the doorway between the saloon and the cockpit. He was of a slighter build than the other two, so not as big a threat.

'Look,' I said, keeping my voice strong. 'You're making a mistake. We don't own this boat and we don't have any money.'

The man in the doorway snickered.

'Shut up,' the other man said. He turned his attention to whatever was going on downstairs. 'Louis, bring Mr Durand upstairs.'

So they knew who Johnny was.

Johnny had mentioned a gun stashed in the navigation station desk. With the man looking away from me, I risked edging toward the desk. When I was poking around, I had noticed that instead of a slide-out drawer, it had a top that had to be raised to reveal its contents. Even in the dark, it would be hard to do that without being noticed. I didn't know how much I could draw on my FBI basic training to help me in this situation. More likely, instinct would serve me. Whatever, I'd have to be quick. I moved closer and slowly reached for the top. I almost had it, but the big man saw me and shoved me away. 'Get away from there.'

Downstairs in the stateroom, I heard the sound of a fist hitting flesh. Johnny grunted. Louis started talking to him, but his voice was so low I couldn't hear what he was saying.

Johnny said, 'I don't have it!'

Louis spoke to him again, louder now, in French. I had learned a fair amount of French in college, and if they spoke more clearly, maybe I could understand what was going on. But I caught only a word here and there. It must be some kind of dialect.

I had been peering down toward the stateroom and turned when I heard a clicking noise. The man standing in the doorway leading to the cockpit flipped a toggle switch next to the door, and suddenly the saloon lights came on. Unlike the other two, this man was thin to the point of emaciation, the muscles of his arms and legs slack. He had long, greasy hair and a crazy look in his eyes. When he saw me looking at him, he grinned. His teeth were stained brown, several missing. A meth addict? What was he doing with these other two?

Repulsed, I looked away, back to the big man. For a few seconds, I was puzzled. I thought I had seen him before. And then I remembered where. He was the man who had been watching Johnny on the docks when he went back to get his backpack. He was all muscle. Around forty, he had the deep tan of someone who spent a lot of time in the sun. His bushy dark hair was flecked with gray, and his bristling mustache barely hid fleshy lips. His arms were heavily tattooed, one arm with an elaborate sailing ship, the other with a wind and sea pattern. No way was I going to overpower him.

I backed away from him and into the galley area. I wished the third man would move away from the door. I envisioned darting onto the deck and diving over the side. He was so thin that I might even be able to knock him down.

Downstairs, there was the sound of another blow, and Johnny cried out.

'Johnny, what's going on?' I yelled. I lunged past the big man, heading for the steps, but he yanked me back.

'Ow!' I yelled, more for the satisfaction of yelling than from pain.

'Don't hurt her. She knows nothing,' Johnny called out from down below. His voice was weak.

'He's right,' I said. 'I just met him. I don't know a thing about what's going on.'

'Louis, get him up here,' the big man said, ignoring me.

Prodded from behind, Johnny staggered up the steps. The side of his head was matted with congealed blood.

Louis's expression was surly, as if he didn't like being ordered around, but when he glanced toward me, his eyes looked panicky. What was he afraid of? These men held all the cards. He pushed Johnny across the room and onto the banquette.

Dazed, his eyes unfocused, Johnny looked in my direction, before he let his head fall back against the back cushion. The bigger, tattooed man started questioning him, speaking loudly. I still didn't understand much of his French, but from his tone of authority, I surmised that he was the leader of this threesome.

While the men were zeroed in on Johnny, I surveyed the saloon for some way to gain the upper hand. Without a weapon, my options were limited. The FBI trainer had laughed when he discussed the possibility of women overpowering men. 'I don't care what the movies show, or how much martial arts training you have, you're at a disadvantage with a strong man. You've got to use your wits and try to find a weapon.' He mentioned aerosol cans, tools, anything heavy, anything sharp. The wine opener lying on the countertop was the only visible utensil, but it was too small to be useful. There had to be knives in the galley. But which drawer held them? The man in the doorway was watching my every move.

The man questioning Johnny was growing increasingly agitated. I understood enough to know that they were looking for something, but the dialect was too strong for me to figure out what it was. Suddenly, the man said something I understood: 'Your friend, Nick.' I tensed. Damn it, I'd known there was something fishy about him.

Johnny's eyes opened at the sound of Nick's name. 'Didier, I don't know what you're talking about.' Then he said something in a clipped voice in French. Whatever it was, the big man, Didier, stepped forward and backhanded him.

I ran toward Didier. 'Stop!' I yelled. 'Tell me what you want. I'll find it.'

Louis came up behind me, threw his arm around my neck and yanked me back to the steps leading down to the stateroom. Didier released a torrent of words to Johnny, and again I heard Nick's name.

I strained against Louis's arm, digging my nails into it to keep him from strangling me.

Didier repeated what he had said, his voice more menacing.

Then he gestured toward me and snapped his fingers at Louis. 'Bring her closer.'

Louis tightened his arm at my throat. I struggled harder, gasping for air, but he held me fast and forced me toward the door to the cockpit, where the emaciated man was standing sentry. When we got close to him, he stepped up to me, grabbed my shirt and ripped it open. Leering, he squeezed my breast and made an obscene gesture at his crotch.

I hit at his arm, shoving him away, and spat at him. He snickered.

Johnny snarled and lunged forward off the sofa. This time when Didier hit him, on the side of the head, he dropped to the floor like a dead weight.

'Jaggo, enough! Get outside,' Didier snapped to the thin man. Jaggo inched his way out the door, his eyes never leaving me.

I wrenched my arms away from Louis, grabbed the ends of my shirt and tied them in a knot.

Didier went to the sink, found a glass in one of the cabinets and filled it with water. He walked over and doused Johnny's head. As soon as Johnny stirred, Didier hauled him back up onto the sofa.

Johnny groaned and opened his eyes, and Didier spoke again, this time his tone more soothing.

Johnny stiffened. 'No,' he said. Blood was leaking out of the wound at his temple, down his cheek.

I started toward them, but Louis grabbed my arms again, so all I could do was look on helplessly as Didier jerked Johnny to his feet. Didier and Louis steered Johnny and me outside into the cockpit. I welcomed the dim light outside after the glare of the lights in the saloon. I waited for my eyes to adjust, still searching for a possible weapon. Johnny ran a tight ship. There was nothing in the open.

If only another boat would come in! If I screamed, maybe someone would hear me.

Why had I ignored all my senses that something wasn't right with Johnny and Nick? I'd been in the islands too long, been lulled into complacency. What good was training if I got myself into a situation through carelessness?

Didier forced Johnny up the couple of steps from the cockpit

onto the deck. Johnny was reeling, barely able to stay upright.
Didier kept haranguing him, and Johnny kept muttering that he
didn't have whatever they were after.

What were they looking for? It sounded as if they were saying,
'That bag.' I recalled the scene before the limbo contest, when
I'd come upon Johnny and Nick in the billiard room. A package
had been sitting on the billiard table between them, next to
Johnny's backpack. And I remembered Johnny's panic when he
remembered that he'd left it behind. Is that what they were after?

The two men's voices grew louder, more agitated. Louis let
go of my arm and began pacing. He pulled out a cigarette and
lit it with quick, anxious motions. The light from the match flared
up, and for a second his face looked devilish.

I eased toward the steps leading up to the deck. If his attention
strayed, I'd be over the side in a heartbeat. But Jaggo moved
closer to me.

Louis had only taken a couple of drags on his cigarette before
Didier called out something. Louis flicked the cigarette onto
the deck and ground it out under his heel, then grabbed my left
arm while Jaggo took my right. The two men forced me up the
steps out of the cockpit and onto the outer deck, then forward,
toward the bow of the boat, where Didier was standing with
Johnny. My eyes were more adjusted now, and I saw the island
lying dead ahead, not that far away. The air was humid and
still. I acted as if I was going along freely, alert for a chance
to wrench myself away from them and dive over the side. If I
did manage to do that, I'd have to swim under the boat in case
they shot at me. And then what? One step at a time. First, into
the water.

Didier turned from Johnny and said to me, 'Miss, you must
tell your friend to cooperate with us. We need certain goods, and
he . . .'

'I don't have it,' Johnny snarled. 'Believe me, it's not important
enough to me to lie about it. If I did, I would tell you.'

'Johnny, if you have what they want, please, now is the time
to give it up,' I said. I was determined to sound resolute and not
as frightened as I felt.

He let his head fall forward and laughed. 'I wish I thought it
would help us.'

'What a pity,' the man said. 'If you had been able to tell us where it was, at least we could have taken care of you quickly.'

At the hint in his words, I turned cold, goosebumps prickling on my skin. There was no mistaking his meaning. Regardless of whether they got what they were looking for, these men were going to kill us. I tried to think of an out. Should I scream? That was stupid. No one was around to help. I glanced toward Johnny and from the light in the salon saw that his eyes were glinting and desperate.

'Leave us on the island,' I said. 'Take the boat.'

'Oh, there is no question we'll take your boat,' Didier said. 'And we will certainly leave you here.'

For a moment, I had a wild hope that they simply planned to leave us here on the island, but then he added, 'Where your bodies won't be found.'

'OK. Wait. I'll tell you where the package is.' Johnny then spoke in the odd dialect again, his voice urgent. He glanced toward me, and I sensed that he was bargaining for my life. I knew he could save his breath. They had no intention of letting me live.

The leader spoke sharply to Jaggo, who went back inside. I considered what I should do. Should I bargain? With what? I refused to plead for my life.

Jaggo came back, laughing out loud. '*Va bien*. It's there.' He walked up to Didier, and the two men conferred in whispers. Jaggo snickered.

Didier said something to Louis, who went all the way forward. I saw him reach down and open a hatch, then I heard the clanking of the anchor chain. They were pulling up the anchor, which meant we were going to leave. No doubt they would pitch us overboard. If they did it as we were leaving, that wouldn't be a problem for me. We weren't that far from the island. It would be a short swim. If they took us out farther into the sound and threw us overboard, that would be a different situation, but still not impossible. The only problem would be if Johnny was too injured to swim. I didn't like the glazed look in his eyes. He had been bashed on the head several times, hard.

The grating sound of the anchor went on for a minute or two, followed by pounding, as if someone was doing something with the anchor chain. Johnny was staring at me, his eyes wild. I tried to smile at him, but his expression scared me.

'Up there,' Didier said. 'Quickly.' He waved toward the bow. Louis pushed me forward. My last vestige of self-preservation kicked into gear. If I was going to have a chance to jump overboard, this was it. I kicked out at Louis, my heel hitting him squarely on the shin. Caught by surprise, he stumbled and I lunged for the side of the boat. But crazy Jaggo was quicker. He snatched my arm and his other arm snaked around my neck. He pulled me back up hard against him and ground his pelvis against me, with a snicker. Didier had a gun to Johnny's head. If Johnny tried to get away, he'd be dead before he hit the water.

'What are you going to do with us?' I asked.

'Jaggo has this little plan,' Didier said, his voice gentle. 'He is a man with a plan. Not a plan I would think of, but an interesting one.'

A man with a plan, a man with a plan, ran crazily through my mind like a children's song. Fear hit me full force, grabbing me in the belly. I clamped my teeth into my bottom lip to keep from howling. I vowed to myself that whatever happened, I wasn't going to beg. I refused to let these men hear me grovel.

At a word from the boss, Jaggo let go of me and Louis took his place. What was Jaggo's plan? Jaggo went to the edge of the bow, and in the light from the salon, I saw that he was standing over a pile of heavy anchor chain, next to a heap of line. I struggled to wrench myself out of Louis's grasp, but he tightened his grip. I turned my head and looked at his face. He wasn't grinning the way Jaggo was. He looked grim and unhappy. But there was no question he would do what he was told to do.

Didier dragged Johnny to my side and shoved him up next to me, my face smashed up against his chest. Louis began winding the thick line around our bodies. They were going to bind us together and throw us overboard! In the shadows, the men couldn't see when I shoved my arms between myself and Johnny so the rope wouldn't be too tight. Maybe if it was loose enough, I could get myself free.

They bound the rope around our legs so it was all we could do to stay upright. But what made me abandon my vow not to beg was when they began to loop the anchor chain around us. 'Please, please, not this,' I begged. A sob rose in my throat.

'Shh, shh,' Johnny whispered. 'Don't give them the satisfaction.'

They wound the heavy chain around us three times, and then the men hauled us to the side of the boat. With the weight of the chain, it took all three of them, grunting and swearing. Then, with a mighty shove, we were tumbling over the rail. The last thing I heard as we hit the water was Jaggo laughing.

FOUR

Nassau was a surprise to Paco Boland. He thought it would be full of rich, white people playing tourist, and that anyone who looked like him, with brown skin, would be serving food, hanging around on street corners to get day labor work, or cleaning the houses or offices of the rich. He wished his brother Diego was here with him, but of course that wasn't possible. His brother was dead.

Paco had copied his brother, deciding that a life of manual labor wasn't for him. He and his friends had found a way of living a bigger life. They were in the business of supplying folks with substances they wanted. It was risky business, no doubt. Paco and his brother and friends had all spent time in prison. But the risk was worth it. It's what had paid for their trip – Paco and his boy Rodney. It paid for them to stay in a nice place and eat in fine restaurants.

Sure, he was here on business, and he'd rather have stayed home and watched the money flow in, hang out with his lady and his crew, and enjoy the good life. But sometimes you had to clean up messes, as they were here to do now. You couldn't let people get away with things. You had to clean up the loose ends. Let everybody know you couldn't be disrespected. Jessie Madison was a loose end.

Still, business or not, he liked Nassau. Black and brown people mingled with white ones, living in style. If he wasn't so caught up in the life back home, he would have considered moving here. Even the white people seemed easy to hang with. They looked him right in the eye, as if he was the same as everybody else.

'I could get comfortable here,' he said to his buddy Rodney. 'Maybe spend a little R and R down here when we're done with our mission.'

They were in a beach bar tossing back their second drink, some touristy thing. Paco had told the waitress this was their first time in the Bahamas and they wanted an island kind of drink.

She'd touched her pink tongue to her wide top lip, cocked her head and pointed her finger at him. 'I think I can fix you right up,' she said.

At first, the drink was too sweet for Paco's taste, but it went down fast, and the second one tasted just right.

Rodney nodded. 'I know what you mean. Maybe we should take a couple of days to kick back before we get serious.'

Rodney was a good guy to have around. Tall, black as eggplant, and with shoulders wide as a truck grill, and a set of teeth to match, he was actually pretty mellow. A guy you could depend on, and attractive to girls so you didn't have to worry that he wasn't going to get with somebody if you did. There was only one thing you had to watch: don't cross him and get his temper revved up.

'We can't take too much vacation time,' he said, frowning at Rodney. They couldn't get off track. His gut tightened, and he suddenly felt hot. He stood up and took off his coat.

Rodney looked him up and down. 'Damn, two of us look like thugs. We need to get us some of them shirts.' He flicked his eyes a couple of tables over where four guys were laughing it up like they didn't have a problem in the world. They were all wearing colorful short-sleeved shirts with palm trees and birds and flowers. 'I like the one with those parrots.'

'Nah, that ain't for me. None of them birds or flowers. I'll get me one in a nice sky blue.'

Rodney sprawled back and sucked up the last of his drink. His big silver and white teeth flared. 'Or maybe I'll get me one with some hula girls on it.'

'Hula girls? That's Hawaii, you lunk. That's the other side of the world.'

'That's what I'm gonna get, though.' Rodney flicked his finger in the air, and their waitress appeared at once.

'Another one?' She smiled.

'Why don't you bring us something to eat? What have you got?'

'You let me take care of you,' she said. She put her palms on the table and leaned toward them, her luscious breasts a quarter-inch from falling out of her halter top. 'I don't even have to guess. No fish for you guys. It's meat, I'll bet.'

Paco didn't even bother to pretend he wasn't taking in every inch of those fine, honey-colored breasts she was so proud of. 'You got that right. Meat.'

She leaned over farther. He could smell her perfume. Paco wanted to bury his face in her cleavage. 'Hamburger or steak?' she said.

'Steak,' Paco said. His voice was thick. 'And fries. And a shrimp cocktail.'

'What about you, sugar?' She pointed her tits in Rodney's direction.

'Sounds fine to me. And I guess another round of those drinks. What do you call those drinks anyway?'

'They don't really have a name.' Her voice was low and sweet. 'I told the bartender to fix you two up so you'd be ready to party in a while. That is, if you're up for it.'

'Like after you get off work?' Rodney worked his grin.

'Exactly like that,' she said. 'Now let me take care of you two.'

She walked away, her hips swaying, her short skirt hiking up just enough to tantalize.

'Oh, oh, oh,' Paco moaned softly.

'Like that, do you?' Rodney grinned. 'We're going to have ourselves some kind of fun tonight. Get ourselves all relaxed before we go find Kayla's sister.'

FIVE

As the water closed over my head, my dive instructor's voice came pulsing out of the past. 'Three minutes, forty-five seconds. Not bad, Jess. Only fifteen seconds to add on before you pass the course.'

Tony insisted that we had to be able to stay under water without taking a breath for four minutes before he would certify us.

'Fifteen seconds!' I gasped. 'It might as well be an hour!'

One guy muttered that Tony was going beyond PADI requirements.

'Listen up, everybody!' Tony roared. 'Four minutes! That's my personal certification program. If you have a problem with that, I'll refund your money and pass you along to somebody else. Somebody who won't save your life someday.'

No one took him up on his offer. He was the best, and everyone knew it. That's why he was top of the FBI's list of dive instructors.

'Jessie, for the benefit of these wimps who had to come up early, how did three minutes, forty-five seconds feel?' Tony was a burly guy with a barrel chest. He swore he could hold his breath for five minutes underwater.

I groaned. 'Like eternity.'

'Exactly. Long enough to get out of whatever trouble you find yourself in.'

Tony could never have imagined that anyone would be in the kind of trouble I was in, tied body to body with an injured man who didn't have the kind of training I'd had.

Johnny had begun to thrash as soon as we hit the water. I wanted to stop him, calm him down. Struggling would use up precious energy and air.

Tony's voice came back to me, stern and unrelenting. 'In a desperate situation, don't let your mind wander. Don't picture your mom crying over your coffin, or how your dog is going to miss you. Focus! Grab on to any tool you can and use it!'

His voice drove me to fight the panic I was barely managing to fend off. What could I use? *Think!* When they were tying us with rope, I'd slipped my arm between Johnny and me so I could loosen it. But with the chain around us, I was bound tight.

The chain was the key. On deck, when the men had finished looping the anchor chain around us, I had noticed that they didn't bother to lock it. I had heard some of it slip off as we went overboard. If we could turn ourselves, maybe we could get it off. Really? I had no idea how much chain still bound us.

Tony: 'Don't let your mind wander! And don't give up!'

Johnny was flailing, using up valuable air. But then I realized he had the same idea; he was trying to turn our bodies, to unwind the chain. Frantically, I flung myself in tandem with him, and we managed to roll. I felt the chain slip once, twice. Despair hit me. It would take too long to unwind it. And even then, we'd still be lying on the bottom, tied up. I thrust the thought away. This was our only chance. Better to die trying to help ourselves than to lie here and drown.

A sudden huge surge of water tumbled us across the shallow reef we were lying on. I clenched my teeth to avoid gasping and taking in water. For a couple of seconds, I was disoriented. The weight of the chain was gone. What had happened? Then it hit me. With the anchor up, the boat had drifted too close to shore. To avoid running aground, the men had revved up the engine and taken off fast, creating the current that had rolled us clear of the chain. I felt a tinge of hope. But we were still tied with rope, lying on our sides.

We had hit bottom fast, so I figured we weren't more than a few feet below the surface. If we could get upright, we might be able to get our heads above water for a quick breath of air.

My lungs were beginning to ache. How long had it been? One minute? Two? I could hold my breath a long time. But how long could Johnny last? *Hold on, hold on*, I thought frantically. I wasn't strong enough to pull us up without his help. But even with the two of us, I didn't know how we were going to do it.

Now that we were free of the chain, I was able to push my arms down from between us, loosening the rope slightly, but there wasn't time to try to wiggle out. I had to think of something else. I drew my legs up as far as they would go and jerked them sideways so that one of my knees slipped between Johnny's, giving us a bit more play. I began to rock from side to side, to try to let Johnny know that we had to pull ourselves upright. His chin touched the top of my head. He understood and began rocking with me.

My lungs were on fire. I felt like my heart was going to burst. We had to get this right the first time. We wouldn't have enough air left to try it again. I tapped his chest once, twice. On three, we strained to pull ourselves upright. The water resisted at first and then seemed to give way.

We made it to our feet but were teetering. Johnny was sagging against me. Being wrapped together made it almost impossible to balance, especially with his weight. The coral was sharp and uneven. And my head was still underwater. I wanted to rip the cords off us, but I was afraid if I moved too much, we'd fall.

Spots were starting to dance behind my eyes. I was sure it had been longer than three minutes. Eternity. Holding my breath for four minutes had never included so much energy expenditure.

The water seemed to speak to me with a seductive murmur. 'Let go. It will be easy. It won't hurt.'

Tony's voice, calm, commanding. 'Surface now! Use all the energy you've got. It's your last chance.'

I won limbo contests because my legs were so strong. Now my legs would have to carry both of us. I gathered my waning strength, crouched and sprang. Hard. I felt as if I were trying to fly.

My face barely came out of the water and I managed only a half gasp before I came down again, planting my feet as wide as I could to take the weight of Johnny's body. Sharp coral cut my feet, and my legs cramped with the effort. I gritted my teeth as the intense pain of the cramp shot through them. I had to hang on.

Again. Don't stop to think. I needed more air, immediately. I forced another jump, this time managing to get a real breath. My oxygen-starved body was humming as if it had been stunned by an electric shock. This time when I came down, I staggered and almost fell. Another cramp hit me, and I groaned, the sound a burble underwater. I had to fight off the pain. Johnny was completely limp now. I could not lose my balance! I'd never be able to get the two of us upright again. Another jump. I had a moment of panic. What if in the dark I was moving us away from the island? Where was the island? In the dark, all I saw was water. That meant the island was behind us.

This time when I came down, I turned slightly in the direction of the island, and shallower water. Johnny's head flopped away, then down, almost toppling us. I wished desperately I could get my hands free of the rope binding us. But I didn't have time. I had to try to move closer to shore.

I knew I had to do it in short hops. No great leaps toward the island. Each time I came down, I risked falling. Crouch, hop. Pause. Crouch, hop. Pause.

Finally, I realized that when I hopped upward, it was taking less time to surface. I was gaining ground. But then I came down against something hard that scraped my shin. What the hell!

'Idiot! It's a ledge. Get up onto it!' Tony's voice had become my own voice. I launched Johnny's and my joined bodies, propelling us up and forward as hard as I could. This time we came down with a jolt a foot higher. I could feel coolness on my forehead, which meant my nose and mouth were almost out of the water. But now Johnny seemed suddenly heavier. Before now, his body had been buoyed by the water. With his shoulders and head out of the water, more weight fell on me. I felt the last of my strength leave me, and I teetered on my feet.

No! I had gotten this far – I couldn't fail now. I took another couple of crouches and hops, but there was no mistaking it – Johnny was dragging me down.

From deep inside I summoned fresh strength and frantically made another awkward lurch toward shore. Within seconds, my head was out. I stood, feet planted, with the dead weight of Johnny's body dragging at me, gasping in air, sobbing between breaths.

Now Johnny was really heavy. His body felt cold next to mine. I had to get him to shore and give him CPR. My legs cramped hard with each hop. And then I did lose my balance. I howled as my head slipped under water. It would be too stupid to drown this close to shore. I'd be damned if I was going to. I wriggled and squirmed and managed to get one arm free of the rope, then tore at the bindings until I got clear of it and loose from Johnny's body. I sat upright and my head popped above the surface. I took in more gulps of air.

I had to get Johnny to land. How long had he been without oxygen? Four minutes? Five? Too long. I crawled to my feet and felt sand under them. We were past the coral, almost to shore. I grabbed the rope that was still tied around his body and dragged him toward the beach.

The last few feet were the hardest, with his dead weight resisting my effort, and my body protesting that too much had been demanded of it. But I couldn't abandon him. When I had most of his body up on the beach, I dropped to his side. He lay absolutely still. His skin was cold, and I couldn't feel a pulse.

'No!' I cried. 'You can't die!'

Suddenly, I remembered the other boat, the one the three guys had arrived on. I'd been so desperate to get out of the water that I'd forgotten it. Was it still out there? Could someone see that we had emerged from the water? I looked out into the cove. But both boats were gone.

I put everything I had left into CPR. Johnny must have water in his lungs, so heart compressions alone wouldn't do. I alternated compressions and quick breaths, over and over and over. After several minutes, I almost gave up, but I remembered that the CPR instructor had told the class you had to do it for at least ten minutes before you even thought of giving up. In a daze, I forced myself again and again. Push, push, push, push, push, breathe, breathe. The rhythm was the only thing that kept me going.

I felt a twitch of his body and heard a gurgle from deep inside him. I gasped and felt for his carotid. A pulse. Faint, but there. I remembered the other thing the instructor had said: that sometimes there was a false pulse brought on by the CPR. 'Don't set yourself up for disappointment,' the woman had said. 'Try to stay detached, so you can be calm.'

To hell with calm! 'Johnny!' My voice came out as a croak. 'Dammit! Wake up! You've got to be alive!' I pushed his body, willing him to stir. But he lay still. The next time I felt for a pulse, there was nothing. I fell across his chest, sobbing.

'I'm so sorry,' I moaned, again and again. If only I had been able to get him out of the water a minute earlier. Finally, I sat up. He was gone. I considered trying more CPR, but I knew it was useless. I started to shiver. My teeth were chattering. The air was warm, so in a detached way, I wondered why I felt so cold.

Then I realized what was happening. I was in shock. Eventually, the sun would come up and warm me, but I had to get warm immediately. I had to find warmth.

I put my hand on Johnny one more time, a sort of benediction. I tried to stand up, but my legs wouldn't hold me. I crawled higher onto dry sand, which was warmer. Then I saw some dark forms of rocks set back from the shoreline. Rocks. They'd maintain warmth. I was shivering so hard I could barely coordinate my movements, but I crawled toward them.

I pulled a few of the larger ones into a heap and lay down on them, wrapping my arms and legs around them, embracing the steadying warmth.

'You're going to be OK,' I whispered. Was that true? I couldn't think beyond right now. Gradually, my shivering subsided and I sank into unconsciousness.

SIX

'Jessica Lee Madison, get out of the sun. You're going to burn up!' My mother's persistent voice was like a nail driving into my skull. 'Wrinkles blah blah blah. Skin cancer blah blah.'

The words penetrated, then faded, repeatedly. She was annoying the hell out of me, and I raised my arm to push her away. The movement shattered my nightmare and made me aware of a different one. I was lying on sharp rocks in the blazing sun. My body was throbbing.

I eased off the rocks, onto my knees, and opened my eyes. I yelped as bright sunlight stabbed my eyeballs. My eyes felt scraped raw. I brought my hands in front of my eyes and peered out, disoriented. The memory of where I was flooded back. And the memory of Johnny.

Johnny. I looked over to where I'd left him. The tide had come in and his body was submerged up to his chest. I whimpered. I had to get him out of the water. Part of me knew that was useless, effort I'd expend for nothing, but another part of me couldn't stand the idea that more damage would be done to his body.

I got to my feet, staggered over and sat down beside him, fantasizing that I'd been wrong, that he was still alive and that I could wake him. But, of course, I couldn't. His skin was pale and gray, and already beginning to bloat in the sun.

'I'm so sorry,' I whispered.

I stared out at the water for a minute, thinking about how little I knew of him. Did he have a family? Siblings? Parents? A girlfriend back home? He was a sweet guy. People who knew him would miss him. Finally, I got to my feet. Now for the hard part.

I grabbed his wrists and dragged him. He was heavy. Sliding him across the sand was hard. But as irrational as I knew it was, I was determined to get him out of the sun. I saw an opening in the brush and pulled him through it, into the shade of some trees. There was a stream under the trees, and I moved him there.

I sat beside him and tried to think of something to do or say to acknowledge his death. I'm not religious and I couldn't think of anything but the Lord's prayer, and that didn't fit.

But then I thought of what I could say. 'Johnny, I promise you I will find who did this. Those men will pay, and if your friend Nick double-crossed you, he will pay too. You didn't deserve this.' My voice broke on the last words. It wasn't as if I'd known him well. But I liked him. I was glad we'd spent the evening together, glad his last night hadn't been spent alone. I hoped it had been good for him. He deserved better. He deserved somebody who cherished him.

I looked up at the sun that was already high in the sky, and wondered what time it was. I looked back at Johnny's body and realized that he was wearing a waterproof watch. I usually wore one similar, but it was back in my room. I had seen no reason to be wearing a watch at the resort.

'Forgive me,' I whispered as I unbuckled the watch and slid it onto my arm. It was ten o'clock.

I looked out at the cove. The sun glancing off the saltwater and sand was achingly bright, and the movement made me dizzy.

Every part of me ached, and the skin on my legs was on fire. Whatever wasn't being blistered by the sun had been scraped raw by coral and rocks or chafed by ropes. I was grateful that I at least had Johnny's shirt on. Gingerly, I pushed myself to my feet.

I needed to get water. The stream where I had brought Johnny's body was muddy, so I followed it farther inland until I came to a pool. I dipped my hands in and tasted the water. It was brackish, but it would do for now.

But now what? The enormity of my situation hit me. No one knew where I was. And I had no way to get back to the island. I walked back to the beach and looked toward Trophy Cay, to the north. It had taken us twenty minutes to get here under motor power, which meant Trophy Cay was approximately three miles away. Normally, I could swim three miles, but in my current state, it didn't feel possible.

Thinking about Trophy Cay, with its luxurious pools and the cheerful beach bar, my spirits sagged. So close, but so far away. Was it possible that people would come here for a side excursion? Then I remembered that today was Sunday. Guests would be leaving. Shelley might wonder where I was, but I had always been independent and she probably wouldn't worry.

I turned my gaze to the south. A hilly peninsula jutted out into the water. The bay and beach where I was standing were on one side of the island; beyond was another bay. Peering in that direction, my eye caught something, and my heart lurched. It was the top of a mast! If I could get to that boat, I'd be saved. But just as quickly, my hope died. What if it was *Island Ice*? It was possible the men who attacked us had merely moved the boat to the next cove.

Irrational fury welled up in me. Who the hell were they anyway? What did they want and how was Nick Garnier involved?

I squeezed my eyes shut, fighting my anger. I couldn't squander energy in anger. If I got out of this mess, there would be more than enough time to investigate how it had happened. Not *if* I got out. *When* I got out.

And the boat might not be *Island Ice*. I took off trotting toward the peninsula. Right away, I ran into trouble. I was barefoot, and the beach was full of coral and rocks that would cut my feet to pieces. I slowed down and walked several yards inland to where the scrub bushes lay, low and thick on the ground, surrounded by sand. It was easier on my feet, but with each step, the thorny vegetation scraped at my legs.

Stop whining, I thought. *Whining is useless. You know that. Besides, you're better off than when you were tied up underwater.* At the memory, I immediately felt nauseous. I had to put what had happened out of my mind. Every time I remembered it, I felt punched in the gut, as if the experience had left me vulnerable in a way I had never been before. Aloud, I said to myself, 'You're just depleted. You're OK. You'll get through this.'

When I reached the shallow backwater of the peninsula, I spotted a Styrofoam cooler with its top still on that had washed ashore. I yanked off the top, willing there to be something to eat or drink inside. But it was empty.

I made my way up the gentle slope of the hilly peninsula as fast as I could, crouching down to avoid being spotted in case the boat was *Island Ice*. At last, I was able to see the sailboat anchored in the next harbor. It was a catamaran, but smaller. Energized with relief, I began flailing my arms and screaming, 'Help, help!'

But even as far away as I was, I heard the sound of the anchor being weighed. There was no way they could hear me screaming over the clatter of the anchor chain. Unless someone happened to look my way, no one would know I was here, trying to get their attention. Despite the odds, I continued to wave my arms, watching, numb, as the boat gradually began to move away out of the cove and into the open water. I continued to signal until the boat was small in the distance.

Exhausted from my effort and the emotional disappointment, I sank to the ground and would have cried if there had been any tears left to cry with. My eyes felt like someone had tried to scratch them out. I sat for several minutes letting my disappointment subside. My body felt as though tiny fires had been set in a dozen places. The scrapes from slamming against the coral ledge were throbbing, and my skin was starting to burn from the intense sun. The bottoms of my feet stung from my clamber up the hill.

'Stop feeling sorry for yourself,' I muttered. I stood up and surveyed the island. From my hilly vantage point, I saw that it was the length of a few football fields. There was too much vegetation for me to see the other side of the island – the Atlantic side.

As I made my way down the hill, I took stock. I had to find some way to get out of here. Maybe I could find something on the island that I could use for flotation. When we took tourists out on dives, we were always retrieving things that had fallen off boats. Anything could be washed up on a beach. I let my imagination run wild and fantasized about finding flares, or an intact dinghy. A cigarette lighter I could start a signal fire with. I could find a cell phone in a waterproof bag! A cache of food!

I came back down to earth. I'd be lucky to come across anything useful. First, I had to figure out where things were likely to be washed ashore. That would be the Atlantic side, with its larger waves. I started walking to the other side of the island, wading in the stream. The water felt wonderful on my feet and legs. Plus, the bottom was sludgy, which was hard to walk in, but also soothing.

The farther inland I walked, the stream grew gradually deeper. Trudging along, my foot kicked something, and I heard a sloshing sound. There in the stream at my feet was a can of orange soda. Unopened, and as far as I could see new enough so that it hadn't rusted out. My mouth puckered and my empty stomach lurched at the thought of the sweet taste. I popped it open and drank in long gulps, my body greedy for the liquid and the jolt of energy. I silently blessed whoever had been exploring here and let the soda slip out of his backpack, into the water.

Another five minutes of wading brought me to a straggly line of stunted island mangroves where the stream opened out and the ropy tendrils of the vegetation led to a brownish, shallow pool. I followed it until it got a couple of feet deeper, and a little clearer. I drank several handfuls and then doused my head in it. I also soaked my shirt in it to cool me down.

On the Atlantic side of the island, the water was much rougher, the waves crashing onto the shore. With such force, it really was possible I could be lucky and find an intact dinghy or Hobie cat that had broken loose from a boat in the more turbulent sea.

I was disappointed to find that the shore was fairly clean of rubbish. That was unusual. I had yet to visit an island that was free of junk that floated in from boats. The currents around the island must be causing flotsam to pile up somewhere specific. At the south side of the island, I saw another cove, and that's where I struck gold. Or at least trash. Floating in the backwater was a stew of garbage. I immediately spotted a dented and scarred windsurfing board. It had been discarded because a chunk of fiberglass was missing. I dragged the board onto land and continued poking around in the heap of junk, hoping to find another soft drink, or maybe a bottle of champagne and some chilled caviar.

I found two dried-up coconuts, an assortment of odd pieces of Styrofoam, a child's T-shirt, frayed rope and two more empty coolers. There was broken crockery, plastic cups and a net bag containing rotting oranges. My heart sank when I saw a small, furry body, but it turned out to be a stuffed dog, not a real one.

Finding nothing more useful, I examined the windsurfing board. It was long, probably ten feet, so if it would stay afloat, I could use it to paddle back to Trophy Cay. But it was heavy, which meant water had soaked into it from the hole in the fiberglass. I pushed it out into the water to judge its flotation. It floated, but the way it wallowed in the water made me leery of how long it would last before it sank altogether. Then I had an idea. I selected some of the larger pieces of Styrofoam floating in the heap of junk. That might help with the flotation if I could find a way to lash it on. But the frayed rope I found was in pieces that were too short. I started looking for more, but then remembered where there was plenty of rope. All I had to do was retrieve it.

I spent another several minutes digging through the detritus and found a relatively good orange and a half-full tube of sunscreen. I gobbled up the orange and slathered sunscreen all over myself, finding the normal activity and the familiar smell of the sunscreen comforting. It brought back thoughts of yesterday, lying around the pool, laughing with my friends. But then I thought of Johnny, and my spirits sank. He had smeared sunscreen on my back. We had teased each other and laughed a lot. Had that only been yesterday? I forced aside those thoughts. They would only drag me down. If I was going to survive, I had to deal with what was right in front of me. Which was a broken-down surfboard and some blocks of Styrofoam, and only a dim idea of how I could put them to use.

The sun was high overhead. It was after noon. Whatever I was going to do, it had to be fast. I didn't want to spend the night here.

Piling my loot onto the board, I walked it through the waves on the Atlantic side until I got back to the stream. I sloshed along, pushing the board. It took a long time. I was all too aware of how depleted my energy was. When I got to the edge of the trees, near where Johnny's body was stashed, I hesitated, wondering if I should visit him once more. I decided not to. What would it accomplish, other than to make me sad? I lay down in the shade and gave myself a twenty-minute rest. I was putting off what I knew I had to do.

When I couldn't bear to stay still any longer, I got up, carried the board to the beach and started to work.

An hour later, I surveyed my strange, awkward vessel. I had waded out onto the reef and found the rope Johnny and I had been tied up with, and used it to lash the Styrofoam to the underside of the boat. It gave me deep satisfaction to turn what had almost succeeded in killing me into something that might save me.

By the time I was finished with my labors, it was two o'clock. I shaded my eyes and stared toward Trophy Cay. Or at least I thought it was Trophy Cay. Was it possible we had come farther, and that the island I was seeing was another one? I watched for several minutes, hoping to see sails or some kind of sign of life I could count on. As I waited, I grew impatient. Why couldn't somebody be sailing around, to at least let me know it was an inhabited island?

And goddammit, why wasn't anyone looking for us? Even if Shelley wasn't worried about me, surely Nick would notice that Johnny was missing. But maybe he assumed that Johnny had gone back to Nassau. He could have told Shelley that. Maybe he'd gone there himself, thinking to meet Johnny there. Or maybe it was something more sinister – maybe he was part of the gang that had attacked us, and he knew what they had done.

I continued to stall, my heart tripping. I already felt wrung out. Did I have the strength to make it to Trophy Cay? Even if I managed to get there, the resort was on the north side of the island. 'Don't be an idiot,' I said aloud. If I made it as far as the island, I could most certainly make it to the resort, even if I had to crawl.

There was one other consideration. In the afternoon, the winds would come up and the water would be choppy, making paddling that much harder. Maybe it would be better to wait until tomorrow morning to set out, when it would be calm. Or maybe it would be better not to try at all. Someone would come eventually.

I shook my head to clear it of the negative thoughts paralyzing me. I couldn't stay here any longer. It was possible that another boat would come in this evening, or tomorrow. But it could also be a week or longer before anyone else would venture here. If another boat didn't come soon, my strength would quickly dissipate even further. I couldn't wait, not even until tomorrow morning.

SEVEN

I stood knee-deep in the water, my breathing ragged, trying to still my fear at what I was setting out to do. What I had to do. Normally, I was not a fearful person; my former FBI trainer John Farrell had even said I was bold. But I knew I'd been ridiculously lucky up until now. Would my luck hold? Could I make it?

'Get on with it,' I said, my voice sounding loud. 'It's not going to get any easier.' I went back to the beach, grabbed the board, and started toward the water. I stopped and looked in the direction of Johnny's body and said one more silent benediction, then continued carrying the board out into the water.

I was satisfied with the way it bobbed on top of the waves for now, but how long could it hold up? If it sank, would I have the strength to swim the rest of the way to the other island? I was a strong swimmer, but even though I knew the island wasn't that far away, it seemed too distant. I couldn't bring myself to look in that direction. Every time I looked at the island, it seemed farther away.

In the detritus on the other side of the island, I had found a decent-sized plank to use for a paddle. It would have been nice to be able to shape it, but I couldn't complain at this point. It had been a gift. Terrified by the prospect of getting a few miles out and losing the paddle, I had spent extra time and, using a shell and a rock, gouged a hole in one end of the board so I could attach a length of rope to it. The other end was tied around my wrist.

I was out of excuses. I was waist-deep with the board bobbing next to me. At the last minute, I turned to look back at the beach and whispered to Johnny, 'I'm going to find them. And they'll pay.'

That promise gave me the extra push I needed. I had waded deep enough that I had to climb up onto the board and start paddling. I sat upright, cross-legged on the board and dipped the paddle in one side, then the other, surging forward.

Because of the way the wind and tide worked, I couldn't aim straight for the cay, which was directly north. The prevailing wind came from the west, and although the winds weren't heavy, the narrow cuts between islands created a current that could pull even large boats off course. I would have to tack, paddling northwest until I was sure I would clear the most powerful part of the current between the islands. If I got caught in the current, my flimsy board would be swept through the cut and out to the Atlantic. The next landfall was Cat Island, a hair under 200 miles east. I slammed the door on that thought.

At first, I paddled mindlessly, intent on keeping the course. Even though I had been physically pushed to my limits, I was fit and strong after several weeks of spending a lot of time in the water. I could do this. Besides, I had no choice.

After I had been paddling a while, I looked back to judge my progress. I shouldn't have looked. It hardly seemed I'd gone any distance. My heart lurched. Seeing the island's relative safety receding behind me slammed me with the enormity of my task. For a moment, I considered whether it was better to go back and hope for rescue. 'No,' I said aloud. 'Just keep paddling.' Looking down into the water reassured me. The water was clear, and I could see the reef below me. It was a familiar sight: a deep, soothing blue. 'You can do this. You'll get there.' It helped me to talk out loud to myself. It eased my anxiety, at least a little.

Searching for some way to keep my mind from sabotaging me, I began to sing. For once, I could sing aloud without someone clapping their hands over their ears and telling me to stop making such a racket. I started on Beyoncé but gave up fast, because I couldn't remember many of the words. I could remember the words to some Katy Perry, but soon I moved to older songs from high school days. Then I sang a few songs from the nineties that my mother had listened to when I was a kid. Finally, I belted out a silly name song my mother had taught me and my sister when we were children. 'Annie, Annie, bo-bany, banana-fanna, fo-fanny.' My mother's name was Annie. I remembered giggling with my sister when we sang 'fanny.'

Our giggles didn't survive my dad's death and my mother's subsequent dependence on alcohol. I paddled on, remembering how scared I was when our mother was on a bender. I had to beg money from her to shop for food and pay the bills. I had to cook and get my sister to school. Mother would sometimes leave us alone for longer than a day. I was determined not to let Kayla see how frightened I was. It was hard, but maybe it's why I had become strong. Letting my mind wander over these thoughts now, I wondered if it would have been better for Kayla if I had shown fear. Maybe Kayla would have learned to navigate the real world better, without depending on drugs and alcohol.

I wondered how she was doing now and thought of how hollow-eyed and fragile she'd looked the day I visited her at the rehab facility. She'd been there for almost three months now. Was she doing well enough that she'd be ready to come home? It was a sobering thought. I was planning to start a job search when I got back. Would I have to put my plans on hold again in order to keep an eye on her? I'd face that decision when I got home. If I got home. My arms were tiring. How much longer could I keep paddling?

Singing made my throat dry, so I stopped. Instead, I started grumbling to myself. Kayla had once said that I had the strongest ability to hold a grudge of anyone in the world. She hadn't intended it as a compliment. But now I used it to spur myself

on, turning all the force of my grudge power onto the image of
the men who had thrown Johnny and me overboard. Which led
back to Nick. The way the guys on the boat had said his name,
with such familiarity, left me no doubt that he was involved with
them somehow. When I got to Trophy Cay, I intended to demand
that he tell me what those men were after.

I had been paddling steadily northwest, and at last, the island
I was aiming for looked closer. I judged that I was not quite
midway between the two islands. So far, I had felt none of the
effects of the current that would run through the cut. Maybe it
wouldn't be as strong as I had feared.

But around four o'clock the wind kicked up higher, as it did
most afternoons. It wasn't heavy winds, but since it was coming
straight from the west, it made it harder to keep the boat headed
out of the current. It also kicked up waves. They were gentle,
but with my strength depleted, the waves made the water feel
like sludge.

When I had started out, I had been sitting out of the water. I
now noticed that the water was lapping at my thighs, which
meant the surfboard was gradually sinking. The board had been
jettisoned because the outer fiberglass was torn. The interior of
the board was made of soft foam, and at the site of the tear, the
foam was soaking up more water, making it gradually heavier,
too heavy for the Styrofoam I had strapped onto it to keep it
buoyant. What would I do if it sank? I was closer to Trophy Cay,
but it still seemed far away.

I gave myself another pep talk. I wasn't paddling over treacherous depths. If the boat did sink, I could ditch the board and
use the rope to strap the Styrofoam around me for flotation.
Normally, I could trust myself to swim long distances, but my
physical reserves were almost gone. For now, I'd keep paddling
until I had to abandon the board. I got myself into a rhythm and
emptied my mind of everything except paddling left, then right,
then left, then right.

Every now and then, I tried to triangulate the distance,
wondering if I had gone far enough to risk turning a few degrees
to the east and starting toward the island, which would make
paddling easier. But fear of getting caught in the current through
the cut kept me heading farther to the north.

Finally, I looked at the island and made the calculation again. 'If you keep on like this,' I said out loud, 'you'll get to Nassau.' For some reason, this seemed outrageously funny and I started giggling. Then I couldn't stop. And before long I was moaning, with dry sobs that wracked my body.

'Stop it,' I yelled. 'You're getting hysterical.' I felt like I was two people, with the stern one fussing at the silly one. But deep in my brain, I knew the stern one was right. I had to get control of myself. I was dehydrated and disoriented. If I didn't keep my cool, all this effort would be for nothing. No matter how frightening the prospect, I had to turn toward the island.

As I adjusted my direction, I wondered when the sun had gotten so low on the horizon. Terrified of being caught in the dark and being swept into the current, I called up some unknown reserve of strength and started paddling like hell. I had let myself go into a sort of stupor, but with fear sparking my adrenaline, I became hyper-aware of my surroundings again. Now it was just me and the paddle. The board seemed to be lurching from side to side, making my efforts harder. I realized that meant I was crossing the current. Fear compelled me to paddle harder. By my reckoning of the angle I was taking toward the island, I was pretty sure I had gone far enough to the north to avoid being swept away, but I wasn't going to let up now.

Suddenly, without warning, the board stopped fighting me and instead surged forward with every stroke. I was out of the current.

'I made it, I made it,' I gasped, glee welling up inside me. The island swarmed forward to meet me. In the light that played at its low angle across the water, I saw that the water was getting shallower by the moment.

I felt giddy with relief. I had made the passage, and if I was wrong, and this wasn't Trophy Cay, and if I had to go another island up, I would. I shoved aside the seed of doubt that said that wouldn't be possible.

I had envisioned a graceful slide of the board onto the land, a leap from my cross-legged position on the board and then prancing across the sand. In reality, the waterlogged board lurched onto the beach and tipped over sideways. I had been sitting so long that my legs were cramped, and I fell over into the water and had to crawl out on my hands and knees. Instead of prancing, I hobbled around like an old woman until my legs stopped trembling.

There was a slight rise of sand dune ahead of me, and when I was able to walk, I made my way to the top of the dune. There, I sank to my knees in relief. I had a trek ahead of me, but at the far end of the island, in the gathering dusk, the resort lights shone bright and inviting.

EIGHT

When I started walking toward the lights, my body let me know how far gone I was. Spots swam in front of my eyes, and my legs kept threatening to give out. I set myself short goals to measure progress, promising I could rest when I reached a goal. 'You only have to get to that tree,' I said. 'Then you can sit down.' But every time I reached the goal, I would press on, afraid that if I sat down, I wouldn't be able to get back up.

Instead of allowing myself to rest, I promised myself treats. Water first, but then, 'A mai tai, a hamburger, a shower, a bed – and some clothes.'

When I finally stumbled out of a stand of scrub trees, onto a section of land that had been cleared and staked out for more building, I leaned against one of the trees, ready to give up. If I lay down now, someone would find me eventually. But vanity won out. I pictured how I must look. My hair felt like ropy seaweed. My legs were scratched and sunburned. If someone found me lying out here, they would assume I'd gotten drunk and passed out. They might even leave me here.

My legs felt like tree stumps, but I forced myself across the empty field, out onto the sandy beach that led down to the water. It was dusk, and lights were on at the bar at the end of the beach. There were no bathers left in the water, and only a couple of people strolling ahead of me, going in for the evening. I wondered where everyone was, but then remembered it was Sunday evening. Most people had returned to Nassau this afternoon. I walked to the water's edge and threw water on my face and hair, smoothing my hair back, and then took a deep breath and headed toward the bar.

Suddenly, I stopped. What was I thinking? I'd been so determined to arrive that I'd forgotten something crucial. Before Johnny and I left the dock, I had seen Didier there on his powerboat. What if he and the other two men had come back here with both boats? What if I ran into them? And what if I ran into Nick? I assumed he'd gone back to Nassau, but what if he hadn't? If he saw me, would he turn me over to Didier?

There were still some chaises left out on the sand and I sank onto one to give myself a chance to think. I was desperate for water, but I couldn't risk walking into a trap. I leaned back and closed my eyes.

'Jessie? What the hell are you doing here?'

I jerked awake. Nick Garnier was standing over me. It was fully dark now. The air had cooled down. Reggae music was coming from down the beach.

I stared at Nick, unable to form an answer.

'Where is Johnny?'

My brain scrambled for purchase. I pulled myself upright, dizzy with the effort. Of course, he didn't know Johnny was dead. Should I tell him, or should I stall? I couldn't trust him. Those men. Saying his name.

'He's . . . uh . . . he'll be here soon.' My voice was a croak.

He frowned. 'Where did you two go?'

'The next island.' I pointed, but then put my hand down, afraid he'd see it shaking.

'When did you get back? I've been waiting at the dock and haven't seen Johnny's boat come back.'

I bit my lip, unsure what to say. To tell him? Not to tell him?

He studied me as if really seeing me. 'What the hell happened to you? You look all torn up.' He crouched down next to me.

The gentleness in his voice made me want to nestle into his arms and sob, but I shrank away. I knew I couldn't trust him. My head was so fuzzy that I couldn't think what to tell him so he'd leave me alone. I wanted to ask him how he knew Didier and Louis, and crazy Jaggo. But if he knew I'd been around them, how would he respond?

He put his hand on my leg. 'How did your legs get all scratched up?'

I flinched. 'I . . . we . . . I had to walk on the island. There was some scrub brush.' I was so thirsty I could barely speak.

'What do you mean, you had to walk? Why did you go ashore?'

I struggled to my feet, pushing off the chaise with my hands. 'I have to go to my room now. We can talk later.'

Nick stood up, still staring at me, his dark eyes puzzled. 'What? No, your roommate checked out of your room.'

'Checked out? You mean she just left without me?' How could Shelley do that?

'I'm sorry. It's my fault. She wasn't sure what to do. The last ferry was leaving. She waited for you so long that she barely made it. I told her that if you got back and missed the ferry, you could get a ride back with Johnny. He was headed for Nassau.'

My mind blanked. No room? 'What did she do with my things? My clothes?' My wallet. My ID. Money.

'I think she took them with her. She was pretty frantic. Maybe she made the wrong decision. Or it's possible she left them with the front desk.'

'I'll find out.' I started to walk away, but teetered on my feet, my head reeling.

Nick grabbed me. 'Jessie, you're not OK. Tell me what happened.'

'I'm fine,' I said. 'I need some water.' My voice sounded far away and Nick's face was shimmering.

Someone was shaking me. I was in a soft bed that cushioned me and I felt warm and safe. But the person shaking me wouldn't leave me alone. 'Jessie, wake up. Talk to me. Where is Johnny?'

I fought my way back to consciousness and found that I wasn't in a nice comfortable bed at all, but still lying on the chaise with a beach towel covering me. Nick Garnier and two other men loomed over me. I tensed, disoriented. Who were these men? What were they planning to do with me? Then I realized that they weren't the men who had boarded the boat. I struggled to sit up.

Nick put a hand on my shoulder and gently pushed me back down. He took my hand and crouched down next to me. 'Take it easy. You're OK.' His voice was reassuring, soothing, but his dark eyes were unreadable. I wanted to trust him, but how could I when the men who had tried to kill Johnny and me had mentioned his name again and again? I reluctantly pulled my hand away from him and appealed to the men standing next to Nick. 'I need something to drink.' My voice didn't sound like my own. 'Juice. Water. Anything.'

One of them, dressed in a short-sleeved bellman's uniform with shiny gold buttons, handed me a bottle of water. I took a big gulp, and the minute it hit my stomach, I felt nauseous. I closed my eyes and gritted my teeth to keep from retching.

Nick pulled my chaise upright. 'Get her some juice,' he snapped to the bellman.

The bellman hurried away. The other man was hovering, wringing his hands. I remembered him. He was the resort manager – Alan something. As long as he was here, Nick couldn't do anything to me.

'Jessie,' Nick said, his voice pleading, 'please tell me what happened.'

An older couple walking by on the beach turned at the urgent sound of his voice. I started to call out to them, but the way they were looking at me, I knew I must look as if I'd been in a catfight. The man put his arm around the woman and steered her away.

Nick saw them and lowered his voice. 'Did Johnny do this to you?'

'Of course not!' How could he even suggest that? His questions brought back everything. The memory set me shivering. I didn't want to tell him what had happened, though.

Nick made an impatient sound and stood up. He pulled the manager aside and the two men conferred. I heard the manager say, 'Too much to drink.'

'I don't think so,' Nick said. His voice was stern. He said something I couldn't hear. The manager nodded and then leaned over to talk to me. 'Miss Madison, I'm sorry you've had a fright. I'll be making a room available to you. Ah, here we are.' He straightened as the bellman appeared with a glass of pink juice. I practically snatched it from him. The fruit punch tasted heavenly, but again it hit my stomach hard. My head ached. I was craving sleep.

I longed to go to the room the manager had offered, but I wasn't sure I was ready to walk. And besides, I didn't want Nick to know what room I was in. I appealed to the manager. 'Can you tell me if my roommate left my things here?'

'I'll go check on that,' the manager said. He hurried away before I could beg him not to leave me alone with Nick.

I took another drink of the juice, not looking at Nick. I didn't want him to know how vulnerable I felt. Even now, those men could be here, on the dock. I looked down the beach in the direction of the docks. There were only a few boats left there. Then I recalled that Nick had said he hadn't seen *Island Ice* return. So maybe they weren't here. But they could come at any time. And they could be on the other boat they'd been on when they commandeered *Island Ice*.

'I wish you would talk to me,' Nick said.

'I'm tired,' I said. 'We can talk in the morning.' By that time, maybe I'd have figured out a way to get out of here without him knowing where I was going.

'I just need to know if Johnny is in trouble. If he needs help.'

I wanted to tell him that Johnny was beyond help. In any other circumstance, I would have been soothed by the concern in his voice, but I kept thinking of the men saying his name. 'Who are you really?' I asked. 'How are you connected to Johnny?'

He hesitated so long that I knew I was right to be suspicious. 'We work together,' he said.

'Doing what?' I found the strength to sit up.

He ran a hand across his forehead, his mouth tight. 'Let's leave that for now. I need to know if Johnny is OK.'

I didn't trust this man. What would he do if he found out Johnny was dead? For a wild moment, I even wondered if he'd been telling the truth when he said Shelley had gone back to the mainland. I squeezed my eyes shut. This was paranoia brought on by exhaustion. Why would he lie about where Shelley had gone? And what could he do to me if he found out Johnny was dead? There were people nearby. He couldn't hurt me. And why would he want to? The men who had killed Johnny had mentioned Nick's name, but all that had nothing to do with me. I was tired of his questions. If I told him what happened, maybe he'd leave me alone.

I took the plunge. 'No, he isn't OK. He's dead.'

'What?' He jerked away, as if I'd slapped him. 'Are you sure? What happened?'

'Of course I'm sure. Some men killed him.'

'What men?'

'Friends of yours.'

He ran his hand across the top of his head. He looked stunned. 'What friends?'

'Johnny and I sailed to a nearby cove. In the night, three men boarded the boat. They were looking for something that Johnny had. And they killed him.'

Nick's face was like stone. He searched my face, frowning. 'Did they get it?'

'That's what you're worried about? If they got whatever you two are smuggling? You're not upset that your friend is dead?'

'Smuggling?' He shook his head. 'No. We weren't smuggling. How did Johnny get killed?'

'Before I answer, I want to know who those guys were.'

He glared at me. 'How am I supposed to know?'

'They kept saying your name. I figured you knew them.'

He was still for a moment, then ran his thumb along the scar on his cheek.

I had an unaccountable urge to touch the scar.

'Did you get their names?'

'I'll never forget them. Didier, Louis and Jaggo.' Saying Jaggo's name sent a spasm of revulsion through me. 'You know who they are, don't you? How do I know you didn't send them to kill us?'

He grimaced, as if I'd hurt him. 'I didn't, OK? How did they kill Johnny?'

My energy was coming back, and with it a fresh wave of anger. 'They tried to kill both of us. They bound us with rope and the anchor chain and threw us overboard.' My voice wobbled and I bit my lip.

I saw skepticism in his eyes. 'How did you manage to get away? And why didn't Johnny get away?'

I gritted my teeth. 'I escaped because I could hold my breath long enough to get out of trouble. Johnny couldn't. He drowned.' I wanted to scream that he'd drowned while he was right next to me. I had felt him drowning, and there'd been nothing I could do to save him.

'That's quite a story.' He doubted me, but I could see from his point of view how crazy it sounded. 'How did you get back here?'

If he had thought the first part was unbelievable, the story of my journey back here would be over the top. I leaned toward him, practically spitting the words. 'If you go to the other end of the island, you'll see how. I found a broken surfboard and paddled it across the cut between the islands.' The full force of how much I had demanded of myself and how lucky I had been to come through the ordeal hit me full force. I clutched the sides of the chaise so Nick wouldn't see my hands shaking.

'Amazing.' He whispered the word, almost to himself. He shook his head, looking past me. 'You're absolutely certain Johnny was dead?'

I saw the manager coming toward us. 'Fuck you,' I said. 'Of course I'm sure.' I eased my legs off the chaise.

Nick looked up and saw the manager and he stood up. 'Mr Christy, did you find Miss Madison's personal effects?'

Alan Christy shook his head. 'Miss Madison, I'm sorry, but your friend didn't leave your belongings.'

I forced myself to stand up. 'Well, I guess I'll have to make do.'

'Oh, no, no,' Christy said. 'I've arranged for the gift shop to extend you credit so you can buy some essentials. I'm afraid it isn't well stocked, but . . .' He looked at the shirt I was wearing – Johnny's shirt – and grimaced.

'Thank you. Is the shop open now?' I had no idea what time it was.

'No, but it opens at nine in the morning. I've arranged for toiletries to be brought to your room.' He handed me a key card. 'I hope you feel better in the morning.'

'Mr Christy, do you mind showing me to my room?'

He looked startled and glanced at Nick. 'Of course.'

'Can I ask you one more thing?' Nick said. He looked at Christy. 'Privately?'

Alan Christy stepped away, and Nick said, 'Look, I just want to know where Johnny's body is.'

I thought of the cold, gray body I'd pulled into the shade. I put my hand across my mouth to keep from wailing. Taking a deep breath, I told Nick where I'd left Johnny. 'He shouldn't be left there,' I whispered. 'Can you go and get him?'

'Don't worry, I'll take care of it,' Nick said. 'First, let's get you to your room.'

'No. I don't want you to come.'

His eyes narrowed. He looked stricken. Then he gave a tired smile. 'You don't trust me. I get it.' He started to walk away and then turned back. 'We'll talk in the morning,' he said.

I had never been so happy to get into a hotel room. All I could think of was showering and sleeping. I tried not to be mad at Shelley for leaving with all my belongings. How could she have not known that if I'd been able to, I would have called her? But I knew Shelley well enough to realize that she'd done the best she could. She wasn't gifted with common sense. Nick had said he was to blame for her decision. I'd have to be very careful with him tomorrow morning.

Before I got into the shower, I sneaked a look in the mirror and couldn't help groaning. My face was sunburned, my lips blistered, and my arms and legs were covered with scratches. It was going to be a while before I felt like myself again.

The hot water in the shower stung, but at least it calmed my shivering. When I emerged from the bathroom, wrapped in the luxurious robe the resort provided, I sat down on the balcony and stared out over the water. The lights of the resort were cheerful, but the water beyond was dark. Where was *Island Ice*? Was Nick lying about it not being here? Was he lying about everything?

NINE

Paco opened the door to Rodney's bedroom. Rodney was sprawled out naked on the bed. 'Rodney. Get up, man. It's morning. We've fooled around long enough. Time for us to take care of business.'

Rodney's eyes sprang open, and he sat up, swinging his legs off the bed. Stretching, he whooshed his breath out and shook himself like a dog. The woman beside him didn't stir.

Paco had seen Rodney do this before: be awake instantly. He admired that. He himself had been lying awake for thirty minutes. It took him time to get his thoughts in order and to be ready to face the world. All things considered, he was surprised he didn't have a worse hangover. Saturday night they'd stayed at the outdoor café until the waitress, whose name was Callie or Cara, or something like that, got off work. Then she took them to a party.

In Newport News, he was used to parties being edgy affairs – heavy on drugs and drinking, and punctuated with hostile confrontations. This party was mellow. Plenty of weed and coke, and everybody easy-going. There were no fights, nobody challenging each other. And such girls! In the early morning, they'd gone home with Callie and her roommate Marla and had spent all day yesterday with them.

After sleeping in yesterday morning, the girls had wanted to go to the beach, but Paco told them he didn't like the sand because it got into his clothes and made him itchy. Instead, they hung out at the dinky pool, drinking rum, lying in the sun, going back to the room for the occasional hit of something. In the afternoon, the girls took them to a tourist store where they bought the island shirts they'd been wanting. Last night had been a repeat of the night before.

He walked back into the bedroom and took one last, regretful, look at the girl he'd ended up with, Marla. Skin the color of seared butter, and it tasted just as good. He was tempted to stay here a few more days. But they'd had their fun. He went and rapped on Rodney's door again.

Rodney stuck his head out of the bedroom and told Paco to give him a few more minutes. Soon Paco heard Rodney and Callie going at it. Her moans got Paco heated up, and he was tempted to go back to the bedroom and wake up Marla. But he'd lost the mood. His brother's ghost was nagging at him. It was time to get down to business. Time to find the bitch who had killed his brother.

He walked into the kitchen, rinsed out a glass and drank some water. The place was a pigsty. He thought his place was a mess!

A half-hour later, he and Rodney were sitting in a café, drinking coffee. Rodney also ordered a cinnamon roll, but Paco didn't like to eat first thing in the morning.

After coffee, they asked the waitress where the dive boats mostly docked. She didn't know, but one of her co-workers said the dive outfits were at four marinas, in different parts of the island.

'Look, bro,' Rodney said. 'I don't know why you're in such a hurry. Let's hang out a few more days. She's not going anywhere.'

They argued, but eventually Rodney wore him down. 'One more day,' he said. 'That's it. Then we get down to business.'

TEN

When I woke up, every muscle ached and my skin was on fire from scratches and sunburn. I saw by Johnny's watch that it was almost ten o'clock, an unheard-of time for me to wake up. I was always an early riser. I lay in bed not wanting to move. I still couldn't quite believe I was alive, much less lying in a luxurious bed. But I was starving. I had been too tired to order food last night.

I called room service and ordered eggs and pancakes. While I waited for the food, I called Jeremy, my boss, to tell him I was sorry I hadn't called to let him know I wouldn't be in today. Of course, he didn't answer his phone. He'd be out on a dive. I left him a message telling him I'd missed the ferry and I'd be back at work as soon as I could. A thought tweaked the back of my mind. When and how was I going to get back? I'd have to address that problem after breakfast.

When the waiter brought the food, I was embarrassed that I had no money for a tip. I signed a generous tip to the room service charge, but doubted if the poor waiter would ever see the money.

It was odd to realize that I had no credit card, no cash, no way to pay for anything. The hotel manager had been generous, so I'd be able to eat and I could pick up a T-shirt and some shorts at the gift shop. But how generous would they be? A week's worth of lodging and food costs a lot. I imagined the manager telling me I'd be washing dishes or waiting tables all week to pay for this bounty. One more reason to find a way off the island.

But there was a more compelling reason that I needed to leave. While I ate, out on the balcony, I remembered the promise I had made to Johnny, and to myself, that I would find the men who had killed him and make them pay. Big words. How was I going to follow through?

Johnny had said he was on his way to Nassau to meet with the owners of *Island Ice*. Would Didier and his men go to Nassau? Even if they did, how would I find them there? I knew so little about the situation. As reluctant as I was to have any more to do with Nick, he was my best chance of finding the men who had killed Johnny.

As soon as I was finished eating, I headed for the gift shop, wearing the same thing I'd been wearing for two days. I was itching to buy something to wear besides my bathing suit and Johnny's shirt.

I didn't remember seeing the gift shop over the weekend, and when I went downstairs to look for it, I discovered why. It was a tiny hole in the wall, not really ready to be open to tourists. In answer to my question, the clerk pointed to a pile of T-shirts and shorts: all hot pink, with the Trophy Cay logo on them – a flamingo and a palm tree, both sequined, along with the resort name. Hot pink. Not exactly my color.

'This is all you've got?' I asked.

'We're not really open yet,' the girl said.

Hot pink it was. They did have a few bathing suits, though, so I added a plain black bikini, too. Feeling only slightly guilty for taking advantage of the manager's generosity, I bought sunscreen, sunglasses and a pair of flip-flops.

I went upstairs to change. I realized that I was still not fully recovered, and before I dressed, I gave in to my longing to soak in the steeping tub. There was even bubble bath. I couldn't entirely relax, though. Every time I started to let go, I found myself feeling the horror of being underwater in chains, struggling. And

Johnny's body resisting, resisting and then going limp. I kept pushing it out of my mind, but I knew it would be a while before I was over it.

Even after the soothing soak, I still felt uneasy and traumatized, but at least I could feel my physical strength returning.

It was time to confront Nick. In search of him, I walked through the lobby, out toward the pool. There were hardly any people in the pool area, because most of the guests had gone back on last night's ferry. I didn't see Nick, so I walked out on the beach. Still no sign of him. I didn't want to go to the dock. Suppose *Island Ice* had come back last night? If it had, and he was with Didier and his crew, finding him most certainly wouldn't be in my best interest.

I went to the front desk and I asked the pouty-lipped desk clerk to connect me with Nick's room.

'He checked out.'

'What?' Dammit. Maybe they'd been exaggerating when they said there were no more ferries. 'Was there an early ferry?'

She looked puzzled. 'No, of course not.'

In that case, there was only one explanation that made sense. Didier's gang had showed up and he went with them.

I started to walk away, wondering what to do next, but then I turned back.

'Is it possible that Mr Garnier left a message for me?'

The desk clerk gave me an eye-roll. 'I'll see.' She turned to the pigeonholes behind her. 'Oh. Are you Jessie Madison?' She handed me an envelope.

I tore it open. The note read: *Jessie, I had to leave early this morning and did not want to disturb you. I hope you are recovered. Don't worry. All is well. Nick.*

I read it again to see if I had missed something in the glib language. 'Don't worry? All is well?' Why hadn't he mentioned Johnny? Had he gone back to the island and retrieved Johnny's body as he said he would?

'If there was no ferry this morning, how could Mr Garnier have gotten off the island?'

'I'm afraid I can't help you with that. Maybe he knew someone with a private yacht. Now, if you'll excuse me.' She pointed to a man waiting behind me. She signaled for the man to step up.

I had no intention of being brushed aside. 'I need to get back to Nassau. How can I do that?'

The man who had stepped up to the counter glared at me as if it was his God-given right to move me out of the way. The clerk raised her eyebrows at him in a 'what-can-I-do?' expression. 'Let me call Mr Christy. He's the manager.'

A few minutes later, the manager walked up. He blinked when he saw me, as if he hadn't thought I'd survive the night.

'Good morning. I hope you had a good night's sleep. What can I do for you?'

'Mr Christy, I need to know what's going on here. How did Nick Garnier get off the island this morning?'

With a clammy hand on my arm, he steered me to the ornate fountain in the middle of the lobby. 'I'm glad to see you've recovered from your, um, ordeal. Mr Garnier wanted to be sure you were taken care of. Is there anything we can do to make your stay more comfortable?'

'Yes, you can answer my question. How did Mr Garnier get off the island if there were no more ferries?'

'I'm, uh, not quite sure. I think he arranged for someone to pick him up.'

Someone? Didier? 'Do you know who it was?'

His smile was strained. 'I'm sorry, I have no idea. I don't really know Mr Garnier. I just met him last night when he was, uh, helping you.'

'Well, I need to get back to Nassau. How can I arrange for transportation?'

His smile was getting strained. 'I don't have any idea. I suppose you could use our business office and look up the water taxis. It will be expensive.'

He was right. And no doubt they'd expect payment in advance. My frustration notched up. 'This is ridiculous. I've got a job to get back to. Surely you have some way for people to get back. What if one of your guests or an employee gets sick?

'We'd have to hire a helicopter. A very expensive proposition. Look, I'm sorry you can't get back to your job, but we made it quite clear in our invitation to the opening that there was only ferry service on weekends.' He stepped closer and lowered his voice. 'I know this must be difficult for you after all you've been through.' His tone was silky. 'Think of it as an enforced vacation. Let me buy you lunch, and afterwards I can give you a behind-the-scenes tour of the resort.'

I thought of a sharp retort, but it wasn't really his fault. I thanked him and told him I'd take a raincheck.

I headed for the marina. There had to be some way to hire a boat to get back to Nassau. I was nervous that the crew that boarded *Island Ice* might have brought her back to Trophy Cay, and I approached the dock gingerly, but there were only a few boats, and it wasn't among them.

The harbormaster, a lean, gray-haired man of fifty, was in his closet of an office, trying to tack up a map of the surrounding cays. When I walked in, he said, 'Good timing. Can you give me some help putting up this map? Tell me if I have it straight.' I directed the operation, which only took a minute.

When he went into a back room to put his supplies away, I studied the map. The island I had escaped from was called Minor Cay. On the map, I saw that it was a pitifully short distance away. It hadn't seemed that short yesterday.

The harbormaster came back out. His nametag read, 'Thad Carson.'

'Thanks for the help. The damn kid who's supposed to help me today never showed up.' He pulled out a handkerchief and wiped his hands.

'Where could he be?' I asked. 'There don't seem to be too many places he could go around here.' Maybe he had found a way to get away from Trophy Cay.

'God knows. He probably partied too much last night and found some guest to keep him company,' Thad said. 'He seemed to attract the ladies. Anyway, what can I do for you?'

'I need to get back to Nassau. Do you have a boat I can hire?'

'Miss, even if I did, it would be really expensive.'

'I'm sure it would be,' I said. 'Look, I have a friend who left this morning. How could he have gotten off the island?'

He shook his head. 'I have no idea. Maybe he had a friend with a boat here.'

Again, I wondered if Nick had even bothered to retrieve Johnny's body. There ought to at least be a dinghy I could hire to take me there to make sure.

I pointed to a row of dinghies with the resort logo, lined up at the near side of the dock. 'Is it possible for me to rent one of those to go over to Minor Cay?'

Thad put his hands on his hips. 'You really are determined, aren't you? Doesn't matter. You can't hire one.'

'Why not?'

'Maybe if you looked closer, you'd see why not.' He seemed amused.

I zeroed in. 'Oh.' None of them had engines. 'Where are the engines?'

'They were supposed to arrive last week, but they didn't.' He shrugged. 'You know how it is in the islands. They'll get here when they get here.'

I sighed. He was right.

'How did you happen to miss the ferry?' Thad asked.

'I ran into some trouble.'

He looked me up and down, wincing when he noticed the scratches and bruises on my legs and arms. 'Sorry to hear it.'

I wondered what fantasy he had about what had happened to leave me with my injuries.

Another idea came to me. 'Do any small planes fly in here?'

'Oh, yes. Or at least, they will eventually. The airstrip is being built.' Which meant, the way things worked in the islands, it was in the planning stages.

'So, I'm really stuck here.'

Thad raised his bushy eyebrows. 'A lot of people would be happy to be in your position. Beautiful beaches, a five-star resort, delicious food. Think of it as an unexpected vacation.'

That seemed to be the party line. And he was right. Most people would be thrilled to be stuck here. But most people didn't have revenge on their minds.

I thanked him and left the office. Now what? I could call my boss, Jeremy, and ask if he would come and pick me up, but he had a business to run, and it was a four-hour trip. He wasn't going to drop everything and come to my rescue. Besides, after I hadn't shown up this morning, he probably considered me fired. I huffed with aggravation. I guess it wouldn't hurt to call and ask him. Maybe he'd have a tourist party that would be interested in coming to Trophy Cay. But first, I had another idea.

There were five boats left at the marina, all catamarans. It was possible somebody would be leaving for Nassau and I could hitch a ride. Of the four boats, I found only one of them occupied. A middle-aged woman came up to the deck from down below when I called out. A hefty woman, she had on a muumuu and was carrying a drink. By her bright eyes, I could see that this wasn't her first drink of the day.

'Nassau? Oh, honey, the only reason we'd go back there is to get provisions, and we're all stocked up. No, we're headed down to Staniel Cay for a few days. Sorry I can't help.'

Something else occurred to me. 'Can I ask you a question?'

'Sure.'

'Did you happen to see a catamaran called *Island Ice* around here last night?'

She gave a throaty laugh. 'Honey, my husband and I shut down the bar last night, and I'm afraid when I got back here, I was in no shape to notice anything.'

'Thanks anyway.'

She pointed to a smaller catamaran down the dock. 'The people on that cat might know. They seem like the kind to keep an eye on things.'

I wasn't able to raise anyone on the boat she had indicated, so I went back to Thad's office and asked for some paper that I could use to write them a note. I left a note on all four of the other boats, asking them to contact me, in case they were going back to Nassau. I said they could find me in the pool area.

Which is where I went next. I was hungry. I ordered a mai tai and a shrimp salad, and waited for someone from one of the boats to come looking for me.

Meanwhile, I fumed. Working on a dive boat, I had come to despise people who seemed entitled. Every now and then, we took out somebody on a dive who didn't find it to their liking and wanted to be taken back – *now!* Told it was impossible, the complainer would mutter dark comments and look daggers at the dive staff. Sometimes they would up the ante, claiming to be too sick to stay on board. They would threaten and bluff, and generally make life unbearable for everyone.

Now, for the first time, I had sympathy for complainers. Regardless of how wonderful the resort was, I was stuck here. I suspected the remaining, happy resort guests would have no sympathy if they knew how desperately I wanted to get the hell off this island.

The mai tai went down easily, and after stuffing myself with the sumptuous salad, I was desperate for a nap. As much as I wanted out of here, an afternoon of lying on a chaise, dozing, was like a siren song. I went into the gift shop and, courtesy of Mr Christy, bought a big hat and a romance novel, and found a chaise. I read for ten minutes before I fell into a deep sleep.

ELEVEN

I awoke with a start, wondering what had jolted me awake. Then I heard it again. The laugh sounded exactly like Jaggo's. I told myself to calm down, that he couldn't be the only person with a maniacal laugh.

But, of course, there was every possibility that my abductors had returned.

I eased off the chaise, and pulling my hat down to obscure my face, I walked out of the sun and into the interior of the bar room where the sound had come from. I sneaked a look at the bar.

For a few seconds, I was sure my heart stopped. Jaggo and Louis were hanging over the bar, chatting to the female bartender. I couldn't hear what they were saying, but by the pained smile on her face, I could tell they were giving her a hard time.

Where was Didier? I felt my neck prickle. He could be here anywhere. I glanced around but didn't see him. *Island Ice* must have docked while I was napping. Where had the boat been until now? And why had they come back here? It occurred to me that they might have heard I had escaped and come here to find me. Had Nick told them?

I fled the bar and went out into the lobby, keeping an eye out for Didier. My breath was ragged. What should I do now? I had wanted to find them, but I intended to do it with the weight of the Nassau police behind me. Here, I was on my own. I glanced at Johnny's watch, mentally thanking him again for providing it to me. It was after four o'clock. I'd slept for three hours.

I couldn't stand being out here, vulnerable to them seeing me, especially since I didn't know where Didier was. Terrified that I might run into him, I headed for my room, taking the stairs instead of the elevator. On the fourth floor, I peeked out into the corridor to make sure no one was there before I started down the hall to the room. But when I got to the door, I stopped cold. Maybe I was thinking about this all wrong. What if Nick had told them I was here? They knew I could identify them, so they might have come to finish off what they started. What if Didier was inside the room waiting for me?

I saw a housekeeping cart down at the other end of the hallway. The housekeeper was vacuuming a room.

'Yes, madam?' she asked, turning off the vacuum cleaner. She was a tall, dark-skinned woman with a Bahamian accent.

I asked her to do me a favor. 'I think there is someone in my room. Would you knock on the door and peek in?'

She looked puzzled. 'Why would someone be in your room?'

It was frustrating not having any cash. If I had been able to offer her a few bucks, she wouldn't have questioned my request. 'I thought I saw someone go in. I'm nervous.'

She shrugged and followed me down the hallway. She knocked briskly. There was no reply. I handed her my key and she opened the door. 'Hello? Housekeeping. Is anyone here?'

No reply.

I thanked her profusely, but she gave me a tight smile as she walked away, probably thinking how demanding I was.

Inside, I double-locked the door and collapsed on the bed, weak with relief. When I recovered enough to breathe, I jumped up and began to pace.

The men might be here for another reason entirely. Maybe they were meeting a drug connection here. Maybe they just wanted to spend the night at a fancy resort. And they might not recognize me even if they saw me. It had been dark when they boarded the boat, and they had been more interested in Johnny and what they were looking for than they were in me. But I couldn't take the chance. I couldn't ignore the possibility that Nick had sent them here to find me.

I had to leave the room and not come back. But until they left the island I was at great risk. What could I do in the meantime?

It wouldn't take much of a disguise to avoid them, but I had nothing to disguise myself with. And then I thought of a way. Poor Mr Christy probably hadn't intended his hospitality to extend to the hair salon, but that's where I headed. I remembered having seen a sign for it, on the other side of the lobby from the bar.

Two hours later, I walked out of the salon as a blond with spiky hair.

Before, my hair had been dark and shoulder-length. Now if my attackers saw me, at a glance they weren't likely to recognize me – unless they were actually looking for me.

I decided to go back to the dock to see if any of the other guests had returned to their boats. Sure enough, *Island Ice* was tied up at the far end. And as I walked toward it, Didier stepped off onto the dock.

I whirled around and headed for the harbormaster's office. It wouldn't be open at this hour, but it was the only structure where I might hide. As I approached it, shivers ran up my spine. I expected at any moment to hear Didier call out, 'Hey, what are you doing here? How did you get away?' I reminded myself that he wouldn't recognize me with spiky blond hair, but fear over-whelmed rational thought. These guys had tried to kill me. And they had succeeded in killing Johnny.

I scooted around the side of the building, where there was barely a foot of space between the building and the edge of the dock. I plastered myself up against the building, listening as Didier's footsteps neared and then passed by. I waited a lot longer than was necessary, nerves fizzing through me. Finally, I risked a peek out. No one was around.

Between the time I'd gone into the hair salon and now, the sun had dipped lower. It was twilight. I heard music start up at the bar. And once again I heard Jaggo's crazy laugh, drifting into the evening air. They were still there, at the bar. I wondered if Didier was with them.

Just then I saw a familiar figure coming toward the dock. The manager. He was walking gingerly, as if he'd been drinking. He'd taken his coat off. He stopped when he saw me. 'Well, look at you with your new hair! Quite a change!' He exuded a cloud of alcohol.

'Yeah, well, I felt like I deserved a treat after what happened.' Was he going to admire it quite so much when he found out he was paying for it?

'What are you doing out here?'

'I could ask you the same thing,' I asked to deflect him.

'A manager's work is never done. I'm checking things out before I call it a day. Making sure the office is locked up.' He walked over and tried the harbormaster's door, which was locked. He flicked his wrist and looked at his watch. 'You have time for a drink?'

'Not right now, but thank you.'

He stepped closer. 'I talked to Thad and he said you were upset that you're stuck here. My wife is here and maybe we could make your stay more pleasant. Take you out to dinner?'

'That's so kind of you. I'd love to meet your wife.' It was the last thing I wanted, to make small talk with Christy and his wife. 'I'm pretty tired tonight. Maybe tomorrow.' I wondered if I should tell him that the men who had abducted me and killed Johnny were in the bar. But no. What could he do, even if he wasn't drunk?

Christy peered down the dock. 'You sure you want to be out here in the dark by yourself?'

I almost laughed. After all I had been through, I was supposed to be afraid of an evening stroll? 'Are you suggesting it isn't safe on the docks?'

'Absolutely not. It's totally safe.' He straightened his tie. 'Tomorrow, then.' He pointed his finger at me. 'I'll hold you to it.' He turned around and went back the way he had come. As I watched him, he was swallowed up in the dusk.

I was alone on the dock. The six boats tied up were dark. Probably the owners had gone for dinner. It was quiet. And deserted. Just like that, I knew what I had to do. And if I was going to do it, I couldn't hesitate. I had to make a move now. I was going to steal *Island Ice*.

I had to work fast. If the three men came back before I got away, they'd kill me.

Heart in my throat, I ran down to the end of the dock where

Island Ice was tied up. Not giving myself time to reconsider, I stepped aboard and down into the rear cockpit. The door to the saloon was slightly ajar. Were these guys not worried that someone would steal their boat? Or was someone aboard? Nick, for example.

'Hello?' I said tentatively, ready to run if anyone replied. But it was quiet.

I ran down and inspected the cabins on both sides of the boat, peeking into them to make sure someone wasn't asleep in one of them. But it was deserted. The three guys had trashed the boat. God, what pigs! When I passed the navigation station, I opened it – there was the gun Johnny had told me he had stashed there. It was a serviceable Sig Sauer pistol. I checked to make sure it was loaded and left a round in the chamber in case I needed to get a shot off fast. At least I could defend myself if they came back before I could cast off. I tucked it into the back of my shorts.

Now to get the boat moving. I was glad I'd had a chance to watch Johnny two nights ago when he drove the boat away from the dock. Since it was tied up at the end, at least I didn't have to dodge other boats when I cast off, before I could get out into the open water.

I ran up to the bridge. My courage almost failed. From this vantage point, the boat seemed huge. I frequently drove a dive boat and had taken the wheel of sailboats a few times, but I had never sailed a boat this size on my own. But I wouldn't be putting up the sails, and the principle of driving it was the same.

I fumbled around where I'd seen Johnny start the motor. Hardly anyone ever removed boat keys, and sure enough, the key was in the ignition. I was confused for a moment. There were two starters. Of course. Two engines. Duh. I made sure the controls were in neutral and started her up. The growl of the engines seemed loud. I hoped the noisy music in the bar would drown out the sound of the boat.

I scrambled below to the deck and cast the lines off the cleats, glancing down the dock to make sure no one had appeared. Then I raced back up to the bridge. Without lines to hold it, the boat immediately drifted away from the dock. I pushed the controls forward, testing them, and gradually the boat responded. I was underway.

TWELVE

It took ten minutes for the stupidity of what I had done to hit me. Before that, I was too eager to get out of sight of Trophy Cay to think of anything but maneuvering the boat. It was big, with powerful engines, and when I pushed the throttles forward, it responded a lot faster than I thought a boat that size would go. I didn't feel like I had full control of it, so I eased the throttles back as much as I dared. The important thing was to put distance between me and Didier's men. I kept glancing back, sure I was going to see them come roaring after me in a dinghy.

After several minutes, the lights of the resort faded, though, and I came face to face with what I'd done. I'd stolen a boat. Even though I felt as though I'd had no choice, the Bahamian Coast Guard probably wouldn't see it that way. I didn't think Didier was likely to call them, but I couldn't be sure. If they did, I'd rather take my chances with the Coast Guard than Didier.

But now that I had committed to grand theft, I had a further problem: I had no charts. They were essential to moving around the shallow Bahamian waters. In some places, the water was no more than marshland. I thought about what I'd learned on our dive trips. The dive boats I worked on usually only went out to islands close to Nassau, but I had been on longer trips to the Exuma Land and Sea Park. I remembered that there were two large areas of marshland near Nassau. One was southwest and shouldn't concern me. The other was directly east. Trophy Cay was southeast, so if I headed northwest of Trophy Cay, I should avoid the shallows.

That didn't mean I was safe from rocky areas and reefs, though. In daylight, you could see the change in color that indicated shallow water, or rocks, and steer to avoid them. But in the dark, with me sitting up high on the flying bridge, all the water looked dark and deep.

In front of me were two computer screens, one of which

probably had an electronic chart plotter, but I didn't know how to turn them on or get the charts I needed. There were probably backup paper charts stowed below, but I hated to leave the wheel to go looking for them.

I began to flip switches on the panel, hoping to figure out how to pull up the charts. The screen lights came on and showed the compass and the depth finder. I had a reasonably good sense of direction and the compass confirmed that I was heading northeast, in the direction of Nassau. The depth finder said I was in three meters of water, which I assumed meant below the keel. I'd have to keep an eye on this screen. It would at least give me warning if I hit shallow waters.

For the next hour, I went as fast as I could, alternating between staring at the dark horizon ahead of me and glancing anxiously at the depth finder. I had to get as much distance as possible between me and the men who had tried to kill me. I wondered where the boat was that they had been on when they boarded *Island Ice*. If it was close by, they could have it pick them up and come after me. It was a smaller boat, a power boat, and would be faster than this catamaran. For all I knew, Nick was on it. I shivered. I usually didn't have so much trouble reading people, but he had me stumped. I didn't know if he was part of Didier's gang, or if he and Johnny had some other scheme going on.

Which brought me back to Johnny. When I got back, I wanted to locate his family. If I could find the owners of *Island Ice*, they'd be able to tell me how to contact his family. Maybe Nick would notify them, but I couldn't count on it.

By nine o'clock, I began to feel less worried that I would be pursued. With my head start, it would be almost impossible for them to find me. The night was pitch back. The moon would rise soon, but I didn't think it was much more than a quarter full. It would be a minor miracle for them to spot one lone boat.

To lower the risk of hitting a reef or rocks in the dark, I now felt I could slow the boat down. I calculated that it would take at least eight hours to get to Nassau, twice the time a high-speed ferry took. I had stolen the boat sometime after seven, which would put me in Nassau harbor in the wee hours of the morning.

And then what? I'd have to wait until it was light to find the public dock. The idea of docking this giant boat gave me a hollow feeling in my gut.

At some point, I realized I hadn't checked whether there was enough gas in the tank to get me to Nassau, but a glance at the indicator told me that I had almost a half tank in each engine. I settled in for the long haul, which meant staying alert. I actually began to enjoy being on a boat, alone, with nothing more to do than watch the water and feel the caress of the breeze.

Even though it was a fine night, after a while the air over the water cooled, and around eleven, I got cold. I slowed the throttle and went down into the starboard cabin to search for a jacket. I found a fleece jacket in the closet of the main stateroom. I shrugged it on and headed back up top, stopping in the galley long enough to grab a bottle of water from the refrigerator. Four long hours to go.

I started considering how to minimize the trouble I would be in for commandeering the boat. As soon as I docked in Nassau, I would turn it over to the Bahamian Coast Guard, explaining why I'd taken it. They could reunite the boat with its owner. Maybe the owners would be grateful if they found out I'd stolen it back from pirates.

Even if they were grateful, the Coast Guard may not be so sanguine. Piracy was a serious matter. Would they send me to jail? At least I'd be safe there. But I doubted things would get that far because I had an ace in the hole. My employer Jeremy LaBreque was a sort of local hero. If anybody could get me out of trouble, it was him.

But after the Coast Guard let me go, then what? Should I go back to work as if nothing had ever happened? Walk away and forget the men who had tried to kill me? Try to find Nick? How would I go about that? As soon as I got back to my apartment, I'd Google him. It would be a start, anyway.

If I did decide to pursue the men who'd tried to kill me, I couldn't tackle it alone. I had gone out a few times with a Nassau cop, Kevin Riley. He was a seasoned police veteran who had moved here from New York, where he'd been a cop for several years. He'd know what to do.

Despite my three-hour nap in the afternoon, I was still tired from my ordeal. My head was throbbing, and a couple of times I nodded off. I needed to find a way to keep myself awake.

If only I had a cell phone, I could at least call someone. Suddenly, I remembered the backpack Johnny had brought aboard with him. Unless the men had taken it off the boat, it must still be here. Maybe there was a cell phone in it. I throttled the engine back until the boat was barely moving and returned to the cabin. I remembered Johnny had stowed the backpack into a closet. But it wasn't there. Didier or one of the others might have taken it with them, since it apparently contained something valuable.

Still, they might have stowed it somewhere. I quickly searched the rest of the big stateroom and then the two smaller ones, tough going, since the owners had filled every space. Clothing, magazines, caches of toiletries, extra linens, blankets, and non-perishable food. The places a backpack could be hidden were endless. I worried that I was taking too long, and ran back upstairs to check out the depth. I was in deeper water, so I had more time to look. I went back to the saloon and started checking the cabinets under the banquette. That's where I found the backpack, along with a package of granola bars. I tore one open.

Johnny's phone was in the front section of the backpack. It only had a fifty percent charge, but that was enough. I put it in the pocket of the jacket I was wearing. Curious to know if whatever the men had been after was still in the pack, I unzipped the main section. I pulled out a T-shirt and a pair of shorts. They gave me a pang. Poor Johnny.

Below the clothing was the package I'd seen sitting on the billiard table between Nick and Johnny when I had found them scowling at each other. I took it out. It felt like a box, and it was heavy. It was wrapped in brown paper, tied up with string, like something you'd mail. Except that there was no address on it; there were no markings at all.

If this was really what had gotten Johnny killed, I couldn't believe the guys had left this behind when they went for dinner on Trophy Cay. Of course, they thought it was safe since they thought Johnny and I were dead.

Should I open it now? I really wanted to know what was in it, what Johnny had died for, and what I'd almost died for. Just as I was fingering the string, the boat lurched.

I leaped up and raced up the steps to the bridge. Sure enough, the depth finder showed a reading of zero meters. My hands went cold. I could easily get stuck, or even put a hole in the hull and sink. I had to get into deeper water. But what direction was deeper? Was I going over a shallow reef? Or was it a big rock formation?

Heart hammering, I stopped the boat and peered out into the darkness. All I could see by the starlight was the water rippling, and it looked the same everywhere up ahead. I held my breath and gradually moved the throttle forward, waiting for another crunch. But whatever I had nudged, it seemed temporary. Gradually, the depth increased. After a few minutes at greater depth, I changed the course back to head for Nassau.

I had learned my lesson. No more fooling around downstairs. The package could wait.

But at least I had the phone. I ate another granola bar and considered whom to call. I couldn't call Jeremy. He'd be in bed, and he had young children. He and his wife wouldn't appreciate a late-night call. And again, what would I tell him?

Not Shelley. She'd still be at work at Feathers. Besides, what would I tell her? *Oh, I'm on my way back to Nassau in a stolen boat. Don't worry about me. And by the way, why the hell did you walk away with my stuff? Didn't it occur to you that I would have called you if I could have?* Thinking of Shelley at work, flirting, serving drinks, laughing, annoyed me. But then I thought, what could she have really done if she was concerned? Who could she have appealed to? Not the manager. He wouldn't have taken her seriously even if she did tell him she was worried. And, of course, there was Nick. Had he encouraged her to take my stuff, because he thought I wouldn't be back for it?

There was one person I could phone. Should phone. I hesitated. It was nearing midnight, and my mother would likely be passed out and wouldn't hear the phone. But sometimes she stayed up late, watching TV. I dialed her number, just to hear it ring, and was startled when she answered on the third ring.

'Mom? It's me.'

'Hello, Jessica.' Hearing her familiar, aggrieved tone of voice, I immediately regretted phoning her. 'Why are you calling so late?'

'I'm checking in to see how you're doing.' I forced false brightness into my voice.

A sniff. 'Why would you care how I'm doing?'

'Mom, please, don't stay mad.'

'Who says I'm mad?'

Drunk or sober, my mother was hard to deal with. Tonight, she sounded sober, which meant her tongue would be sharpened for battle. 'You were angry when I wouldn't tell you where Kayla was. I was hoping you'd gotten over it. I had to keep it secret, you know.'

A crackle on the line. 'I didn't hear you. You're breaking up. Where are you?'

'I said, you seemed angry when I wouldn't tell you where Kayla was. I don't want you to stay mad.'

'And *I* said, where are you?' Her voice hardened.

'I'm on a boat near Nassau.'

'How nice for you. Living the good life.'

I couldn't help laughing. 'Not exactly.'

'I suppose you want me to thank you for sending money.'

'That's not necessary. I just called to hear your voice.'

A pause. 'You wanted to see if I've been drinking.'

'Mom, no.'

'I know you think you're pretty smart, but you might be surprised.'

'Surprised about what?'

'Oh, some things.'

My heart sank. My mother played some nasty games, and who knew what she meant? Whatever it was, it couldn't be good. 'Mom, what do you mean?'

'The best-laid plans don't always go your way.' Her voice was sing-song.

I groaned inwardly. When my mother was drunk, she wallowed in self-pity; when she was sober, she spoke in innuendo. It made for hard going in conversation. 'Look, I don't want to fight. I want you to know if anything happens to me, that I love you.'

She snorted. 'Such a drama queen! What do you think is going to happen to you?'

That, coming from the queen of drama queens. 'I hope, nothing.'

Silence.

'Mom, I was thinking I might come back to the mainland before too long. If it's OK, I'd like to stay with you until I get a few things sorted out.'

'Any old port in a storm, is that it?'

I gritted my teeth to keep from saying something sharp in return. 'Look, Mom, if you don't want me there, say so. I can make other arrangements.'

'Do what you want. That's what you'll do anyway.'

I was always tired of the game long before she was. 'I have to go now. I'll be in touch. Bye, Mom.' I hung up before I said something I regretted.

The conversation with my mother had darkened my mood. I was tempted to go down to the saloon and mix myself a drink – a strong drink. If I was lucky, maybe I could find some scotch. I savored the thought, imagining the peaty, mellow flavor. But it was a fantasy. Alcohol would slow down my reflexes and make me sleepy. Better to stay irritated and anxious. I had a lot of hours to get through before I could turn the boat over to the authorities in Nassau, and I needed to stay alert.

Staring out at the dark water, I went back over the conversation, as I so often did, wondering how I could have steered it in a different direction. I still felt helpless against her moods. One comment had made me uneasy. What did she mean when she said the best-laid plans weren't going my way? One thing came to mind. Could she have found out where Kayla was in rehab? Surely not. *Oh, really? Was I that sure?* She had sounded awfully vindictive and pleased with herself.

She'd been angry when she found out I'd arranged once again for Kayla to go into rehab, but this time I wouldn't tell her where she was. She never admitted that she enabled my sister's drug problems. Every other time she was in rehab, Kayla had called home, crying, and our mother had rushed to retrieve her. No matter how much I pleaded with her to be tough with my younger sister, she insisted that 'this time' Kayla really would shape up on her own. I sometimes wondered if she wanted Kayla to fail so she could feel better about her own failures.

I had never told her exactly what happened the night I went to Kayla's rescue. I tried not to think about it. But now, with nothing more to occupy my thought, the memory crowded in.

If Kayla's plea for help had come two weeks later, I would have been through the induction ceremony and been a full-fledged FBI agent. I would have had a badge and a gun and the might of the FBI behind me. That night, I knew if I went to Kayla's rescue, if she had done what she said she did, her whole sordid story would likely come out and I'd be booted from the training program. The FBI didn't take kindly to recruits with serious family issues.

I had thought Kayla was doing OK, that her last rehab had set her straight. Then, my mother dropped the news that Kayla was living with Diego. I did a search on him and wasn't surprised to find that Diego Boland was a drug dealer with a criminal record and a coterie of loyal "associates," including two brothers who were also criminals. I kicked myself now. Why didn't I step in at that time and force Kayla to leave him, and go back to rehab? How could I have let the situation drag on? I knew why. Because I was afraid that if I disclosed it to my trainer, he would immediately pull the plug on my candidacy. I hoped to sneak in under the radar and deal with the situation once I was an FBI agent for real.

When Kayla called and told me she'd killed Diego, I remembered hoping that in her drug-addled state she'd made a mistake. But there was no mistake. I arrived to find Diego Boland sprawled on his back, a kitchen knife sticking out of his chest. It made me sick to remember all that blood.

I managed to haul Kayla out of the house, sure Diego's brothers would kill us if they came home and found us. But there was no way I could keep Kayla from being arrested for Diego's murder.

Now, plowing on through the night, reliving that nightmare, I could hardly bear to think of the next morning when I went to my trainer, John Farrell, and pled my case. But he said there was nothing he could do. He was furious with me and said it wasn't so much what Kayla had done that would get me booted, but that I'd failed to come to him for help when she got involved with Diego. I was out. His one concession was helping Kayla get into a good rehab program.

I also suspected that John had a hand in having Kayla's case dismissed by the DA in Newport News, declaring it was a case of self-defense.

I had come to the Bahamas to recover from my world being upended. And now, here I was on a stolen boat in the middle of the night, being pursued by people who wanted to kill me.

I remembered my first thought when Didier's men had boarded the boat – that the men were Diego Boland's brothers who had found me and were out for revenge. It wasn't out of the question. In my exit interview my FBI trainer had warned me that Paco would come after me if he found out where I was. In retrospect, I would have preferred to take my chances with Paco and his gang rather than Didier. Jaggo's laugh would never leave me.

Planning to return to the US, I had shied away from considering whether Paco was still a threat. Island life had lulled me into complacency. *Was* Paco still a threat? I hadn't talked to John Farrell since I got here. Maybe it would be a good idea to check in with him and ask him to find out what Paco was up to.

My thoughts had gone way too dark. I needed to stretch my legs. I was hungry and I was tired of granola bars, so after checking to make sure I was in deep water, I went below and rummaged around in the galley. I found cheese and salami in the refrigerator, and some crackers in the pantry, and took them back upstairs.

While I munched, I flipped on the VHS radio and turned to channel sixteen to monitor the radio traffic. At first, it was quiet, but a few minutes later, I jumped when a man's voice spoke loud and clear. 'Hey, babe, are you still with me? This is Matterhorn.' A woman replied that she was there, and they should switch to another channel. Hearing the voices, speaking normal, everyday things was comforting. For a while, I listened to random bursts of talk: people at anchor planning to come in or go out of Nassau the next day, people out on the Atlantic side moving in the deeper waters outside the shelf. It helped keep me awake. Eventually, the talk died down as people went to bed.

It was almost two o'clock when a quarter-moon showed up to the east, casting a silvery gleam on the water. It was a welcome change from the complete darkness.

Staying awake got harder. In the pre-dawn hours, my thoughts strayed to places in my mind that I usually tried to keep at bay to keep despair from creeping in. Consideration of how my life would have been different if my dad hadn't died, gunned down on his way home from work on the docks.

After he died, I barely had time to mourn. Somebody had to keep the family moving forward, and at the age of fourteen it fell to me. Getting my sister and myself to school, sending my hungover mother off to work in the morning, putting meals on the table, wrestling enough money from my mother's paycheck to pay the bills. Often, the only thing that kept me going was my determination that one day I was going to do what the cops had failed to do – find out who killed my dad. It's what led to my decision to apply to the FBI.

I told myself that eventually my sister would be an adult and my mother would learn to deal with life without me, and then I'd be free. That had been a fantasy. When I was a senior in high school, I realized that there was no way she and my sister were ready to function without me. I had to go to college close by so I could keep them from falling apart.

College was one more hurdle to get over. It meant juggling the teenaged Kayla, who was more and more difficult, my mother's increasing disfunction and my studies. Along with working as many hours a week as I could cram in at the local Starbucks.

No matter how hard it got, I clung to the thought that eventually my plans would work out. After college, I would work for a year or two and then enter the FBI training program. I hadn't reckoned on my sister and mother refusing to move on. Never considered they might drag me down.

Why couldn't I force myself to get beyond the burden of my family? Other people walked away; why couldn't I? No amount of planning or determination seemed to kick my habit of being the rock for my sister and my mother. No question that it was unhealthy, but knowing that didn't stop me from continuing the sacrifice.

Now, because of my sister's chaotic life, and the bad decision I'd made on her behalf, my life was in total disarray. I was determined not to let it stay that way. In my exit interview, John Farrell had suggested I apply at ATF – Alcohol, Tobacco and Firearms, or the Secret Service or the US Marshals Service. 'They investigate a lot of interesting cases. And their rules aren't as rigid as the FBI's. I'll put in a word for you.' He also suggested the Treasury Department, which had an investigative arm.

Another possibility was becoming a cop. That was my least favorite option. I'd never forgiven the Newport News PD for their listless pursuit of my dad's killer. But in a way, that made it somewhat attractive. It would give me a chance to poke into what they'd found – and what they'd let slide.

I shook myself out of my mood and took stock of my surroundings. Nothing had changed. Dark night, dark water punctuated by a path of moonlight. I was beginning to wonder whether I'd badly miscalculated my course. It was almost three o'clock, so surely by now I should be approaching Nassau. To keep my mood from tanking further, I did a few brisk exercises, and then took a turn around the deck. When I got back up to the bridge, I noticed a lightening of the sky on the horizon. Could it be possible? Yes, it had to be lights from the city of Nassau.

Like an idiot, I began hooting and dancing around. I had gone far enough west to escape the marshes. Now I could turn directly north and head for the city. And after that, it was a matter of staying awake long enough for dawn. I swung the boat to starboard, and as if to reward my diligence, the depth suddenly went to five meters.

But the ordeal wasn't over. The next two hours trying to stay awake was torture. I wanted desperately to close my eyes. 'Just for a few minutes,' I grumbled out loud.

'Stop being a baby,' I replied. I punished myself with sets of fifteen jumping jacks at a time.

I must have dozed, because with a shock I realized that I could actually see the island of New Providence looming, a big lump on the horizon. Now I really did have to slow down. It would be stupid if I got this far and ran aground on the marshes outside the island. It was five o'clock. Another hour and the sky would begin to lighten.

By six a.m., I had steered the boat around to the northeast side of New Providence and was idling outside the biggest marina in Nassau. Apparently, it was still too early for anyone to be at work on the docks. I had concluded that it was stupid to try to dock the boat by myself. I had managed to come this far, but there was no way in hell I could dock a twenty-five-foot-wide catamaran alone without tearing up either the dock or the boat. I'd have to notify the marina that I needed help bringing her in. A couple of boats ghosted past me in the early light. I thought of calling out to ask for help. But it was better to reach the marina staff. They were equipped to take care of someone who didn't know what they were doing.

I spent an hour steering lazy circles in the harbor before someone finally answered my call on the VHS and gave me a cell number to call. I told them my dilemma and asked if someone could come out in a dinghy and come aboard to dock the boat.

'There is no one here who can come out to you.' I could see the young black man standing on the dock with the cell phone to his ear.

'Somebody has to; otherwise, I'm likely to take out your dock.'

'I'm sorry, miss, but there's really no one. But I assure you, if you can bring your boat in close, very slowly, and toss me a line, I can secure her. We'll take our time. You can do this.'

I smiled at the man's sweet, lilting voice. He was right. All I had to do was put the boat in reasonable proximity to the dock and he'd do the rest. Dockhands were used to providing help to inexperienced sailors.

A half-hour later, I was tied up on the end of one of the docks. I couldn't wait to get off the boat and hand it over to the Royal Bahamian Defense Force. The RBDF was the Bahamian equivalent of the US Coast Guard. The young man who had helped me dock had explained that the RBDF was the proper authority to notify when a boat was in trouble. He had contacted them for me. It would be somebody else's problem now.

I ran downstairs to wash my face. Looking in the mirror was a jolt. I had forgotten my spiky blond hair. Well, at least my hair didn't need combing.

I shouldered Johnny's backpack and then remembered the gun in the nav station. I decided not to leave it on the boat and ran back upstairs to retrieve it. I stuffed it into the backpack.

When I stepped down off the boat, the guy who had helped me dock came hurrying up. 'Wait. Miss, the RBDF has directed me to tell you to remain with the boat until they arrive.'

I turned and looked back at the boat. By now, I loathed it.

'I'll stay, but I'm going to sit here on the dock, not on the boat. Can you find me some coffee?'

He grinned and said he could do that.

THIRTEEN

'What do you mean, how do I know her name is *Island Ice*? It's painted right on the side!' I grumped at the young naval officer interrogating me. I felt like a toddler who hadn't had enough sleep. Which I hadn't.

It didn't help that the officer, Lieutenant Amos Cooley, seemed to think his trim white-and-green uniform gave him the right to treat me like a criminal. Peering down at me from his skinny six-foot-two height, he had taken me through my story again and again, as if he suspected I had stolen the boat for nefarious reasons and then had second thoughts.

'No, it is not, Miss. The name has been painted over.'

'No, it . . .,' I frowned, trying to remember if I'd had actually seen the name on the boat or if I had just recognized it. Maybe I hadn't actually seen the name. 'Look, I know that's the name of the boat. I was on it before. I told you.'

It was ten a.m., and I was still being held captive in the Nassau Marina harbormaster's office. I had waited two endless hours for the naval officer to show up so I could tell him a strongly edited story of how I had come to be in possession of a forty-five-foot catamaran. Leaving out all mention of the island and my escape, I told him the men had come aboard *Island Ice* in the night, forced me off the boat and left, taking Johnny with them. When they returned without Johnny, I was scared that they had come back for me, so I escaped the only way I could – by taking the boat. It seemed like a sound story to me. But he clearly didn't believe me. I wondered what he would have thought if I'd told him the truth, that the men hadn't taken Johnny with them; that he had died. I thought involving the Coast Guard in Johnny's death would get me in worse trouble. I hoped that Nick had done as he promised and retrieved Johnny's body.

The sticking point with the officer seemed to be that no one had reported the boat missing. That made sense, since Johnny had told me the owners were in New York. They didn't know that the boat had been hijacked. But did they know it had been used for illegal purposes? I wasn't even sure myself. I thought of the backpack. Was whatever the men had been looking for still inside it? Was it drugs? Despite the freezing air conditioning, I started to sweat. The backpack was by the chair I was sitting in. Suppose Lieutenant Cooley insisted on examining it? If he found drugs, I might as well kiss the next few years of my life goodbye.

'How do you account for the fact that no one reported the boat missing?' He had asked that same question three different ways. It would have been easier if I'd been able to tell him that the last time I'd seen the boat's captain, he was dead, so there's no way he could have notified the owners that it had been hijacked. Johnny's death was a complication I didn't want to bring into the matter.

I knew why Lieutenant Cooley was so suspicious. Too many boats in the Bahamas were involved in the drug trade. In the few months I'd been here, half a dozen boat raids had netted millions of dollars in cocaine, heroin, and cannabis. You couldn't blame him for suspecting that my predicament was the result of a drug deal gone sour.

I told him once again that the owners were in New York and most likely unaware that it had been stolen. I got up and peered out the tiny window to where the boat was tied up. A Coast Guard officer stood sentry next to it. Sure enough, where there should have been a name, it was blank.

'OK, I see the name isn't there. The people who stole the boat must have painted over it. I didn't notice the name wasn't there. But it was the same boat! I recognized the furnishings. Look at the boat papers. That'll give you her name.'

He smirked. 'A clever idea. But there are no boat papers aboard. Do you think we're stupid?'

'No papers? They've got to be there somewhere.' I was so tired that I was nauseous. I wanted to get this over with, but we seemed to be stuck at an impasse. 'All I know is it's the same boat I was on when three men abducted my friend.' I had left out the part where I was chained up and tossed overboard. It seemed too complicated. Now I wondered if I should have told the whole story.

Suddenly, the door burst open. 'Jessie, I'm here. Sorry it took so long.' My boss, Jeremy LaBreque, stopped short. 'What happened to your hair?' He looked down at my pink shorts and gaudy T-shirt and shook his head, grinning. 'You've gone tourist!'

I leaped up and flung myself at Jeremy, throwing my arms around him. 'I've never been so happy to see anybody! Can you please get me out of here?'

Earlier, while I had been waiting for the RBDF officer to arrive, I had called Jeremy. At first, he had yelled at me for not showing up yesterday, saying I was selfish, and that I had screwed up the schedule and pissed off the other members of the staff who had to work short-handed.

After all I had been through, the tirade coming from Jeremy sounded like music. When he finally wound down and listened to my story, one that bore only a passing resemblance to the real story, he sounded skeptical but said he would come and pick me up as soon as he could. And now here he was. He could yell at me all he wanted to.

He held me at arm's length and said in his lilting island accent, 'Whoa, Mama, wait until the tourist boys get a load of you.'

'Believe me, I didn't do it on purpose. I'll tell you about it later.'

'OK, let's find out what has to happen for this nice man to let you go.'

Dive boat owners didn't usually have a lot of clout with the Bahamian Coast Guard, but Jeremy was well known. His nickname was Hat Trick because he'd gone to the local high school and been a star on the only-time-ever winning cricket team. His specialty was said to be a 'hat trick,' whatever that was. A tall, muscular black man, he was still athletic and had a cheerful personality. He'd be one of the people I'd truly miss when I left the islands.

After he identified himself to the officer, things went my way. I had to sign a ream of paper that I hoped didn't admit to my being responsible for the shape of the boat.

Jeremy whisked me away and drove me to my apartment. I filled him in more on what had happened, but I left out the worst parts. When he stopped outside, he said, 'I need you back at work, Jessie. Like tomorrow.'

I'd been through hell, and right now I felt as though I could sleep for a week, but I owed Jeremy for getting me out of hot water with the RBDF. 'I'll do my best to be there,' I said.

My apartment keys were in my tote, which Shelley had brought back with her, so I stopped at the office of the so-called manager. The only thing he 'managed,' as far as I could tell, was to drink himself into oblivion every day, helped along with significant quantities of weed. But at least he came to the door when I knocked, and he didn't question me when I said I needed to be let into my apartment. He handed me the master key and said to bring it back when I could.

'Shelley?' I called out when I let myself in. No answer. I tapped on Shelley's bedroom door, but there was no reply. Part of me was disappointed not to find her there. I was still miffed at her for absconding with my belongings, but in the scheme of things it was a minor problem. I craved the company of someone I could have a normal conversation with.

I needed to decide what to say to account for where I'd been since Saturday night. I wasn't ready to tell her that Johnny was dead. That would bring up too many questions. But I wanted to ask her some things about Nick. Maybe she'd learned something useful about him. I hoped she at least knew how to get in touch with him. He had a lot to answer for.

I took a long, hot shower and got dressed in shorts and a T-shirt. The pink shorts and T-shirt went into the trash bin under the sink. I never wanted to see them again.

I had just made myself a turkey sandwich when Shelley breezed in. 'Jessie!' She ran to me and hugged me so hard I felt all my bruises light up. 'Where have you been? I've been out of my mind.' Without pausing for my answer, she squealed, 'Oh, my God! Look at your hair! It looks so cool. What made you decide to do that?'

The question was so normal, so at the other extreme from the last few hours, that I felt hysterical laughter bubble up. I swallowed it down and said, 'Seemed like a good idea.' *And it seemed like a good way to save my life.*

'It must have cost a fortune.' She stopped, frowning. I realized she was working out the timing. 'Where did you get it done?'

I took a bite of my sandwich, trying to think of the best explanation. 'Umm, at the resort salon.'

'Really?' She cocked her head. 'When?'

'Yesterday afternoon.'

'Wait a minute. You were there and didn't call me? I was worried half to death.' She looked stricken.

'I'm so sorry, Shelley. Things got a little crazy. And I didn't have my cell phone.'

She crossed her arms. 'You have a lot to answer for. You really scared me. I didn't know what to do, you know – whether I should come back or wait for you. And whether I should bring your stuff with me.'

'Look, you did the right thing.'

'Why didn't you come back on Sunday?'

'Johnny and I went to another island; we had trouble with the boat and we couldn't get back.'

She chewed her lip, looking like a hurt child. 'I don't understand why you didn't call. When you didn't come home last night, I started to panic and thought maybe I should have stayed until you got back. How did you get back here? I thought there wasn't another ferry until next weekend.' Shelley's frantic questions cast everything I had been through in a surreal light. In her wildest imagination, Shelley couldn't have guessed what really happened.

'I got a ride back to Nassau this morning.'

'With Johnny?'

'No.' I finished the sandwich, set the plate in the sink and poured myself a glass of water. I couldn't seem to drink enough water since being stranded on the island. 'Look, I'm really sorry I didn't call.'

She rummaged around in her bag and came out with a few sample bottles of booze. She often lifted samples from the bar where she worked. She lined them up with the others on the end of the kitchen cabinet that served as our bar. 'Well, you're here now, and that's what counts.'

'Forgive me?'

'Sure. Nick said you two must have gotten involved and forgot what time it was.' She gave a suggestive grin.

'Something like that.'

She was staring at my legs. 'What happened to your legs? They're all scratched. You look like you were in a fight with a cat.'

'I got tangled up in some bushes.'

'What?' She shook her head and gave an exasperated huff. 'Oh, whatever. You need to put something on the scratches so they don't get infected.' She disappeared into her bedroom and came back with a tube of Neosporin, plus bright orange nail polish, polish remover, and cotton balls. She handed me the medication, then sat down on the sofa, pulled a foot up close and examined her toenails critically.

I thanked her for the Neosporin. Shelley might be ditsy, but she was thoughtful. I sat down in our rickety side chair and doctored the scratches.

She started swabbing off her old polish, the polish remover pungent in the air. 'Your boss Jeremy called this morning, asking if I knew where you were. He was really pissed when you didn't show up.'

'I talked to him. We're good now.' Time to ease into the subject of Nick. 'Did you have a good time after I left?'

'Ugh, no. After you guys left, the party went downhill.' She switched feet and started on the other toes without looking up at me. 'Nick was annoying, and I was bored.'

Here was my opening. 'What do you mean, annoying? What did he do?'

Shelley shook the nail polish bottle. 'Nothing bad. He was nice to me but not, like, very exciting. It was like his head was somewhere else, you know?'

'Mmm. Have you seen him since you got back?'

Shelley had started polishing one toenail and paused, looking at me with wide eyes. 'Why would I see him? We didn't hit it off at all.'

'Right. I don't know. I thought maybe he'd called or something.' I licked my lips. 'Do you happen to have his phone number?'

'No, and I didn't give him mine either.' Shelley went back to her nails.

'Did he tell you anything about himself?'

'No. He was Silent Sam.'

'Well, what did you talk about?'

'*Nothing!*' She looked up and rolled her eyes at me. 'He asked the usual: what I did for a living and where I was from.'

'Did you ask him where he was from?'

'No, or maybe. I don't remember.' Suddenly, she glared at me, frowning. 'He actually asked a lot of questions about you.'

'Like what?'

She shrugged. 'Like, where you worked. I told him you worked on a dive boat, and he asked how long you had been here in the islands.' She huffed. 'He was a lot more interested in you than he was in me.' She went back to work, polishing the toenails with swift strokes.

'What else did he ask?'

'Jessie, why are you asking all these questions? Are you attracted to him?'

If I said no, Shelley would dismiss my questions. 'Maybe. Sort of.'

'Oh.' She capped the bottle of nail polish. 'Well, he was sort of good-looking, if you like the unsociable type.'

'What else did he ask about me?'

'He asked where you came from. And what you had done before you got here.'

The idea of Nick asking about me was alarming. I'd escaped from his pals. Maybe he was planning to hunt me down, and Shelley easily told him how to find me. 'What did you tell him?'

'I told him we were roommates, not BFFs, and if he wanted to know more about you, he should ask.'

From her sulky tone, I knew she was pouting because Nick had shown more interest in me than in her.

'Well, I'll probably never see him again anyway. Did he happen to say how long he had been here?'

'No, Jessie, he didn't. Now can we please stop talking about him? Are you seeing Johnny again?'

'Not really.' There was no way to tell her he was dead without inviting a flood of questions. I was glad I had stowed Johnny's backpack in my room. If Shelley had seen it, she'd want to know what I was doing with it.

'I thought Johnny was cute.' Shelley picked up a magazine and fanned her toes. 'What do you think of the color?'

'I like it. Very tropical.' I yawned and stood up. 'I'm pretty tired. I think I'll take a nap.'

In my room, I sat on the bed and tried to think how to find Nick. I fired up my elderly computer and Googled his name. There were a few entries for Nick Garnier, but he wasn't one of them. I tried variations on his name, but there was nothing. That was odd. Maybe he had given me a false name.

But his number might be on Johnny's cell phone. I retrieved the phone from Johnny's backpack. It was out of juice. His was a Samsung, while I had an Apple, so the plugs were different.

There were some phone cords in our kitchen catchall drawer. I went back into the kitchen and rummaged through the drawer. Shelley was standing at the refrigerator eating ice cream from a carton. She said, 'What are you looking for?'

'A charging cord for a Samsung.'

'I thought you had an Apple.'

'This is an old phone.' My reply didn't make sense, but it seemed to satisfy Shelley.

I tried a couple of charging cords before I found one that fit the Samsung. 'Got it!' I ran back to my room before Shelley could ask any more questions. I plugged in Johnny's phone and it started charging. Now I was in business.

While I waited for the phone to charge, I thought about whether I should call the Nassau Police Department and tell them about Johnny. I had a friend in the department who I could speak to. But I didn't know if Johnny's body was even still on the island. It was possible Nick had brought the body back here or notified the authorities himself. I'd ask him before I got the police involved.

As soon as I was able to check the phone, right away I found Nick's number under Johnny's contacts. I stared at it. Could it be that easy? I hesitated. If I called and he answered, what would I say? I was so wiped out that I couldn't think clearly. My head was buzzing. The bed beckoned, soft and cool. I lay down, promising myself I would only lie there long enough to decide what I should say to Nick.

FOURTEEN

When I woke, it was dark outside. At some point, without being aware of it, I'd crawled under the covers, still in my clothes.

I was famished, but as usual, I didn't feel like cooking. Not that there was anything to cook. Shelley and I agreed that cooking was overrated.

Our apartment was near the wharf, so I walked over to Papa Joe's – my home-away-from-home eatery. The one decent café in this port, it was always busy. The crowd in the café tonight were mostly people I recognized. A gay couple I saw there a lot waved and pointed to an empty chair at their table, but I called out, 'Next time,' and headed for an empty booth near the back.

I knew the menu by heart, and I didn't even look at it, just ordered a cheeseburger and a Red Hook. Such a luxury. Less than twenty-four hours ago, I'd been steering a stolen boat through treacherous waters. I sat back and took a deep breath, savoring being back in familiar territory. My respite wouldn't last long. I was determined to find Nick Garnier. But for now, I'd give myself a break.

My gaze fell on a middle-aged couple sitting side by side a few tables away from me. Most people in the café were cheerful, but these two looked gloomy and restless. They also tugged at my memory. I had seen them somewhere before. I didn't think they'd been on one of our dives, but it was possible. The woman was around fifty, with a helmet of ash-blond hair, and thirty extra pounds stuffed into Capri pants and a sequin-studded T-shirt. The man was several years older, lean and leathery, like someone who spent a lot of time on a boat, which made sense given that boaters kept this place going. They both had cocktails in front of them. I wondered what had gone wrong on their vacation to put them in such a funk. They kept glancing toward the front door. Maybe they were mad because they were waiting for someone who was late.

Suddenly, their faces brightened and the woman waved.

Idly curious, I glanced at the front door, and when I saw who they were waving at, I felt as if I'd been punched in the stomach. It was Nick Garnier. He spied the couple and started toward their table. I quickly turned my head away, hoping he hadn't seen me. What was he doing here? Who was that couple?

Then I remembered exactly who they were. I hadn't actually met them; Johnny had pointed them out to me at the party where I met him. They were the owners of *Island Ice*. Why was Nick meeting with them? Did they know what had happened to their boat? Did they know that Nick and Johnny had been using it to transport contraband? One thing I doubt they knew was that their captain was dead.

I wondered if I should leave before Nick saw me. I'd changed my look drastically, so maybe he wouldn't recognize me. I took a sip of my beer, my mind whirling with confusion.

My burger arrived. I could ask the waitress to box it up so I could sneak out. But that might bring attention to me. Better to keep my head down. I ate a few fries and had taken my first bite of my burger when I felt a presence at my side. 'Move over.'

It was Nick. Instinctively, I scooted over in the booth. He sat down and I glanced at him, feeling a rush of anger. 'What are you doing here?' I said.

'More to the point, what are you doing here? How did you get off Trophy Cay?'

'I come here all the time,' I said. 'And it's a hell of a coincidence for you to show up here.'

He fiddled with the silverware, not looking at me. 'Shelley told me you come here a lot. I was meeting some people, and they're staying close by, so I suggested it. But I'm asking again: how did you get off Trophy Cay?' His voice was quiet and angry. Why was he angry? Because I wasn't dead?

'It damn sure wasn't with your help. How did you get away? Leaving me stranded, I might add.'

His face was flushed, his eyes glittering. 'It was best for you to stay there.'

I was suddenly trembling with fury. 'Oh, really? Where your friends could find me? They showed up at Trophy Cay again.'

'What friends? You mean Didier and that crew?'

'That's exactly who I mean. For all I knew, you told them where I was and sent them to kill me.'

He glared at me, his lips a thin line of anger. 'Of course I didn't. Don't be a fool.'

'You still haven't told me how you know them.'

'Jesus, I can't believe they showed up . . .' His voice trailed away. He could have been talking to himself. Then he looked back at me, his dark eyes searching mine as if he had a question he didn't know how to ask. He put his hand on my arm. In spite of my anger at him, the gesture felt like a caress, and I had an unexpected surge of desire. 'Look,' he said. 'It's complicated. I don't have time to talk right now, but we do have things to discuss.' He slid out of the booth and stood up. 'I'll be in touch.'

Then he did something strange. When he got out of the booth, he looked down at me, bared his teeth in a big, friendly grin and reached out to ruffle my hair. 'I like the new look,' he said, his voice loud enough to carry.

Hands shaking, I picked up my cheeseburger and set it back down, too confused to think straight. I took a few sips of beer and eventually calmed down. When I finished my burger, I ordered a slice of key lime pie. Nick and the couple still hadn't left. I wished I could be a fly on the wall to hear what they were discussing.

Although the food and beer settled me down, I was too keyed up to sleep, so I walked along the dock, wondering what kind of story Nick would conjure up to explain his involvement with the men who'd abducted Johnny and me. His odd turnaround of behavior at the café made me nervous. Anyone who didn't know the situation would think the two of us were good friends. So, if my body washed up somewhere a week from now, no one would think to suspect Nick Garnier.

There was one way to deal with this. I could call Kevin Riley, my friend the Nassau cop.

Kevin met me at Feathers, the bar where Shelley worked. He was good-looking in a tough-guy way. Only his puppy-dog eyes softened the hard line of his jaw and his perpetually serious expression. He had told me he moved to Nassau from New York City, to start over after a messy divorce.

We'd gone out a few times after we met, but there was no chemistry, and he seemed vulnerable. I didn't want to encourage him and then have to tell him I was only here short-term.

It was ten o'clock, and Feathers was hopping, even though it was Monday night. There was nothing special about the bar that would explain why it was so popular. The interior was shabby, with scarred wooden tables and scruffy walls plastered with posters of the island. The room opened out onto a big wood porch dotted with fake palm trees. The food was your regular Nassau fare – hamburgers, fried conch, curly fries, pizza, and fried chicken or fish. But they were known for an honest pour, which made them unusual.

Kevin and I sat out on the porch, under fairy lights. The music was deafening inside and only slightly better outside. We ordered a gin and tonic for me; a beer for him.

Now that we were sitting across the table from each other, I was having trouble getting started telling him what had happened to me, and I could tell he was puzzled. He complimented me on my new blond hair for the third time.

'I'm glad you like it.' I sipped my drink.

'I mean you looked great before, but this is like a new you! What made you decide to change it?'

This was my opening. 'Someone was after me who wanted to kill me and I needed a disguise.' I had to raise my voice to be heard.

He chuckled. 'Right. I didn't mean to pry. I guess you don't really need a reason.'

'I'm serious. That's exactly what happened. And that's why I need to talk to you.'

His smile faltered. 'That sounds pretty strange.'

'Yes, it was.' I traced moisture on the side of the glass.

'Are you sure they intended to kill you?'

'I'm really sure. One hundred percent.' I finally met his gaze and saw that he was dubious.

He swigged his beer. 'Uh, OK. You want to tell me about it?'

I squared my shoulders and leaned closer across the table. 'Do you want the long version or the short version?'

His eyes skidded from my face to our surroundings and back. 'Give me a summary, and then you can fill in the details.'

'Summary? Sure.' I lowered my voice. 'You heard about that big opening on Trophy Cay last weekend?'

He nodded.

'I was there. I went out on a boat with a friend. Three men boarded the boat, tied us up, and threw us overboard. Then they left with the boat. I managed to get away, but my friend died.' My voice wavered, and I took a breath to steady myself. 'Last night, I stole the boat back and brought it to Nassau. That's the short version.'

He stared at me for several seconds, scowling. 'I don't know where to begin. Is this for real?'

I ignored his doubtful tone. 'I didn't make it up. It's true.'

'How does the blond hair come in?'

'When I got back to the resort from the island, I saw the guys who threw me overboard. I was afraid they would recognize me, so I had my hair dyed and cut short. Afterwards, I stole their boat and brought it back here.'

A tentative smile played around the corners of his mouth, and I knew he still wasn't convinced. He took another sip of his beer and sat back, folding his hands across his stomach. 'Maybe you'd better give me the long version.'

So I did. The only time I felt shaky as I described what happened was when I thought of Johnny's lifeless body smashed up against me as I struggled to escape the last of the rope that bound us.

Kevin's face grew stern as I spoke. He no longer looked at me as though he thought I was telling a fairy tale.

When I wound down, he reached over and laid his hand flat on the table between us. 'I don't know what to say. I'm sorry I didn't believe you earlier. You must have been terrified. Where is the boat now?'

'I handed it over to the Coast Guard this morning.'

Kevin barked a laugh. 'I can't believe you risked stealing their boat. And drove it for what, six hours? Do you know how insane that was?'

'Of course I do! And it was eight hours. Kevin, I didn't have any choice. I knew exactly what they would do if they found me alive.' Until now, I had been unsure what I wanted from Kevin, or from the situation. I didn't know whether to step away and hope never to see the three men again, or pursue them and make sure they were caught and punished. But now I knew. 'Kevin, I want to find those guys. I want them in prison.'

Kevin cocked his head. I could tell he was hesitant. 'I'll do what I can, but finding them isn't going to be easy.'

'I know it isn't. I'm going on the assumption that sooner or later they'll come here. Especially now that their boat was stolen.'

He nodded and leaned in close. 'Which brings me to the next point. I want you to stay out of it. It's up to the police to find them and deal with them.' For the first time, he sounded like a real cop. His voice had taken on a ring of authority.

He took out a black notebook and a pen and jotted down the name of the boat, and Nick's and Johnny's names. 'And you mentioned your roommate, Shelley. I'd like to talk to her, too.'

'She wasn't there. She won't know anything.'

'Yes, but she was on Trophy Cay with you, and she met your friends Nick and Johnny. In fact, she spent some time with this guy Nick. He sounds shady to me.'

I blew out a breath. 'God, Kevin, you don't know how good it feels to talk to you,' I said. My gaze swung around the room. I caught two guys watching me intently. Not my three 'friends,' anyway. It was the blond hair. I was tempted to go straight home and dye it back.

Kevin had me repeat everything I had told him, jotting down notes while I talked. 'You were right to call me. And now you need to leave it alone. These guys sound like they're big trouble. It's probably a drug ring. You don't want to get involved with people like that.'

I didn't make any promises. He didn't know about my FBI connection. Or, rather, my ex-connection. And I was going to keep it that way.

He tucked away his notebook and pen and rose. 'Come on, let's get you home. You need to get a good night's sleep. Tomorrow I'll tackle this.'

At the door to my apartment, there was that awkward moment – to kiss or not to kiss – but thankfully Kevin was all business. 'Get some rest. We'll talk tomorrow.'

I barely had the strength to make it to bed. The next thing I knew, it was six a.m. and my alarm was buzzing. I turned my phone on to see if Nick had called. He hadn't. Had he gotten the message? Or was he stonewalling me?

FIFTEEN

My workday was torture. Someone had called in sick, so Jeremy scheduled me for a real dive, not a snorkel adventure. The tank seemed to weigh twice as much as usual, and it took all the spirit I could muster to be reasonably friendly to the tourists. Even the water fought me. Every encounter I'd had with the ocean in the last few days had been dangerous, so it seemed forbidding and alien. And in the back of my mind, I kept wondering whether Didier and Louis were looking for me. I wouldn't be that hard to find. I was trembling with physical and mental exhaustion by the time all the gear was put away.

Jeremy followed me off the boat and onto the dock. 'You OK? You struggled today.'

I hitched my duffle up higher on my shoulder. 'I'm fine, Jeremy. Just tired. What have we got on for tomorrow?'

'I'm sorry I had to have you come in today. Maybe you should take a day off tomorrow,' he said.

'Oh, right. Did you see the looks I got from the crew this morning? You'd think I had stolen their paychecks.' I sounded petulant, but I couldn't help it.

'They'll get over it. But I'm worried about you. I didn't want to pry, but if you want to talk . . .'

He was bending over backwards to be kind. I hadn't yet given him an explanation for why I'd been absent on Monday. I lowered my duffle to the dock and tried to smile. 'Thanks, Jeremy, but it's something I have to work out for myself. You're right, I am tired. Any chance I can do a half-day snorkel tomorrow?'

'I'll make it happen.'

I took a step toward him. 'Jeremy, you've been really good to me. I do appreciate it.' I had to tell him I'd be leaving. And maybe sooner than I had thought. But not this minute, not after he'd gone out of his way to support me.

'No big thing.' He put out his fist for a bump.

'I'll be back in form soon.' I picked up my duffle again, took a step past Jeremy and froze. Nick was in the parking lot, leaning against my old Toyota, waiting for me.

For a second, I balked and thought of asking Jeremy to walk me to my car. But I wasn't in the mood to be rescued. I was ready to take Nick on myself. 'See you,' I said to Jeremy. While I walked toward Nick, I checked my phone. Kevin hadn't gotten back to me. It would have been nice to tell Nick that the cops were coming for him and his friends.

Going on the offensive, as soon as I was near enough, I called out, 'I'm glad you're here. We need to talk.'

Nick straightened and shoved his hands into his back pockets. 'You're right, we have things to discuss.'

I motioned him away from the car, opened the trunk and threw my duffle in. Then I met his gaze straight on. 'Let's start with Johnny. Where did you take his body? Has his family been notified? I'd like to meet them.'

Up close, Nick looked tense. There were dark circles under his eyes. 'I've arranged for his body to be shipped home.'

'Where is home?'

'Canada.'

'And I'm supposed to take your word for all this?'

'I don't know what choice you have.'

'Oh, I can poke around. I have resources.'

He suddenly seized my arm, his eyes fierce. 'Look, you can't do that. You're asking for trouble.'

I jerked away and crossed my arms across my chest. 'I can take care of myself.'

'No, you can't. You don't know what you've gotten yourself into. Those people almost killed you, and if they find you, this time they'll succeed.'

'Then why don't you tell me what I've gotten into? You can start by explaining why you abandoned me on Trophy Cay.'

He snorted and put his hands on his hips. 'Abandoned you? I

left you there so you'd be safe. And after what happened to you, I thought you could use the time.'

'Safe? Really? You think so? How safe was I when your buddy Didier and his friends showed up there?'

He sighed. 'OK, I hadn't figured on that. And I repeat, they aren't my buddies.' He sounded distracted.

'Really? Then why did they keep bringing up your name?'

Nick glanced around the parking lot, and I couldn't help but do the same. Except for stragglers from the dive boat, the lot was deserted. 'Let's get in my car,' he said. He looked at my car and smirked. 'It's nicer than your rust bucket.'

We both looked at my car. It was a 1982 Toyota that could have won a contest for most ancient and rusted on an island where seventy-five percent of the cars were ancient and rusted. I'd bought it for $500 and had overpaid.

'Don't be rude about my car. It gets me where I need to go. Why can't we talk outside?'

'We'll be safer out of sight.' He walked around to the driver's side of a dark, late-model SUV parked a couple of rows over. 'Come on, get in.'

The last thing I wanted was to get into the car with this guy. He was stalking me. He had shown up at the café last night and had quizzed Shelley about where I worked. It wouldn't be hard to phone the dive shops and find out which one I worked in.

'I'll get in your car if you'll give me the keys,' I said. And immediately thought to myself that if he had a gun, having his keys wouldn't do me much good.

He hit the fob that opened the doors and then tossed the keys to me.

I caught them. 'Hold on,' I said. 'I forgot something at the dive boat. I need to run back for a minute.'

'Wait, what? Where are you going with my keys?'

'I'll be back.' I ran back to the shop, hoping Jeremy hadn't left yet.

Luckily, he had stayed behind to work on a faulty regulator. He looked up. 'Forget something?'

'Listen, Jeremy, I need your help. I can't take time to tell you what's happening, but I'm going to be sitting in a car in the parking lot talking to a guy that I don't trust. When you come out, will you find me and mention tomorrow's dive? If I'm in trouble, I'll say I'm not sure I can come in tomorrow. That's your signal to call the police.'

'The police? No need for that. I can handle your guy.'

All Bahamians seemed to have a fundamental distrust of the police. Too bad. There was no way I was going to put Jeremy in a position for Nick to hurt him. He had a wife and three kids. 'Just do it my way, OK? It'll probably be fine. I only want some backup.'

Jeremy shrugged. 'Whatever.' When an American said 'whatever,' it sounded sulky. When Jeremy said it with his island accent, it sounded like anything was possible.

When I got back to Nick, he was scowling.

I went to the passenger side and climbed into the SUV.

As soon as we were in the car, I said, 'All right, what's with all the cloak-and-dagger stuff?'

He put his hands on the steering wheel and gazed straight ahead for several seconds. A muscle was working in his jaw. Finally, he sighed deeply and turned to look at me. 'Last night, you said Didier's crew came to Trophy Cay. Clearly, they didn't find you, so what happened? How did you get away from them? How did you get here?'

I considered what I should tell him. Should I tell him the truth? What difference did it make? And deep down it gave me perverse pleasure to let him know how resourceful I'd been.

'I stole *Island Ice*.'

He shook his head. 'Get serious!'

'I am serious. I stole the catamaran and motored it back here to Nassau.'

He moved to sit sideways, leaning against the door to look at me. 'You mind filling in the details?'

'Louis and Jaggo were having dinner, and I saw Didier get off the boat. I figured he'd gone to join them, which meant they left the boat unguarded. So I stole her and brought her back here.'

'Alone.' He was staring at me, his dark eyes intense. In other circumstances, I would have been attracted to a man who looked at me that way.

'Yes, alone. It wasn't that hard. Well, not technically. It was hard staying awake all night.'

'Start at the beginning and tell me exactly what happened from the time you saw Didier and his men.' Seeing my stubborn look, he added, 'Please.'

I told him how horrified I had been when I heard Jaggo's laugh. 'That was the last thing I heard when they pitched us overboard. I'll hear that in my nightmares.' I shuddered. I went into greater detail describing seeing Didier get off the boat and deciding to take the chance that he wouldn't come back soon. I realized there was an element of bragging to the story.

'Why didn't you go to your room and wait for them to leave?'

'For all I knew, you had sent them and told them what room I was in.'

He shook his head and looked out the front window. I couldn't tell if he was amused or angry. 'Go on. You panicked when you saw them, so you took the boat. Then what?'

I detailed the journey back to Nassau. He didn't interrupt. When I was done, he said, 'You didn't happen to spot Johnny's backpack while you were on the boat, did you?'

That damned backpack again. What was in it? 'No. I didn't have time to be rummaging around. I had to stay at the wheel. I was scared I'd run aground.' Lying to him about the backpack came easily. I had no intention of turning it over to him. I had yet to open the package. Last night, I had fallen into bed right away, and this morning I had been in too much of a hurry to get to work.

'What happened when you got here? Were you magically able to dock the boat?'

I ignored his sarcasm and told him I'd gotten help from the dockhand, and then I described the annoying ordeal with the Coast Guard.

'I have to admit that's quite a story.'

'You don't believe me?'

He gave a sharp bark of laughter. 'Would you believe it if somebody told you they had driven a catamaran back here by themselves in the dark? After stealing it from three guys who tried to kill you?'

'It's the truth!'

'Shit, I'm beginning to think you're brazen enough to have pulled it off.'

'I'll prove it. Let's walk over to the dock and talk to the deck-hand who helped me bring her in. It's the next dock over from here.' I reached for the door handle.

'That won't prove anything. You could have been with those three guys and come back with them.'

It took me a second to realize what he was implying. My cheeks grew hot, and I threw myself back into the seat and glared at him. 'You think I'm with them? Are you crazy? They tried to kill me.'

'That's what you said. But I don't know whether you're telling the truth. There's no one to corroborate the story. You could have planned the whole thing.'

'Even killing Johnny?'

'Even that.'

'That's ridiculous. Why would I go off with him and then . . .?' My voice trailed away as I realized it wasn't ridiculous, and that going off with him might look as if I had lured him away to steal whatever those guys were after.

Nick was drumming his fingers on the steering wheel. 'Look, for all I knew, you and those guys arranged the whole scenario, and you had some way of escaping that Johnny knew nothing about.'

'Oh, please. That's ridiculous. Why would I do that? If I was with them, all we had to do was kill Johnny and sail off into the sunset.'

He shrugged. 'I didn't say it was a perfect idea.'

But it made sense from his point of view if he thought he was the target of a double-cross. I thought back to seeing him last night with the owners of *Island Ice*. Something had been nagging at the back of my head. *Island Ice* had been at the dock all day yesterday. The owners were obviously staying nearby, so why hadn't they seen the boat? Hadn't the Coast Guard contacted them to say it had been returned? 'Why were you talking to the owners of *Island Ice* last night?'

He rubbed his hand across his forehead. 'They wanted to know . . .' He stopped abruptly. 'Look, you've told me enough. If you're telling the truth, then you have to get out of here.'

'Hey, hey, hey!' I glared at him, furious. 'You can't tell me what to do.'

'Jessie, if you really aren't connected with those guys, you're in deep trouble. If they find you, they will kill you. They won't stop to talk to you, they won't ask questions, they won't pay attention to anything you say. They'll kill you.' He spoke with such intensity that jitters ran down my spine.

'Believe me, you don't have to tell me the men were dangerous. I know it. They already tried to kill me once.'

'Exactly. That should tell you something. Look, if it's a matter of money, I can get you a plane ticket. You need to go somewhere safe. Do you have somewhere to go?'

The offer was tempting, but why would he make it? Why should he care about me? It sounded an awful lot like he wanted me out of the way. 'No way,' I said. 'I've already told the police what happened to me. If they catch the guys, they'll need me to ID them.'

'You what? Oh, Christ!'

Bingo. If he was hooked up with Didier's crew, he sure as hell wouldn't want the police involved. 'What's the problem?' I asked, mocking him. 'Why do you mind if I went to the police?'

He sighed. 'It's complicated.'

'You keep saying that. It's time for you to give me some real answers. How did you get over to Minor Cay to retrieve Johnny's body?'

He started to say something, but I powered on.

'You said you hitched a ride back to Nassau with a boat coming back. How did you explain that you were also bringing a body?'

He made an exasperated noise. 'OK, I lied. I'm not going into details, but I hired a hydrofoil from Nassau.'

'That must have cost you.' I remembered wondering how he could afford to pay for a weekend at the opening of Trophy Cay. 'You're playing fast and loose with money. The stakes must be high.'

'They are. I had to get back here.'

'Just like I did.'

We were at a standoff, glaring at each other.

Finally, he put his hand out. 'Give me the keys. If you won't leave, as least I can take you where you'll be safe.'

'What do you mean, where I'll be safe? Like on an island that I can't get off?'

'Give me the goddamn keys!' he shouted. 'You have no idea what you've gotten yourself into.'

I reached back and opened the door behind me.

He grabbed my arm and twisted it upwards. 'The keys!'

The door was open, and I threw the keys onto the pavement. 'Get them yourself.' I wrenched my arm away from him and leaped out of the car.

I headed for the dock where I'd left *Island Ice*. Worried that he might follow me, I glanced back and saw that Jeremy had Nick pinned up against the car. Even though Jeremy was a lot bigger than Nick, I had the feeling Nick was more dangerous. I stopped, hoping Nick wouldn't hurt Jeremy. Nick twisted around and saw me watching.

'You're acting stupid,' he yelled.

I kept walking. Anything to get away from him.

SIXTEEN

When I reached the dock where I'd left the catamaran, I intended to ask the dockhand why the owners of *Island Ice* hadn't picked her up.

The catamaran wasn't there. After twenty minutes of searching the docks, I had to admit that it was gone. The Coast Guard had probably moved it. I wanted to know if that was the case, or if someone else had taken charge of it – maybe Didier. Or even Nick.

The young guy who had helped me bring the boat in yesterday morning was in the harbormaster's office. He sent me down the street to the Royal Bahamian Defense Force office. There, the officer on duty told me it was routine for confiscated boats to be taken to an inspection dock on the other side of the island.

'Why was she confiscated?' I asked.

The guy looked through papers on his desk until he found what he was looking for. 'Says here, she didn't have any papers.' He set the paper down. 'Is she your boat?' He smiled.

'Belongs to a friend,' I said. Some friend!

'Tell them it could take a couple of days before they can retrieve it. And there will be paperwork. Here's where they can contact us.' He rummaged in a drawer and found a card and handed it over.

I started to leave, but at the door turned back. 'Do you know if anyone has been asking about the boat?'

He shook his head. 'I've been here since ten a.m. and no one has come by.'

As I walked back to my car, the things Nick had said rushed back to me. I wasn't safe. I found myself eyeing with suspicion every person I saw on the docks. By the time I got to my car, I was tense with nerves.

I had just arrived at my apartment building when my cell phone rang. It was Shelley, asking if I wanted to come over to Feathers Bar to have a few drinks. 'There's a fun group here.'

I could hear people chattering in the background. 'I'm wasted. We had a full dive today.'

'Maybe later?'

'I'll see.'

There was a long pause, and then Shelley's voice was distant. 'Jessie, you have been so weird lately. I don't know if I can room with somebody who has so many issues.'

I muttered something about PMS and hung up. I'd be out of here before long anyway, but I didn't want to leave with a bad feeling between me and Shelley. I let myself into my apartment, went into the kitchen and pulled a pint of mint chocolate chip ice cream out of the freezer. There were only a few tablespoons left, with freezer fuzz on it. I ate it anyway.

I should call Jeremy. I was curious to know what had happened between him and Nick after I fled. But I didn't want to bother him at home. I'd ask him tomorrow.

Still hungry, I rummaged in the freezer and found a frozen pizza crusted with ice. There was also a half-pint of rum raisin ice cream. It was Shelley's favorite, and therefore off limits. But I had gotten used to living dangerously. I ate the ice cream while the pizza cooked.

It was only eight o'clock, and my body wanted to go to bed and sleep until morning, but it was time to find out what was in Johnny's backpack. I'd told Nick it was still *on Island Ice*, so at least he wouldn't be breaking into my apartment and demanding I hand it over. Still, I should figure out what to do with it. I went to my bedroom, pulling my T-shirt off on the way.

I picked up the backpack and put it on my bed, ready to open it when the phone rang. It was Kevin.

'I'm sorry as hell I couldn't get back to you.' He sounded tired. 'I guess you heard there was a shootout in the casino at Atlantis. I've been over there all day.'

I was glad to hear that Kevin hadn't blown me off. 'Shootout? No, I've been out on a dive and hadn't heard. Did you just get home?'

'Who's at home? I'll be here at the station all night.'

'I guess that means someone was killed.'

'A tourist got caught in the crossfire. One of the shooters was wounded and the other one got away. Anytime something like this happens, the tourist industry here goes nuts. I thought New York politicians were sensitive! The powers-that-be are demanding that we find out what happened, like *now*. I'm sorry that means I don't know when I'll have time to deal with your situation.'

'Look, I appreciate you calling. I know you'll get to it when you can.' I wanted it to be now, but he had his hands full.

'I mentioned what happened to you to my partner. He said you should talk to the Bahamian Navy – you know, the RBDF. Stealing boats is really their concern.'

'Maybe I'll do that.'

Kevin didn't have a contact name, but he said if I had trouble getting help, to call him back. I hung up, feeling defeated. No way was I going to call the RBDF. I had already told them my story, and they had tried to twist it so that I seemed guilty of something. Something besides commandeering a boat that didn't belong to me. I'd either have to wait until Kevin was free to pursue the investigation or investigate on my own. Starting with the backpack.

I unzipped the backpack and lifted out the package. It was small, the size of a cigar box. I took a deep breath. Here was the moment of truth.

I took the tape off the package carefully, in case I decided to wrap it back up. It had a familiar odor that I couldn't quite place. When I had the wrapping off, I blinked. It was a cigar box! Bigger than most cigar boxes, it was something like twelve inches on each side and another twelve inches deep. The box was ebony, finely polished with intricate engraving on the sides. The words 'Nicaragua Supremo' were stamped on the top in gold. Surely the cargo the men were looking for wasn't a box of cigars! But this was most definitely a cigar box. People were always bragging that they had bought Cuban cigars in the islands. You could find them for sale in some of the more exclusive shops, discreetly tucked into out-of-the-way showcases. But how valuable could they be?

I opened the box. Five cigars of different varieties lay nestled on a velvet cloth. I stared at them, stunned. This is what they were willing to murder for? Maybe there were cigars that went for thousands of dollars. How would I know?

Or maybe the cigars were laced with cocaine or some exotic drug. I picked up one of them and sniffed it, turning it over. Then I realized that the box was too deep to simply have one layer. I scooped up the other four cigars and took off the velvet cloth they were sitting on. I had expected to see another layer of cigars; instead, there was a bulging leather pouch crammed into the box. I lifted out the pouch. It was heavy.

It was tied with a leather thong that took some undoing to unknot. Inside were at least a dozen black velvet bags of various sizes. They looked like the kind of bags that expensive jewelry came in. I opened a small one and shook the contents into my hand. A pair of diamond earrings. But these were no ordinary earrings. They were large teardrop diamonds, surrounded by dark-blue stones. Sapphire? No, these were the color of the ocean. I tucked them back into their bag and opened another. This one contained a diamond cuff bracelet, with large stones, interspersed with what looked like rubies.

Stunned, on automatic, I opened one bag after another. Each piece of jewelry was more magnificent than the one before it. The ultimate was a necklace that made me gasp in awe. It was like something you would see at the Academy Awards, or in pictures of extremely wealthy people at a New York gala. Nests of diamonds clustered around outsized red stones, all set in pale gold.

Outside a jewelry store, I had never seen such an array of jewelry. I couldn't possibly know the value of a haul like this; I had never owned anything more expensive than a pair of sterling silver earrings. But I was pretty sure what was in the backpack amounted to millions of dollars' worth of jewelry. Where could it have come from? Maybe from France. The pirates, Johnny, and Nick all spoke French. I could imagine jewelry like this being displayed in some fancy Paris boutique. Had there been any recent robberies? Surely a theft like that would have made international news.

Hands shaking, I stuffed the bags back into the pouch, and the pouch into the cigar box. As if by putting them back I could forget I knew they were there.

How could Didier's gang have been so careless to leave the backpack where it was easy to find? I knew the answer from FBI training. Criminals may be crafty, but they were also arrogant. The three men thought they were home free. They'd killed witnesses to their theft. They had foiled what they took to be a plot by Johnny to steal the jewelry. They had celebrated with a fine dinner at Trophy Cay. And felt secure in their assurance that the backpack was a perfect hiding place for the stash.

I had been naïve to think Johnny was merely involved in smuggling drugs. The jewelry was a whole different ballgame. Small, portable, unexpected. Easily overlooked when authorities were focused on the drug trade.

So, what was Johnny doing with it, and how had Didier known he had it? And how did Nick fit into the picture? I could picture Nick Garnier as an international jewelry thief. But Johnny? Not so much. Maybe he'd been telling the truth when he said he worked for Nick. Maybe he had no idea what was in the package. Maybe he was delivering it to the couple who owned *Island Ice* and Nick was supposed to provide security. If that were the case, why was he reluctant to tell me? It would have made an easy explanation.

Now that I knew what the gang had been after – what was worth risking lives for, and worth killing for – I understood what Nick had meant by telling me to stay out of it. Didier, Louis, and Jaggo would be looking for this package relentlessly. And they would have no problem killing anyone who got in their way. Namely, me.

I couldn't keep possession of such dangerous cargo. My heart was skittering. My impulse was to drive straight to the police station and hand the jewelry over. But I was reluctant. I had heard stories of evidence being turned over to the cops and subsequently disappearing. I wanted to give the box directly to Kevin, and unfortunately there was no way to get in touch with him right now.

But the package wasn't safe with me, either. If the guys found out I was alive, and that the backpack was missing, they'd know that I had taken it. I got up and paced around, trying to order my racing thoughts. How would Didier and his gang know that I was alive or that the pack was gone? The Coast Guard had confiscated the boat right away, so even if Didier's crew was back in Nassau, they wouldn't have been able to get on the boat, so they wouldn't know the backpack was missing. They would assume it was right where they had left it, with the jewelry package intact. And they shouldn't even know I was alive. That is, unless Nick had told them. He was the key to this.

Was he involved? It didn't quite make sense. He had had plenty of opportunity to get rid of me. And something told me he wasn't soft-hearted. This jewelry was a huge haul. If he thought I could expose him and the others, he'd have no compunction about killing me. So why hadn't he? I didn't trust him, but I couldn't figure out what game he was playing.

Thank goodness my instincts had led me not to tell Nick I'd taken the backpack. Unless Didier's crew somehow found out I'd commandeered the boat and were able to get on it and search for the backpack, for now I was safe.

It was too late tonight, but tomorrow morning I'd have to either get in touch with Kevin or find someplace to stash the cigar box and its contents.

SEVENTEEN

Jeremy cornered me as soon as I arrived at the dive dock the next morning. 'I need to talk to you.' Then he smiled. He had a great smile, wide and generous to go with soft brown eyes. 'You look more like yourself this morning. You feeling better?'

'A lot better.' I had slept more soundly than I had in days and felt like my old self. 'What did you want to talk about?'

His expression grew serious. 'What was going on with that dude after work yesterday?'

'I'm sorry, I should have called and thanked you. It wasn't such a big deal after all. Just a guy I met.'

'A guy you met?' He studied me. 'Well, you be careful. He doesn't look like a righteous guy to me.'

'What do you mean?'

'Type of man like him, he's either a gangster or a cop. Did you know he had a gun on him?'

My heart speeded up. 'Are you sure? How do you know?' I wondered what Jeremy would say if I told him I had a gun stowed at my apartment. I hadn't figured out what to do with the gun I'd taken from *Island Ice*.

'After you left, we had a few words – maybe it got a little physical, you know? When I pushed him, I felt the gun under his jacket.'

I assured him that I would be careful. As I was getting the equipment ready for the snorkel trip, I mulled over what Jeremy had said. If Nick had had a gun with him, why hadn't he pulled it on me when he wanted to get me into the car? Or later, when I refused to stay and hear him out?

On the half-day snorkel, I was partnered with a guy I'd worked with before who knew how to do his job. It was a beautiful day, a 'paradise kind of day' as they called it in the islands. The water was clear, and the fish performed as advertised.

When I got back to the dock, I looked around anxiously but saw no sign of Nick. I didn't want to take a chance of him sneaking up on me with no one around, so I waited until my co-worker was leaving and walked to my car with him.

On the way home, I stopped at the grocery store to replenish the pitiful stock of food left in the apartment, in particular a large carton of rum raisin ice cream for Shelley.

At the check-out counter, I spied the headline on the island newspaper: 'One Dead, Two Wounded in Casino Shootout.' I opened the paper, looking for news of a body found on Minor Cay, but I didn't have time to look carefully, so I bought one of the papers and stuffed it into my grocery bag. After I loaded groceries into the car, I fished the newspaper out of the bag, wondering if the lead article mentioned Kevin's name. I glanced at the two grainy pictures at the top of the article and then flicked my eyes to the text. But I only read the first few lines before something tugged at my subconscious. I looked back up at the two pictures and gasped. It couldn't be! Next to the photo of the middle-aged blond tourist who had been killed was a picture of Jaggo. The photo was fuzzy, but there was no mistaking the guy's stringy hair and crazed eyes.

Shaken, I read the rest of the article. Jaggo, whose real name was Jacques Monard, had been badly wounded. I didn't feel sorry for him, but if he died, it meant whatever the cops could get out of him died with him.

Apparently, a fight had started in the casino over a craps game, and two men had drawn guns. The tourist who died had been the victim of a stray bullet. The man who got away was described as around five foot ten inches, stocky build, bald, in his fifties.

That didn't sound like either of Jaggo's partners, but that didn't mean anything. In the FBI Academy, I'd learned that witnesses were notoriously unreliable. Two different people could be within a few feet of a crime and come away with completely different descriptions of what happened and what the perpetrators looked like.

I looked through the rest of the paper more closely but saw nothing about Johnny's body being found. Had Nick reported it to the authorities like he said he would?

I started the car. Now it was urgent to get in touch with Kevin to tell him that the injured man was one of my abductors. And maybe I should mention the body on Minor Cay to see if the police had been informed. I raced home, put away the perishables and sat down at the kitchen table to phone Kevin.

But reaching him wasn't that easy. 'He's in a meeting, and I don't know when he'll be available,' the duty cop said.

'Look, could you tell him it's important? It's related to the casino shooting.'

'Miss, if you have information, I'll be glad to take it.'

'It's actually concerning another case, but they may be connected. Could you tell him that? He'll know what it means. He has my number.'

I wanted to get cleaned up and change clothes, but I was afraid Kevin would call while I was in the shower. I paced around the apartment, returning again and again to look at the picture of Jaggo. Even knowing he was in critical condition, I still felt a ripple of fear and disgust every time I looked at the photo. But I couldn't seem to stay away from it. I flung the newspaper down and picked up my purse, tucking my phone into it. I had to get out of here.

The night before, I had decided to contact the owners of *Island Ice* and tell them everything that had happened on their catamaran. Finding them might be difficult. I didn't even know their names. But I'd ask around. The boating community was gossipy, and someone would probably know where they were. Also, without their boat, they had to be staying somewhere. There was one high-end 'boatel' on the wharf, and if inquiries around the docks didn't work, I could try there.

I was having second thoughts about reaching out to them. Suppose they were involved in smuggling the jewelry? Then they'd probably already know that things had gone wrong. But if they weren't part of the plot, they deserved to know that their boat was back in Nassau in the possession of the Coast Guard, and that Johnny, their captain, was dead.

I still didn't know what Nick was doing with them in the café. When he met them, he hadn't known that the boat was back in Nassau. Now that he did, he might already have told them.

Either way, maybe I could find out more about Nick from them. I'd have to be careful how I approached them. If they were involved in jewelry theft, they were as guilty as Didier and his gang. And most likely just as dangerous. Still, they didn't know who I was.

I decided not to tell them Johnny was dead. Instead, I would approach them by saying that I had met Johnny and had noticed their boat at the dock and wondered if he was around. If they already knew he had died, they'd tell me. If they didn't know, that meant Nick was keeping the information from them, for who knew what reason.

I remembered where Johnny had said the boat was docked. When I had met him the first time at the party, he had urged me to come and visit, and told me where the boat's slip was located. Maybe someone in a berth nearby would be able to tell me more.

The 'docks' were a series of boat marinas, some private, some public, that lay along a mile-long stretch of the water between the mainland and Paradise Island. It was quiet on the docks this afternoon. Most people who were usually near boats were out on the water, at the beach, or indoors seeking refuge from the afternoon heat. The dock where Johnny had told me *Island Ice* was usually berthed was reserved for big boats, including a couple of mega yachts. Even at this time of day, crews swarmed over some of those huge crafts, polishing every piece of chrome, swabbing decks, making sure not a speck of dirt could despoil the pristine shoes of their megabucks owners. Those weren't the boat people I was looking for.

On a nearby, less prestigious dock, I spotted a trawler that looked as if it had been there for a while. The waterline of the boat was dark with scum. The water around it was oily and contained a lot of backwashed junk.

'Hello,' I called out. 'Anybody home?'

A muscular, island-tanned woman in her fifties poked her head up from the gangway. 'What can I do for you?'

I told her I was looking for the owners of *Island Ice*.

The woman frowned, searching her memory. 'You mean the Turpins. That's a nice cat they've got. It left here a week ago with their captain.' Her eyes twinkled. 'Cute guy with great buns. Is that who you're really looking for?'

I shrugged. 'Him, too.'

'I think Betty and Carl flew to the mainland for a few days. But I heard they're back. I haven't seen them around here, though.'

'I need to talk to them. Do you know where they would be staying if they're not on the boat?'

'Hold on, let me ask my husband. He makes it his business to know everything that happens around here. And they say women are busybodies.' She raised her eyebrows and grinned.

She retreated into the cabin, and when she came back, she said, 'Jack says he ran into them yesterday. They're staying over at the boat hotel.'

The boat hotel was an upscale Marriott that catered to boat

owners who were having repairs made, or who needed to be pampered after being out on their boats too long.

There was no one at the front desk, so I rang the bell. An elegant, dark-skinned island woman appeared from an inner office and confirmed that the Turpins were staying there, but she said she'd seen them go out an hour ago.

I was thinking of waiting in the lobby until they returned, but I was thirsty and there was an outdoor bar a few hundred feet down the dockside. I could watch for them there and waylay them when they came back to their hotel. As I turned from the desk to walk to the front door, it opened and the Turpins walked in. I waited to approach, since they were speaking to someone behind them, and I didn't want to barge in.

'Let's talk in the coffee shop.' The woman had the strident voice I remembered, which carried through the room. She led her entourage in the direction of the café. That's when I got a good look at the men following her. My throat constricted. One of them was Didier. Well, that certainly answered one question.

I turned and hurried in the other direction, toward the elevators, feeling the back of my neck prickle with fear that Didier would recognize me. When I glanced back, they were gone. At that moment, the elevator opened and I jumped back. At this rate, I'd have a nervous fit. The couple that got off gave me a curious look.

Heart racing, I eased back into the lobby, ready to run if Didier returned. I looked out the front window, worried that Louis would be waiting outside. I didn't see him, so I could safely get away. But now that I had had a moment to calm down, I hesitated. Did I dare follow them into the coffee shop and try to eavesdrop on them? Could I risk being recognized? With my hair so different, and sunglasses on, I didn't think Didier would recognize me. Nick had spotted me easily enough when he saw me in the café, but he had known I was alive. Didier thought I was dead. I slipped my sunglasses on and headed for the café.

The café was small and intimate, with only a dozen tables. It was typical island décor, a mural of a beach scene, tables decorated with conch shells, seashell-patterned curtains at the windows. Even though the café was air-conditioned, ceiling fans whirred lazily, keeping up the charade that the hotel was an island resort instead of a cookie-cutter motel.

Didier was sitting with his back to the door, so I was safe from his scrutiny. I chose a window seat as close to their table as I dared and sat with my back to them.

Carl Turpin was speaking, but his voice was so low that I couldn't hear what he was saying.

When he was finished, the other man spoke. I didn't recognize his voice, but like Didier, he had a heavy French accent. 'I am sure we can get this matter taken care of.'

'Of course we will,' Betty Turpin said. Even if I couldn't hear everything the others said, I could count on her loud voice to carry.

Carl said something in a soothing tone, but all I caught was '. . . boat back.'

Didier growled something in reply. My skin prickled at the sound of his voice.

The other man said clearly, 'Mr and Mrs Turpin would not try to cheat us, Didier. They know that would be a mistake.' Cheat them? What did that mean?

'Look,' Carl Turpin said, his voice louder now, sounding tense, '*Island Ice* was stopping at Trophy Cay, but – *mumble, mumble* – this weekend. But now – *mumble, mumble* – back here today or tomorrow.'

'Ah, here we are,' Didier's companion said.

The waitress had arrived with a clatter of dishes. Betty Turpin demanded cream, and the server said she'd be right back with it.

'And why exactly is your captain held up?' the unknown man said. His tone was overly polite.

I had risked a glance at him when I came in. He was a stocky man with sagging jowls and heavy bags under his eyes. In contrast to the others, who were casually dressed, the man had on cream-colored linen pants, a silk shirt, and leather shoes. What did he mean, the captain was held up? Maybe that's why Nick had met with them at the café – to give them some BS about the boat being delayed. But why?

'He had some trouble with the boat,' Betty said. Oh my God, they still thought Johnny had the boat and was bringing it back.

But that made no sense. Didier had hijacked the boat, so he knew
the Turpins didn't have it. Unless he hadn't told them.

'How did you find out about this trouble he was supposedly
having?'

'What do you mean, *supposedly?*' Betty said sharply. 'A friend
of his told us.'

'Who is this friend?'

'His name is Nick Garnier.'

So Nick still hadn't told them the boat was back in Nassau.
He had had plenty of time, so why hadn't he? And why hadn't
the Coast Guard notified them? That made more sense. Even
though the name had been painted over and I hadn't found the
boat's papers, there was plenty of identification on the engine of
a boat. That information was with the US Coast Guard, and it
might take a day or two for the Bahamian Coast Guard to get it
from them. Besides, like most government entities in the islands,
they probably weren't in any hurry.

'Nick Garnier? How interesting. And you believe him?' The
unknown man's voice was cold.

With bad timing, the waitress showed up at my table. 'Iced
tea, please,' I said and thrust the menu at her.

When the waitress walked away, the foursome was speaking
more quietly. Maybe they had noticed that I was nearby. To give
the impression that I wasn't paying attention to them, I dug my
cell phone out of my bag and pretended to punch in numbers.
'Hey,' I said. 'What's up?' I pretended to listen for a few seconds
and then giggled. I wasn't a giggler, and it sounded fake even
to me.

When I picked up the conversation again, Carl was speaking,
but again I couldn't make out what he said, just that he sounded
cowed.

Betty said, 'He'll be here, and you'll get your money as soon
as he arrives.'

There was a long pause. I wished there was some way I could
see them. I hunched down over the phone as if I was saying
something I didn't want overheard.

Didier's companion said something I couldn't hear, and then,
'But your information and our information don't quite agree.'

'What do you mean?' Betty asked.

'Didier, would you care to tell Mrs Turpin what happened?' He spoke to Didier as if he were speaking to a minion.

Didier explained that Johnny had unexpectedly left Trophy Cay with 'a friend' on board. 'A woman. We had no idea who she was, so we began to worry that he was planning to double-cross you and take the package.'

'Wait. How did you know this? You were following the boat?'

'And a good thing we did, too.'

Betty interrupted. 'Carl, I told you I didn't like the look of that Johnny guy when you hired him. Now look what he's gotten us into.'

'I'm sure Johnny will be here,' Carl said, louder. 'We were told it would be today or tomorrow.'

The man with Didier said, 'I sincerely doubt it, no matter what your friend Garnier said.'

Betty gasped audibly, but the man ignored her and continued. 'Didier acted on his suspicions and he boarded the boat and took care of your captain and his friend. Wherever the boat is, your captain is not with it.'

I almost dropped my phone.

'What do you mean, *took care of them*?' Betty's bullying voice had gone up a notch to a squeak. Even at a whisper, Betty Turpin's voice carried. 'Wait. You killed Johnny? And took the package?' As easily as that, they had dismissed Johnny's dead friend – me.

My heart was hammering, and I had an irrational fantasy of standing up and screaming, 'You're wrong! I'm not dead! I got away.' My cheeks burned with horror that I would even have a fantasy of doing something so crazy. I was seized by a wave of nausea. I gulped down tea to keep from retching.

'What did you mean when you said "wherever the boat is?"' Her voice had lost its screech and was more a gasp.

Suddenly, a chair was pushed back and Didier said, 'That's what we would like to know.' I could tell from the direction of his voice that he had gotten up and was standing near Betty Turpin. 'My crew and I left your boat on the dock at Trophy Cay for an hour to have dinner, and when we came back, it was gone.'

'Gone?' Betty sputtered. 'What do you mean, *gone*?'

'Disappeared. Hijacked.'

'Well, it's your fault if you left it untended!'

The other man spoke. 'If you know who took the boat and where it is now, I suggest you say so.'

'How could we know anything?' Carl Turpin blustered. I could hear him scramble to his feet. 'We weren't even here.'

I clutched my phone tightly to my ear, holding my breath.

'It's always possible that you changed your mind and arranged with Mr Garnier to confiscate the boat.'

'We don't even know who Nick Garnier is! He said he was our captain's friend. He doesn't know Johnny is dead,' Betty said.

'I seriously doubt that. I repeat, if you know where your boat is, you would be advised to tell us.'

'We're telling you the truth; we don't know,' Carl said.

'Then you'd better start looking.' The man's voice grew menacing. 'And perhaps you could start by asking your good friend Mr Garnier what he knows.' Footsteps, as the men walked toward the door. I was terrified that Didier's gaze would fall on me and that he would somehow guess who I was. I felt like a rabbit out in an open field with a hunter.

'Wait!' Betty called out. 'We'll find the boat. How do we get in touch with you?'

The man with Didier called back, 'Don't worry, we'll be in touch.'

The Turpins were silent for several seconds after the men left, and then Betty Turpin said, 'I told you we shouldn't leave him to go to Georgetown on his own. I didn't trust him. You're the one who thought he was so wonderful.'

'Betty, I had to go back to New York because something came up with the money end of things. You could have gone to Georgetown with him if you were so worried.'

'Whatever! But now we've got to find that goddam boat.' They scraped their chairs back and walked out.

I sat transfixed for several minutes after they had gone. Hearing the two men speak so casually of murdering me and Johnny had hit me once again with the stark knowledge that I truly had barely escaped dying. I took deep, measured breaths and talked myself down. *You survived. You're tough. Remember that.*

Seeing Didier and hearing him talk had revived the terror of my near-death. I had considered getting out of here and leaving the police to clean up the mess. But hearing the foursome talk, I changed my mind. No way was I leaving. Didier and his pals had tried to kill me. I wasn't going to let them get away with my attempted murder. And I had made a promise to Johnny.

I had gained one thing from listening to the foursome. I knew that Nick was involved, too. Not only did he know Didier's crew, but he also knew the owners of the boat. What was he up to? Was he double-crossing them, maneuvering to get the jewelry for himself?

I fled the hotel and went to the dockside bar nearby. I ordered a rum and tonic and sat staring out at the boats, mulling over what I knew, and what I didn't know.

Johnny had been carrying the contraband jewelry to take back to the Turpins. That was pretty straightforward. He and Nick were somehow hooked up together. But Didier disrupted the plans. Maybe Didier had made a deal with Nick Garnier to cut out the Turpins. Nick had seemed upset at Johnny's death, but maybe he had only intended for the jewels to be stolen – not that murder would be involved.

I struggled to remember exactly what I had seen in the billiard room at the resort between Nick and Johnny. Johnny's backpack had been open between them. But I distinctly remembered that Nick had the package in his hands. He handed it back to Johnny. If Nick and Didier had been planning to cut out the Turpins, why hadn't Nick simply told Johnny he was taking the package back to Nassau himself? How could Johnny have stopped him? So why did he give it back to Johnny? My head was starting to hurt.

All I knew is that whatever they were all playing at, I had introduced chaos by stealing the boat. I should feel satisfaction, but I was wary of what I had set in motion, and afraid that this time the attempt on my life might be successful.

I headed back to the lot where I'd left my car and headed for home.

EIGHTEEN

Rodney was unhappy. He was fine with whatever they had to do to avenge Paco's brother; he was all in. But when he got here and saw what a nice place it was, he wanted to have some fun first. 'I've never been to a place like Nassau and I want to get a taste of it.'

Paco had agreed to hang out for a few days, but he barely hid his impatience. He complained that he wanted to get the job done and go back home.

Paco was a home boy, no question. Rodney appreciated that Paco had tried to let him have some fun, but now that they had been here a while, Rodney wanted more. He wasn't ready to leave. 'What's the hurry? The women on this island are too fine to waste,' he argued.

'No, man, I can't relax until we take care of business. Afterwards, we can hang longer.'

But Rodney knew Paco well enough to know that once they had gotten rid of the girl, he wouldn't want to stay. 'What's one more day?' he asked.

Paco held him to his promise, though, and this morning they had gone on the hunt. He and Rodney agreed to split up, even though it meant renting a second car. Neither man complained about having to search the whole island. They were used to being patient to get what they were after.

They knew Jessie Madison was working as a diving instructor, but they didn't know where. So they had set out to question the dive shops. The shops were located all over the island, but Paco finally found the one where Jessie worked. When they met back up, he bragged that he managed to talk the girl behind the counter into telling him where Jessie lived. Now it was evening, and they were sitting in their rented convertible outside her apartment building waiting for her.

'That's her!' Paco jerked his chin at a girl getting out of her car.

'Driving that rust bucket?' The ancient Corona had arrived spewing smoke. It looked like if you poked it, the frame would crumple.

'Yeah.'

'You sure? I thought she was a brunette.'

'Yeah, well, chicks dye their hair, genius.'

'She's a babe.'

'Not for much longer. Not after I get through with her.'

'We gotta make sure, though. We don't want to mess with the wrong person.'

'What, you want to go over and ask if she's Jessie Madison? There were pictures of all the dive people at the shop, and I took a look. It's her. She looks like her sister.' He nudged Rodney, excited. 'Look, she's taking a wetsuit and a sports bag out of the car. I'm telling you, it's her.'

Rodney grunted. He considered protesting that it seemed a shame to kill somebody who looked that good, but he knew Paco well enough to know anything he said would be wasted energy. Paco wasn't going to change his mind. Rodney figured if he was in Paco's shoes, he'd probably feel the same way. 'You ready to go get her?'

'No hurry.' He was watching the girl intently. He turned to Rodney with a leer. 'Anticipation is half the fun.'

Rodney started to give him some smart mouth, asking why they couldn't hang out a few more days if he liked anticipation so much, but he didn't want to waste his breath.

Paco insisted on sitting, waiting for the girl to come back out. 'She's not the kind of girl to stay in at night. We'll see where she goes.'

After a while, Rodney got out of the car and paced. He couldn't stand inaction. He wasn't as patient as Paco. If it had been him, he would have done the girl and moved on.

NINETEEN

When I got home, Shelley was watching a rerun of *America's Top Model* and painting her toenails again, this time chartreuse.

I wanted to smooth things over with her. I sank onto the sofa next to her, groaning.

'Hey! Careful. You'll mess up my pedicure.' Shelley shot a sidelong glance at me. 'Where have you been? You smell like a brewery.'

'I just had one drink,' I said. 'Listen, Shelley, I'm sorry. You were right. I have been acting weird. I've been stressed lately. But it won't last forever. Are we OK?'

Shelley made a pouty noise. 'I don't know. When you came to live at my place, you said you liked to party. I don't want to always worry that you're going to rube out on me.'

I couldn't help laughing. 'Rube out? What the hell is that?' Shelley was always picking up odd expressions because she served tourists from all over.

Shelley cut her eyes at me, a grin playing on her lips. 'Some guy sitting at the bar said it. I thought it sounded good. You know, like a redneck is a rube, and they don't know what's up?' Her smile flitted away. 'But I mean, really, Jessie. Shape up!'

'I hear you. I had a kind of strange experience, and it's taking me a couple of days to get over it.'

Shelley screwed the top back on the polish. 'What strange experience?' She didn't even look at me. She wasn't that interested.

Oh, nothing. Some people tried to kill me and I had to steal a boat. No big thing. No way I could explain it to Shelley. 'Something odd that happened on Trophy Cay. Don't worry. I'll be fine.'

'On Trophy Cay? You mean after I left? Did sweet Johnny get rough?' She zeroed in on me for good gossip.

The words stabbed me. 'No, nothing like that.'

With no prospect of juicy details, she went back to her polish. We stared at the screen, where the models were being shot in various poses on outdoor sculptures.

'I could do that,' Shelley stretched one leg into the air. 'My legs are as good as hers, don't you think?'

'No question. You've got better hair, too.'

Shelley fluffed out her blond mane.

My cell phone rang, and I saw that it was Kevin. I couldn't talk to him in front of Shelley, so I headed for my room and shut the door behind me, hoping she wouldn't take it as a snub.

'You called and said it was important. What's up?' Kevin had on his official cop voice. And he sounded rushed.

I cut to the chase. 'The guy wounded in the casino shootout? I saw a picture of him in the paper. He's one of the guys who tried to kill me. Maybe you can find out from him what's going on.'

There was a moment of silence. 'You're kidding. Goddammit!'

I was startled at the fury in his voice. 'Why, what's the problem?'

'He didn't make it. He died this afternoon.'

'Oh, Kevin.' I groaned.

'Yeah, I'd like to have questioned him. I'd also like to have known what the hell he was doing at the casino. We can't figure out what went down in that shootout.' He was talking low and fast, as if he was thinking out loud.

'Who was the shooter?'

'We haven't ID'd him. Listen, I can't stay on the phone. We've got a meeting starting right now. I thought I'd give you a quick call and make sure you were OK.'

'Yes, I'm OK, but . . .'

In the background, I heard someone say, 'Kevin, you're holding us up.'

'Wait! There's more.' I needed to tell him about the jewelry.

'Can't talk now. I'll get back to you.'

'Kevin! This is important.' But I was talking to dead air. I punched his number back in. I had to make him listen. But my call went to voicemail. Frustrated, I tossed the cell phone onto the bed and paced to the window. It was dusk. I saw a guy pacing in the parking lot. He kept glancing at the building. I felt uneasy.

Could Didier have found out where I lived? I was too far away to recognize the man. Was I being paranoid? God, I wished I could talk to Kevin and get this whole thing over with. My plan of exacting revenge on Didier for killing Johnny seemed more and more remote. Eventually, I sat down on the bed.

I'd counted on turning the jewelry over to Kevin tonight. I could wait until tomorrow, but the longer I had it, the more nervous it made me. The Turpins thought the backpack with the jewelry was aboard *Island Ice*. When they got the boat back and didn't find the pack, they'd be desperate to find it. And eventually, they'd find me. Maybe through Nick. He knew I was the last person to be on the boat. Even though I had told him I didn't have the backpack, he'd probably suspect I was lying. I lay back on my bed and stared at the ceiling. Maybe it was best if I returned the jewelry to the boat. It wasn't my business anyway. It was police business. I could tell Kevin where it was when I spoke to him.

I rejected that idea. Returning the jewelry meant I'd be giving up. I sat up, feeling like I was at a dead end. It was dangerous for me to keep the jewelry, but I didn't want to give it back either. Then I had an idea. I could sneak the backpack onto the boat, without the package in it. When they found the backpack empty, the Turpins might think one of Didier's crew had stolen the package. I'd be off the hook. Now all I had to do was find someplace safe to stash the jewelry and get the backpack back onto the catamaran. The first part would be easy enough, but returning the backpack to the boat would be something else entirely.

I tackled the jewelry problem first. Where could I stow it where no one would suspect? Certainly not in my apartment or my car. I didn't have a safety deposit box – I barely had a bank account. I could ask Jeremy to hold the package for me, but I didn't want to put him in danger. Same with Shelley. Besides, she'd want to know what was in it, and I couldn't trust her not to open it.

And then I realized the perfect place: one of the dive boats. No one would think of the package being there. And I'd be close to it. It didn't have to stay there long. Just until I talked to Kevin.

I'd hide the jewelry on the dive boat, and after that, I'd find out where the Coast Guard kept their confiscated boats and figure out a way to return the pack.

TWENTY

During the day, the dock where the dive boats were berthed bustled with activity, but now it was deserted and I couldn't help feeling vulnerable, given what I was carrying. It was dusk, and the afternoon wind had died down. The dive boats, four in Jeremy's fleet, hulked in the shadows, spooky and unwelcoming. My imagination was working overtime. I surveyed them, trying to decide which one to hide the jewelry on. They were basically all alike, but dive instructors tended to gravitate toward the same boat every day.

The one I usually worked on was called *J-Diver2*. If someone did suspect I had stashed the jewelry on one of these boats, anybody could tell them I usually worked on *J-Diver2*. Maybe I should hide the pouch on one of the others. But I preferred to be near the stash when I went out on the boat tomorrow. If I was lucky, Kevin would call tonight and I could bring him here to retrieve it, but if I had to wait, I wanted to know the package was where I could keep an eye on it.

I stepped aboard *J-Diver2*, feeling jittery. There was still a hint of light low on the western horizon, but under the canopy of the dive boat, it was pitch black. I heard the crunch of gravel and saw light beams as a car drove into the parking lot a few hundred yards away. The engine switched off. I waited, but I didn't hear a car door. Whoever it was couldn't see me in the gloom of the boat, much less what I was up to. One car had already come in behind me, but they had parked near the entrance. I hoped nobody was planning to come here to the dive boats. It could even be Jeremy, checking on something. Maybe it would be best if I tried this later. I went back out and stood on the stern of the boat, looking down the dock, but no one appeared.

I moved back up under the boat's canopy, turned on the penlight

on my keyring and looked around for a place to put the pouch.
A dive boat was a basic craft, intended only for ferrying divers
and snorkelers back and forth to dive sites. There were no refine-
ments for people's comfort. There were crude benches for people
to sit on while they were underway, but no storage lockers. There
were pegs for holding equipment, and a spacious holding area
for the tanks, which were stashed overnight in a shed. I flashed
the light on the instrument panel. Next to the wheel was a cabinet
door marked 'First Aid.' Diving was a rigorous sport, but I had
rarely seen the First Aid kit brought out. It was one of the few
places on the boat where I could hide something.

I opened the door. The bin was small and crammed with
different kinds of medical emergency items, everything from
packets of Band-aids and antiseptic cream to a big plastic bag
at the bottom of the bin that held a defibrillator. The defib bag
was much roomier than it needed to be. I took the pouch out of
the backpack and was able to fit the pouch into the defib bag
with room to spare.

After I shut the bin, I sat down on one of the benches in the
dark, debating whether I was doing the right thing by leaving it
here. But I couldn't think of anyplace better. It would have to
do for now. I'd be in touch with Kevin soon, and then the jewelry
would be out of my hands.

When I walked down the dock toward my car, I saw that the
two other cars were still in the lot. One, a convertible with two
men in it, was parked close to my car. The other was a white
SUV near the entrance to the lot. I was probably being paranoid,
but I was worried that one of the men from *Island Ice* had either
recognized me, or Nick had told them where I was, and they had
followed me here.

I walked faster as I got near my car, ready to run if I needed
to. But whoever it was made no move to get out of the convertible or the SUV.

Still, I was glad when my car started right away and I was on
my way to the other side of the island, to dispose of the
backpack.

From what the Bahamian Coast Guard officer had told me, I
knew vaguely where the boat was being kept. What I didn't know
was whether I would be able to get onto it. If the boat was with

others that were being held as evidence, it would likely be under the watchful eye of a security guard, or behind a physical barricade.

The traffic was heavy this time of evening, with tourists cruising the island looking for action, and it took me almost an hour to drive to the other side of the island. There was never a time when the traffic was light in Nassau, even on weeknights. There weren't that many cars on the island, but there weren't enough roads to take care of them.

Following the GPS on my phone, I saw that the Coast Guard's main station was located in a warehouse area. I turned off the main road into a maze of pot-holed roads snaking between hulking buildings. This was where cargo going to and from the island was stored until it could be distributed or loaded on a cargo barge. If I had thought the dock where the dive boats were moored was spooky, this was worse. It was a working area, not kept up for looks. There was junk everywhere; old, discarded equipment, broken packing crates, giant trash bins overflowing with plastic, and coils of wire.

I drove slowly, searching for the building, until I reached an area that was better kept, and finally spotted the Bahamian Coast Guard office. It was closed for the night. One hundred feet away, a ramp led up to a dock secured with a high chain-link fence topped with razor wire. This must be where confiscated boats were kept.

I didn't want to park in front of the Coast Guard office in case there was a night watchman on duty. He might be curious why someone was parked there. I drove a block away and tucked in next to a warehouse, between two forklifts. I heard another car stop down the street and looked back, but it turned off into another warehouse lot.

When I got back to the Coast Guard dock, I slipped behind a stinky dumpster close to a nearby warehouse and waited to see if a security guard came by. I had been lurking there for five minutes when a rat came scuttling across the open area toward me. I shuddered and stamped my foot at it. It stopped and looked right at me. I waved my arms. 'Beat it,' I whispered. For a minute, I thought it was going to ignore me, but just then a car drove up and stopped near the dock, and the rat darted back the way it had come.

From my position behind the dumpster, I watched a portly, uniformed man with a flashlight get out of the car and stroll up the ramp. He continued to the far end of the dock, where he paused. I couldn't see what he was doing, but I could hear it. He'd taken the opportunity in the dark to relieve himself off the dock. After a minute, he strolled back, humming to himself. He got back in his car and drove away.

As soon as he left, I ran up the ramp to the gate to see if I could get inside. The gate was located midway between the two ends of the dock. To the right, a small spotlight illuminated the berths. There, I saw only Coast Guard vessels – a couple of big ocean-going trawlers and a few smaller cutters. The left-hand side was ill-lit. From the outline of the boats, I could see that there were various shapes and sizes. I walked down to the end and spotted *Island Ice* on a side-tie at the end of the dock. How was I going to get to the boat? Besides the razor wire that would be impossible to climb over, the fence extended five feet beyond the dock and then wrapped around. Lights from across the water showed that the fence wrapped around the back, too. They were serious about keeping these boats impounded. I supposed I could swim to it, if I couldn't find any other way, but that held no appeal.

The security was tighter than I had imagined it might be, but then most of the boats confiscated were part of drug arrests. People involved with drugs probably had a lot of determination to get their boats back, even if they had to do so by stealing them.

I returned to the gate. Idly, I tried the handle and was startled when it turned and the gate opened. Someone had left the lock unsecured. But I soon discovered why. I pushed the door further, but it stopped cold, only a few inches open. Not nearly enough space for me to squeeze through.

I looked up at the top of the gate. Just beyond my reach, a chain with a heavy lock secured the gate. That's why it barely opened. I pushed harder. All I needed was ten inches to be able to squeeze through the opening. But it simply wouldn't give. I glared up at the chain. When had chains become the bane of my existence?

I considered whether I should find the watchman and try to

sweet talk him into letting me in, but something told me he'd heard it all before.

I wondered how often the watchman came around. He hadn't seemed particularly alert, but it wouldn't be a great idea to let him catch me here. I walked back down the ramp to the side of the warehouse where he'd parked before and made sure he wasn't lurking anywhere. It was utterly still.

Maybe it wasn't such a good idea to be doing this. I could come back tomorrow morning and try to talk my way onto the boat.

I wasn't ready to give up yet, though. I had one more idea. Near the dumpster, I spied a sturdy wooden crate. It was bashed in on one side, but still strong enough to hold my 125 pounds. I carried it to the gate and stepped onto it so I could reach up to examine the lock and chain. I found that a portion of the chain hung back behind the gate, probably for the convenience of whoever had put the lock on. That left more free links than were apparent from the front. I put my fingers through the links and tugged, and the chain slipped toward me. Now the gate would open a little farther.

Hopping down from the crate, I tried the gate again, and this time it opened several more inches, enough for me to squeeze through. I returned the crate to where I had gotten it, ran back to my car and retrieved the backpack, and slipped inside the fence.

Now, if there wasn't a giant, toothy dog guarding the interior dock, I was home free. Even if the boat was locked up, I could find someplace on the deck to put the backpack. But apparently the Coast Guard trusted its security system – the boat wasn't locked. I pulled open the sliding door into the saloon and crept inside. Dim light from outside lit up the saloon, but it didn't penetrate the cabin area. I stashed the backpack in the storage under one of the seats in the saloon where I'd found it. The hard part was done.

I listened for the watchman but heard nothing. With the back-pack safely stowed, I suddenly felt more frightened than I had been during the whole venture. I had been so busy working out the quandary of how to get into the boat that it hadn't occurred to me that if Didier had found out where the boat was being kept, he might be looking for a way to get onto it, too. It would be crazy to get the backpack securely aboard and then run into one of my abductors.

I ran along the dock inside the fence, pulled open the gate and squeezed out. Now at least if the security guard or anyone else found me, I could claim I never got aboard. Nevertheless, the prospect of running into anyone compelled me to race for the car. As I rounded the corner of the warehouse, I ran smack into a man. He grabbed my arm and twisted it behind me.

'What are you doing here, Missy?'

I turned my head and saw that it was the security guard. He hiked my arm up higher. 'How come you were sneaking around here?'

'Ow! I'm not doing anything wrong. I came to see if the Coast Guard had a boat I'm looking for.'

'Funny time of day to be doing it.' He was breathing heavily, and I got a faint whiff of alcohol.

I didn't reply.

Suddenly, I felt his free hand between my legs. 'I think we can work it out so I don't have to turn you in.'

'Get away from me, you pervert!' I lashed out with my free hand, hitting his arm, but he tightened his grip.

'I'm not the one walking around in the dark looking for trouble.'

He had one hand on my arm, the other between my legs. Which meant he wasn't holding a weapon on me. I bent my knees and dropped my weight straight down and drove my elbow into his crotch.

'Oww,' he howled. 'You devil!' He lost his grip on my arm, but was still on his feet, although he staggered. I punched him in the throat. He clutched his throat with both hands, his eyes widening as he fought for air. I took off running toward my car.

Just as I opened the car door, a figure stepped out of the shadows. 'That was a tidy move.'

I gave a yelp before I recognized the voice. 'Nick! You scared the hell out of me. What are you doing here?'

'I could ask you the same thing. Are you begging for trouble? Or are you accident prone, or what?' I couldn't see his face in the shadows, but he sounded like he was laughing at me.

'I remembered that I left something on *Island Ice* and I thought

I could come and get it.' I gestured toward the dock. 'But it's impossible to get in.'

Nick snorted. 'Really. Must have been something pretty important. You couldn't have waited until tomorrow and asked the Coast Guard to let you aboard? Or waited until the owners got her back and asked them for your valuable property?'

My laugh sounded hollow. 'Oh, it was just a whim. I happened to be on this side of the island, and it didn't occur to me they'd keep the boat locked up.'

Nick took a step closer to me, pinning me up against the car. For the first time, I could see his face in the light of a security beam. His jaw was tight, and his dark eyes furious. 'I followed you here and I saw you take the backpack onto the boat. Why did you do that? You told me you didn't have it, that you left it there.'

'OK, so I lied. Sue me. But now it's back on board.' My heart was hammering so hard I could barely hear myself talk. First the security guard, and now Nick. Of the two, I would have preferred to take my chances with the guard. I was pretty sure Nick wouldn't fall for any sudden moves on my part if I tried to get away from him.

'How lucky that you had the backpack with you when you came over to this side of the island.'

'What's your excuse for being here?' I asked.

'Trying to keep you out of trouble.'

'I can take care of myself.'

'Look, Jessie, luck has been with you so far, but it isn't going to last forever. You need to get out of here. Nassau is a dangerous place for you to be right now.'

'And it isn't dangerous for you?'

He glanced around. 'We can't talk here. Have you had dinner? We can talk over dinner.'

'What?' I was hungry, but I didn't know if I wanted to have a meal with him. I started to refuse but then realized this was my chance to find out more about him: what he was up to and how he knew the men who had abducted me. I didn't trust him, but at a restaurant there would be other people around, and he couldn't hurt me.

'Dinner?' he said. 'A meal? A chance for me to persuade you to make an intelligent decision for once?'

'I guess dinner's OK.'

'We'll take my car,' he said.

Oh, right. No way was I going to get into the car with him. 'No. Let's meet somewhere.'

'You know Bud's Seafood Shack?'

'Yes. It's a terrible place.'

'It's close by.'

'I'll follow you.'

He shrugged. 'Suit yourself.' He watched me get into my car. 'Promise me you won't run away.'

'Of course I won't. I'm hungry. And dinner's on you.'

I waited until a white SUV pulled out. Nick stuck his hand out the window and waved. When had he changed cars? I fell in line behind him.

TWENTY-ONE

On the ten-minute drive to Bud's, I fought the impulse to veer off onto another road and make a quick getaway. I didn't do it because Nick was driving a much more powerful, newer vehicle, and he would overtake me in no time. Plus, this was an opportunity to quiz him on his involvement with the men who had abducted me. From the conversation I'd overheard at the café, I knew he was in deep. But deep into what, exactly? I was determined to find out.

Bud's Seafood Shack was in a block of restaurants that catered to tourists as 'authentic Bahamian food,' with names like Papi's Big Plate, Aunt Suki's, and The Deep Dive. Islanders came here because the food was cheap and plentiful. The place was crowded, but we were able to get a table indoors at the back. The tables were big rustic picnic tables, scarred and dented from years of use.

Nick and I slid into a wooden booth across from each other.

Between stashing the jewelry and sneaking onto the boat, my nerves were jangling, and the deafening noise didn't help. I wondered why Nick had chosen this place. It didn't seem like his type. I could imagine him more in a bistro. French.

A huge waiter named Benedict came to take our orders right away. I ordered a beer and Nick said he'd have the same.

'And a bottle of water,' I said.

While the waiter went off to get our drinks, Nick studied the menu, and I studied him. Despite my mistrust of him, I couldn't help being attracted to him. His dark hair and eyes gave him a brooding, mysterious look. He had a shadow of beard along his jawline that accentuated his scar. His muscles stood out defined inside the chest-hugging T-shirt, a definite turn-on.

He was dressed in black – long pants, a long-sleeved T-shirt and black shoes. It looked good on him, but something told me he hadn't dressed that way for looks. Dressed in dark clothing, he would be harder to see at night. So, what had he been doing near the Coast Guard dock? Had he planned to sneak onto *Island Ice* and steal the jewelry? He didn't know that I knew what was in the backpack, so I wondered what he thought I was doing with it.

He threw down the menu. I liked his hands. They were square and strong-looking, with dark hair on his wrists and the backs of his hands.

'What are you ordering?' he asked.

'Doesn't matter. It will all taste the same. Fish. It will be served on huge mounds of island dirty rice with plantains, tomatoes, onions, cucumbers and whatever else they can heap onto a plate.'

'That good, huh?'

'It will fill us up.'

The waiter brought the beer and water, and we gave him our order. I drank half the bottle of water. When I put it down, I looked down at my clothes. I was dressed in cargo shorts and a formerly white T-shirt. My activities at the dock had left me with smudges and cobwebs on my clothes. My hands were grimy. I went off to the bathroom to wash them.

I laughed when I looked in the mirror. Even though my hair was short, it was sticking out at funny angles. I fussed with it and washed my hands and dusted off my clothes and put on some lipstick.

'Much better,' Nick said dryly when I sat back down.

'Glad you approve.' We both picked up our beers and took sips at the same time.

He smiled. 'How do you like living in the Bahamas?'

'I thought we were going to talk about you,' I said. 'For starters, what you are doing here in Nassau?'

'I do some international business,' he said, and without pausing, 'How do you come to be here?'

I refused to let myself be diverted this time. 'That doesn't tell me why you're involved with those men who attacked Johnny and me.'

'No, I guess it doesn't.' He sipped his beer and looked out over the diners before he brought his attention back. 'I'm here to retrieve something they stole.'

'From?'

'That isn't important. The important thing is that I was hired to get control of it.'

What did he mean? He had had the jewelry when we were on Trophy Cay. I had seen it lying between him and Johnny in the billiard room.

I decided to go along with his charade for now. 'What are you supposed to do with it?'

'Take it back where it belongs.'

'How did Johnny fit in?'

His gaze slipped past me, and I saw the muscle in his jaw tighten. 'I probably shouldn't have involved him. I don't think he took seriously the danger he was in.' His eyes flashed to mine. 'Sort of like you.'

'How was he involved?'

Nick hesitated, his eyes calculating. 'He was transporting the items I was supposed to retrieve.'

'That makes no sense. If you hired him, how did he get the goods? And why didn't you get them instead?' It seemed silly to be dancing around the subject, but Nick didn't know that I knew what was in the package.

'It's complicated.' Nick looked relieved when the waiter appeared with our plates, overloaded, as I'd predicted. Nick's eyes widened.

'Dare you to eat it all.' I snickered.

'I've lost my appetite just looking at it.' He stabbed a piece of fried plantain and stuck it in his mouth. 'Have you been here before?'

'Don't try to change the subject. You said it's complicated, so let me ask you a simple question. If you've been hired to get something from those guys, how come they know who you are? Wouldn't it be better for your employers to send someone the thieves didn't know to retrieve it?'

Nick grimaced. 'Do we really need to go into this now? Why don't we enjoy the meal? Besides, I'd like to get to know you better.' He leaned toward me with an ingratiating smile that I took to be partly mocking.

'All you need to know is that those men tried to kill me, and they kept mentioning your name. If what you say is true, how come they knew who you were?'

'Let's just say it's a cat-and-mouse game.'

I poked a fork into the mound of rice. 'But who is the cat and who is the mouse?'

He blew out a breath. 'Sometimes I'm not sure.' He sounded sincere.

'Why was it only the two of you on the job? It seems like a risk to send a couple of men to do such a big job. Your employers must have a lot of faith in you.'

He paused, fork halfway to his mouth, his expression going blank. He laid his fork down. 'It wasn't supposed to be just the two of us.'

'Who else?'

His face hardened. 'A guy who was on the boat with the crew that jumped you. He'd been checking in until the night you and Johnny were boarded. I haven't heard from him, and I suspect the worst.'

I remembered the loud bang I'd heard minutes before Didier's men came aboard. A gunshot? 'I think you're right.' I told him about hearing the noise.

'Now do you understand why I want you to stay out of this? You've already seen good evidence that they won't hesitate to kill you.'

I stalled while I toyed with my food. I did consider it. Maybe he was right. But I remembered the conversation I'd overheard this afternoon. The satisfaction in Didier's voice when he said he'd taken care of Johnny and me. I felt my jaw tighten. I was afraid of those guys, but I refused to let fear drive me away. I owed them revenge not only for Johnny but for myself. 'I have no plans to be chased out of here by those men.'

He set his beer down so carefully that I had a feeling he would have preferred to throw it at me. 'Don't be ridiculous. You had a narrow escape, and they aren't going to let you get away with that again.'

'As if I didn't already know that. Let me tell you what happened this afternoon.'

He sighed. 'What now?'

'I overheard an interesting conversation between one of the men who tried to kill me and Betty and Carl Turpin.'

He tensed. 'How do you know who they are?'

'I never actually met them, but Johnny pointed them out to me the first time I met him a few weeks ago. And then, strangely enough, I saw you with them the night after I brought *Island Ice* back from Trophy Cay.'

He watched me, his eyes calculating, while he rubbed his thumb across the scar on his lip. 'Where did you overhear them?'

'I'll get to that. Why were you with them when I saw you in the café that night?' I asked.

'I needed to stall them. I told them I knew Johnny and that he had called and asked me to contact them, to tell them he was delayed.'

'Well, at least you have a plausible story.' I stabbed a piece of fish and put it in my mouth. It was the consistency of rubber.

'You said you overheard something this afternoon. Where were you?'

I described eavesdropping on them in the restaurant. 'I heard them say they had killed me and Johnny.'

'Are you crazy?' Nick said, his voice raised. 'Do you realize what would have happened if they had recognized you?'

People at the neighboring table were glancing curiously at us. Our waiter materialized. 'Everything OK?' He eyed our barely touched plates.

'I'll have another beer,' Nick snapped. 'You want one?' He asked me.

'Sure.'

'I was really careful,' I said as soon as the waiter was gone.

'I kept my back to them and the only time Didier ever saw me, he was more interested in Johnny.'

Nick shook his head and poked at his food.

I ate a few bites of rice, feeling smug that I had rattled him. 'When I was listening, I also heard them say that the Turpins didn't know where their boat was. How come you didn't tell them it's back here?'

He waved a hand dismissing my question. 'What did the guy with Didier look like?'

I described him. 'Do you know who he is?'

He nodded.

'Tell me,' I said.

The waiter plopped our beers down.

'I'm not going to encourage you by telling you anything you don't already know. You've got to get off this island until these men are caught. This man . . .' He shook his head. 'He's worse than the others.'

I wavered again. I had been planning to leave soon anyway. Speeding up the process by a couple of weeks wouldn't be a problem. I almost laughed. Who was I kidding? I had no intention of leaving.

I leaned forward and spoke sweetly. 'It seems to me like you're the one in danger, with both of the men you were working with dead.'

'There will be reinforcements. Soon.'

'Until then, I'll stay.'

Nick clamped his jaw. He gave a low growl. 'He said you were stubborn.'

'Who? Johnny?'

'No. John Farrell.'

Hearing the name of my ex-trainer at the FBI, my jaw dropped. 'Who?'

'You heard me. I talked to your ex-trainer. He said you were smart and resourceful, but that you were stubborn and didn't work well with others.'

I started to speak, but he held up a hand to stop me. 'He didn't mean you didn't get along with people. He meant you thought you could do everything yourself, that you didn't need help from anyone.'

My fork clattered to my plate. My head was spinning. 'How did you know I was a trainee? Did you check up on me? How long have you known?'

Nick laid his fork down and put his elbows on the table. 'I told you I didn't trust you. But if your story was true, it meant you had some impressive skills. I asked my boss in New York to find out who you were. He called me back this afternoon and told me some very interesting facts. After that, I called Farrell.'

'Who is your boss?' I leaned forward, so mad I was seeing him through a film of red. 'And don't give me any more bullshit,' I added.

He sighed. 'No more BS. Got it. Farrell said I could share this with you. I work for a private security firm connected with the Jeweler's Security Alliance. I'll bet you've never heard of them.'

'No, I haven't.'

'Nobody has. And they prefer to keep it that way. It's a loose association of jewelry industry experts set up to fight jewelry theft around the world.'

'Jewelry theft? Like from jewelry stores or from private owners?'

'Retail stores mostly.'

'How big a deal is the theft?'

'Really big. Billions of dollars' worth of jewelry is stolen from stores every year.'

'Like the jewelry I found? It's magnificent. Is it from France? Didier's gang spoke French.'

'This jewelry happens to be from France, but they work all over.'

'How do they get away with it?'

'Most stores don't have enough security. The thefts are kept quiet because jewelers don't want gangsters to know how easy it is to do a jewel heist. That where the alliance comes come in.'

'And your job is to find the thieves and arrest them?'

He hesitated. 'We arrest them if we can. We try to work with local law enforcement, or even the FBI, but sometimes the alliance has to act on its own.'

I could see he was choosing his words carefully, which alerted my antennae.

'You mean it's like a vigilante group?'

He had piqued my interest. A private security firm that worked with the FBI. Imagine.

He laughed. 'That's a little harsh. It's just that we've found that the police and government law enforcement agencies don't always prioritize jewelry theft, so the alliance has an arm called I and R which works a little faster.'

'I and R stands for?'

'Investigation and Retrieval. That's what I do.'

I thought about it. There was something he wasn't revealing. 'Retrieval. So your main job is to retrieve the jewelry even if you can't arrest the thieves?'

He grimaced. 'You do know how to ask questions, don't you?'

'What's the answer?'

'That's not the main job, although sometimes all we can do is grab the goods and get out. But in this case, Didier's gang has been plaguing us so we set up the scheme to trap them. And then you showed up.'

'Really? You're blaming me? I didn't exactly ask for this.'

'I know you didn't. But here we are. Look, this gang is well organized and brutal. You got a taste of that. Now do you see why I want you out of the way?'

'I've done all right so far.'

'Yes, you're clever.' He gave a short bark of laughter. 'Anybody else would be dead by now. But you can't keep on trusting that cleverness will be enough.'

I wavered. He was making sense. Maybe it was time to bail.

He saw my indecision. 'My offer still stands. I'm prepared to get you on a plane out of here tomorrow morning.'

'All right,' I said. 'I can pack tonight. But I can't leave first thing. I need to clean up a couple of loose ends.'

'Good. I'm glad you've come to your senses.' Nick's jaw was tight, his mouth in a grim line. He pushed his plate away. 'We should get out of here.'

'Not so fast. I have a couple of other things to tell you. Did you know that Jaggo is dead?'

He blinked. 'He is? How did that happen? And how did you know?'

I had a twinge of satisfaction, knowing something he didn't know. I told him I had seen Jaggo's photo in the local newspaper.

'Remember I told you I called my cop friend and told him I'd
been abducted? He's been assigned to the case.'

'Maybe you should give me this cop's name. I need to have
a talk with him and ask him to back off. The local cops could
screw things up.'

'I trust Kevin. He's an ex-NYPD cop and a straight-up guy.'

'Yeah, well, we've had trouble with the Bahamian cops getting
in the way.'

'You can try getting in touch with him, but he's swamped.' I
wrote down Kevin's name and the station where we worked.
'There's something else.'

'What now?' He didn't try to hide his exasperation.

'I have the jewelry.'

He started laughing and dropped his head into his hands. 'And
you let me rattle on about the jewelry. I should have known you'd
be too nosy not to open the package.'

'It was kind of fun, actually. For a wild minute, I considered
hopping on a plane and disappearing with it.'

'Why didn't you?'

I shrugged. 'You know. Conscience and all that.'

'Overrated.' He laughed but sobered quickly. 'If you knew the
jewelry was in the backpack, why did you put it back on the boat?'

'Because the jewelry isn't in it. I thought if they found the
backpack, they might blame each other for the missing package.'

'Possible.' He stood up and counted out a wad of bills on the
table. 'I mean it this time. Let's get out of here.'

I was walking ahead of him, and at the doorway, he put his
hand on my waist. It felt like an electric shock. I'd begun to actually like him as we talked. And not just like him but get a buzz
from him. And I realized the attraction had been there all along.

Out on the street, we walked toward my car.

It was a fine night, warm but not too humid. There were a lot
of people milling around, some watching a steel band in the
vacant lot across the street. A few Bahamian women were dancing,
dressed in colorful skirts, with their heads wrapped in matching
fabric. I wondered if the cafés hired them to entertain tourists.

When we got to my car, he said, 'So whose car are we taking
to get the jewelry? Mine or yours?'

'I didn't know we were doing that. I thought I'd hand it over to Kevin.' I put up a hand to stop his protest. 'That was before I knew who you were. But I'd still feel more confident if I checked out your story.'

'How are you going to do that?'

'First, I'm going to Google Jeweler's Security Alliance. And if there really is such an organization, I'm going to call John Farrell and ask him to return the favor and corroborate your story.'

'Can we do that tonight? I'll feel a lot better when I have the jewelry in my hands.'

'I only have his work number, not his private number. It'll have to wait until the morning. But trust me, the jewelry is secure.'

He made an exasperated sound. 'OK. Then we can go and get the jewelry when I bring you your plane ticket, right? Where can we meet for that?'

'Remember the café where I saw you with the Turpins? I'll meet you there. Early, before work.'

'Good.' I reached to open my car door. There was a squeal of brakes and a popping sound. Nick grunted and flung himself against me. Another popping sound that I realized was a gunshot when it pinged against my car. I dropped to the pavement, and Nick went down next to me.

People were screaming, and I heard the car speed away.

A couple of men ran over to us. 'What happened? Did they hit you?'

I lifted my head and looked past Nick's shoulder to make sure the car was gone. 'I'm fine,' I said, sitting up.

Nick groaned and pushed himself upright, to lean back against the car. That's when I saw the dark stain on his shoulder. I touched it and my hand came away bloody.

TWENTY-TWO

'What the hell did you do that for?' Paco yelled. He sped away, dodging the gawking spectators, and careened onto a side street.

'You said you wanted to scare her,' Rodney said.

Paco slammed his hand on the steering wheel. 'This is *my* call! You had no right.'

Rodney didn't say any more. He was too busy hanging on as Paco swerved recklessly through back streets, barely missing a few parked cars.

Finally, Paco pulled onto a side road that led to a beach. He let the car roll to a stop and sat with both hands gripping the wheel. He turned to glare at Rodney.

'You know what?' Paco said. 'You're an idiot. Shooting at somebody to scare them won't work if they don't know who's shooting.'

Rodney shrugged. He couldn't figure out what had gotten into Paco. Usually, he didn't mind gunplay. 'Hey, man, I didn't shoot her. At least now she'll know somebody is after her.'

'I think you hit the guy,' Paco said. 'I told you, nobody else. Just her.'

Rodney opened his car door. 'You're getting to be a real pussy, you know it? Like a control freak. I didn't come down here to have you push me around.' He got out of the car, slammed the door behind him and strode toward the beach. He didn't like to fight with one of his best friends, but he had to keep his dignity.

After a while, he heard Paco's door open and close. Soon he sensed Paco standing next to him. They stood not speaking for a while, watching the waves. As they foamed up near the shore, something made them sparkle. He wondered if it was a trick of the light from houses along the shore, or some kind of weird substance in the water.

Finally, Paco said, 'You're right, man. I shouldn't have gotten on your case.'

'It's all good,' Rodney said. 'I can see where you're coming from. You want to get it done, but you want to do it right.'

'Listen. Something has me freaked out. I mean, what is this bitch up to? First, she's sneaking around at the dive dock, then she goes down to that warehouse. All the time hauling that back-pack around. I mean, is she leaving something off or picking it up?' He was quiet some more.

'I told you we should have grabbed her at the warehouse.'

'You know, you were right. But I thought whatever she was up to, we might be able to make some money off it.'

'It could still work,' Rodney said.

'Dude!' Paco said. 'We'll find out when we make a move on her. And that's going to be tomorrow morning. At her place.'

Rodney held his fist out for a bump. 'Right on, brother. I'm with you.' They weren't real brothers, but with Paco's brother Diego gone, Rodney felt as though he ought to step in and fill that gap.

TWENTY-THREE

'Not too much damage,' Dr Emily Bastian said, patting Nick's arm. The young emergency room doctor had lively eyes and a halo of dark, bushy hair. 'Without an X-ray, I can't guarantee the bullet didn't chip a bone.' The X-ray machine was broken, and Nick had refused an MRI. We were at a small urgent care clinic, and the doctor had suggested we go to a larger hospital, but Nick said he just wanted to be patched up.

'I'll be fine,' Nick muttered.

'You should have it checked in a week or so to make sure it's healing properly,' she insisted.

'I'll make sure he does,' I said, drawing a glare from Nick.

'The nurse is getting you a sling to make you more comfortable. And here is a prescription for painkillers,' the doctor said.

'I'll take care of that, too,' I said, intercepting the scrip before Nick could grab it.

'Don't bother,' Nick said. 'I won't take them.' He slid off the bed, but when he tried to stand, he staggered and had to lean against the bed. Beads of sweat stood out on his forehead. He shook his head to clear it.

'Careful,' the doctor said sharply. 'The pain medication I gave you will make you woozy for a while.'

'I told you, I'll be OK,' he said. It came out a snarl. I had a feeling he was humiliated for letting himself get shot.

'I'm sure you will, but I would advise you to have the prescription filled. In the early morning hours, you will wish you had something stronger. Don't be a martyr, Mr LeBreque.' She took a step back and then said, 'And by the way, we have notified the police that you were the victim of a gunshot. They said it will take some time to get here and to ask you to wait.' She whisked out of the room.

'Good luck with that,' he grumbled when she was gone.

'LeBreque?' I lifted an eyebrow.

'You didn't think I'd give them my real name, did you?'

Nick picked up his T-shirt, where it had been tossed onto a chair, but when he saw the dried blood, he dropped it again.

'Why don't you get back on the bed for a few minutes,' I said. 'I'll go out and find something for you to wear.'

'Whatever.' He attempted a shrug, wincing when the motion made him freshly aware of his wound. 'Where are you going to find something this time of night?'

'In case you don't remember, I'm famous for being resourceful.'

I helped him back onto the bed. He lay back and closed his eyes. 'Give me a minute,' he said, 'and I'll go with you. We can't hang out here long. The cops will be a problem.'

'Don't be stupid. Rest a little longer. I'll be right back. Trust me, it will take hours before they show up.' I left the room before he could try any more heroic moves.

A half-hour later, I parted the curtain and saw that he was awake. His face was pale, but he looked less groggy.

'I brought you this.' I held out a garish tropical shirt featuring parrots in bright yellow, orange, and green.

'Jesus, that's ugly.'

'It's all I could find, and it's better than that.' I nodded toward the ruined black shirt still lying on the chair.

He gave a wan smile.

'How are you feeling?'

'Angry. I was stupid to let my guard down.'

'You couldn't have known somebody was going to drive by and shoot you. Who do you think they were?'

'I'm not sure. I was hoping you knew.' Nick took the shirt from me with his good hand. 'Where did you manage to find something this awful?'

I grinned. 'Strip mall down the street. An all-night drugstore. It had some of everything. Here let me help you.' When he had it on, I stepped back and surveyed him, and couldn't help laughing. 'Worth every penny of the ten dollars. Which you owe me, by the way.'

'Let's get out of here,' Nick said. 'I'd like to be gone before the police show up.'

I moved to his side, took hold of his good arm and helped him off the bed.

We had left my car where it was parked back at the restaurant, and I had brought him to the ER in his SUV because it was bigger and more reliable. Even though his vehicle was roomier, it was still hard for me to get him into it. He had to stop a couple of times to catch his breath. Although the bullet had hit his shoulder, he admitted that the whole side of his torso was aching. When he was settled, he leaned back against the seat and wiped the sweat from his brow. 'You can take me to pick up your car, and I'll get back to my hotel on my own.' His voice was ragged.

'The doctor said no driving tonight. I'll take you to your hotel room.'

'No! I can drive.'

'That's not an option.' I slammed the car door and went around to the driver's side. I started the car and backed out of the space. 'Where are you staying?' I asked.

'Just go get your car,' he snapped.

'OK, if you don't want to tell me where you're staying, you can sleep at my place. Shelley will be glad to see you.' I snickered.

He sighed. 'You are probably the stubbornest woman I've ever met.'

'Yep. I'm famous for being stubborn. As my ex-trainer told you.' I pulled out of the lot onto the busy road.

It was almost midnight, and the traffic was sporadic but sprinkled with reckless drivers. I had to pay attention. The next time I looked over, he was dozing. After a while, I heard his breathing change and knew he was awake again. 'Do you know where you are?'

He sighed. 'More or less. I can't believe it's only midnight. Seems like it ought to be at least two in the morning.'

'You really conked out.'

He took a sharp breath as I passed a car with inches to spare. 'Do you always drive like a wild woman?'

'So they tell me. How's the shoulder?'

'I'll live. Did you manage to get a look at whoever shot me?'

I drove onto the verge to pass someone turning left. 'No. There were two men and they were driving a convertible.'

'A convertible? Did you get the make of the car or the color?'

'It was red, probably a Mazda. Sports car, anyway. Why, do you think you might know who it is?'

'It might have been the guys who were watching you at the dive boat tonight.'

'What? What do you mean, watching me? And how do you know that?'

Now that he mentioned it, I remembered the two vehicles in the parking lot when I'd taken the jewelry to hide on the dive boat. One was a red convertible. The other was a white SUV. 'That was you parked near them?'

'Busted.'

'You changed cars.'

'Yep. I turned in the black SUV and got a different color.'

'Why were you there?'

'Keeping an eye on you. And no, not because I'm suspicious. Like I said, I'm worried that you're in danger.'

'Oh, yeah? Look who got shot.'

As I turned into the parking lot at my apartment building, Nick sighed. 'All right, I give up. I'm not staying at your place. Shelley's chatter is more than I can handle. Take me to my hotel. I'm at the Marriott. You know the one.'

'Where the Turpins are staying?'

'That's the one. And no, I'm not staying there because I'm connected with them. I told you the truth. I am who I said I am. So get that out of your head.' He sounded so grumpy that I knew he must be in pain.

At the hotel entrance, I jumped out of the car and went around to open his door, waving away the valet who sprang to action. 'I'm dropping him off,' I said.

'Do you need me to help you get to your room?' I asked.

'No, I can do that.'

'I'll park your car and leave the keys at the desk.'

'I'll see you first thing tomorrow.'

'Look, I've decided to go to the dive boat and get the jewelry tomorrow morning. I'll call you as soon as I'm back.'

'And then you're leaving the island.' He said it like it was a fact.

I hesitated. 'I've been giving that more thought. I don't think those guys are looking for me.'

'Of course they are. You can identify them.'

We were in an exposed place under the canopy at the hotel's entrance. Anyone could see us, including the Turpins or Didier and his men. And the valet seemed to be listening. 'Think about it,' I whispered. 'I can only identify them if they get caught. For all they know, I'm some ditzy girl who was at the wrong place at the wrong time and pose no threat to them.'

'I can't believe you,' he growled. 'Most people would be screaming to get away from the situation.'

'I'm not most people. Look, you need to get some rest. We'll talk in the morning.' He was pale and sweating. 'You sure you don't need me to go upstairs with you?'

'No. I can get there on my own.'

'Wait. I almost forgot.' I leaned into the car and brought out a prescription vial. 'When I bought that fine shirt, I also got the prescription filled. Like the doctor said, take the medication. Don't be a martyr.'

Before I parked Nick's car in the hotel parking lot, I drove to Feathers to find Shelley, thinking she might be willing to follow me to get my car. While I drove, I tried to conjure up an image of the men who had shot Nick. I had been deep in conversation with Nick and not paying attention to my surroundings. All I knew for sure was that they weren't part of the crew that abducted me. I would have zeroed in on them without fail.

I supposed it was possible that they had hired a couple of men from the island to get rid of me. But why would they do that when they were perfectly capable of doing it themselves? And it made no sense for them to be in a showy convertible. That was something tourists did. Someone from the mainland who wanted to show off. And then a thought stabbed me. Someone like a petty drug dealer: someone like Paco Boland.

I'd been in the islands long enough to have been lulled into complacency about Diego Boland's brother and his friends. Not to mention that I'd been focused on the events with Didier's gang.

Had Paco located where I was? I sat in the car outside Feathers and let the possibility take root. How could they have found me? Then I remembered my conversation with my mother. Her innuendo about best-laid plans. Surely, she wouldn't deliberately tell them where I was, but I could imagine one of them wheedling the information out of her.

On the other hand, maybe it wasn't them. If it was Diego's friends, why hadn't they confronted me in the parking lot at the dive dock? Or killed me? And why had they shot Nick instead of me?

But the men in the parking lot at the dive boats had been in a convertible. I focused on remembering exactly what I had seen when I left the dive boat. I remembered walking toward my car and seeing the convertible and noticing a second car. I knew now that the second car belonged to Nick. Maybe that's why they hadn't shot me then, because Nick was a witness who could identify them.

But that didn't make sense. Tonight, they had sprayed random shots at us in an open setting. Maybe they had been trying to scare me and hit Nick by accident. But why? Why not just kill me? Again, maybe it was because Nick was there. If Nick had walked away from me when we left the café, would I be dead now?

Shelley was with a crowd of people at Feathers. She had gotten off early, but she was still partying. She looked alarmed when I told her what I wanted. 'Come on, Jessie, get serious! It'll take forever to drive all the way across the island this time of night. Why did you leave your car there, anyway?'

'Mmm, I came back with a friend.'

'Well, why doesn't your friend take you to get it?'

'He couldn't do it.' No way I could tell Shelley that Nick was involved and that he had been shot. It would open up a volley of questions, not only about how he had gotten shot but what I was doing with Nick in the first place.

Shelley got up and signaled me to follow her. I realized that she was unsteady on her feet. She pulled me close. 'Listen, Jessie, I've had too much to drink to be driving on that road. Do you think you can find somebody else?'

'No problem. You go back to your friends.'

She hesitated. 'I don't want to leave you stranded. I can take you to work tomorrow if you need me to.'

'I'll be fine, Shelley. You're right. Too many crazy drivers on the road this time of night.'

She toddled back to her table.

I didn't see anyone else I knew in the noisy bar, and I couldn't think of anyone who might be willing to do me such a big favor. I could have taken an Uber, but it was too expensive. Shelley had offered to drop me off at the dive dock in the morning, and Nick could take me to get my car later.

I drove Nick's SUV to the hotel and walked back to my apartment. With time to think, I gave some more consideration to the guys who had shot Nick. If they really were Diego Boland's friends, how had they known I would be at the dive dock? They must have been following me. I kicked myself mentally. I'd been so caught up in my other drama that I'd let my guard down. If I had been paying attention, I would have noticed two men in a convertible following me.

Something else I needed to put Kevin on to – if he ever called me back.

TWENTY-FOUR

'Why isn't her car here?' Rodney's voice was furry in the early-morning hour.

'How the fuck should I know?' In spite of their truce, Paco was still pissed off at Rodney for shooting that guy last night. He had been awake half the night going over and over the incident. If someone had seen them and given their license number to the cops, they'd be sitting in jail now trying to explain not only the shooting but how they'd gotten hold of a gun in the first place.

Rodney yawned. 'Probably shacked up with the guy she was with in the restaurant. I wouldn't mind a piece of her myself.'

'You've already had plenty.' Paco was also in a funk because of what happened afterwards. Rodney had insisted on going back to Marla and Callie's apartment. Marla had welcomed Rodney with all systems go, but Callie was out. Marla called Callie to come home, but she never returned. Paco sat and watched some stupid chick flick on TV and drank beer all evening, trying to tune out Rodney and Marla in the bedroom.

'Hey, man, I'm sorry Callie flaked on you. We'll go back there tonight, and Marla said she'll make sure Callie is around. Yo, d'you think you could hang out here while I find us some coffee? I saw a coffee shop a block back.'

'Yeah, but keep your phone on. If she comes out of the apartment, I want you back here.'

TWENTY-FIVE

After waking at two a.m. and again at four thirty and tossing and turning in between, I finally got up at six and made a piece of toast and some coffee. and sat in front of the living-room window which overlooked the parking lot. Sitting with my knees tucked up under my chin, I watched the sky turn from dark gray to light gray, then become streaked with gold.

At six thirty, I made the phone call I didn't want to make, to Jeremy, telling him I couldn't make it to work. I'd lied when I told Nick I was leaving the island today, but I still couldn't go to work. I had other plans.

'I'm trying to cut you some slack, Jessie. I know you've had a lot going on in the past week. I hate to say it, but I may have to replace you. I can't run a business not being able to count on people.'

'I understand. You've been terrific, Jeremy. I couldn't have worked for anybody better.'

'Hmm, sounds like you're ready to call it quits.'

'Honestly? I don't know.'

'I hate to lose you, but I always figured you for a short-timer.'

'Jeremy, I'm really sorry. After I've taken care of a few things, I'll make a time for us to talk. I have some explaining to do.'

I had considered whether I should get the jewelry off the boat before it was taken out today, but maybe it would be safer to leave it there for now.

Next, I dialed Kevin's number. When I had returned with Nick's car last night, I checked my messages and saw that Kevin had phoned while I was in the hospital waiting for Nick. His message said, 'I need to talk to you about the guy who died. Something funny going on there. Call me tomorrow morning.'

Kevin's phone rang several times before a sleepy voice answered. But when he heard my voice, he became alert. 'Hey, yeah, listen,' he said. 'What do you know about this guy who died in the casino shooting?'

'I told you, he was one of the men who tried to kill me.'

'But you don't know what he was doing here in the islands?'

'Well, actually, since I talked to you, I have found out more. Can we meet?'

'I'll be at the station by nine.'

I felt better knowing that I'd soon be able to lay everything at Kevin's feet, including turning the jewelry over to him. It was still only seven a.m. which meant I had time to get over there and retrieve the jewelry before the boats left. Then I remembered I didn't have my car. Dammit. I could take an Uber to the dive dock. Or I could beg Shelley. As long as I got to the dive boat before eight thirty, when the boats went out for the day, I'd be fine. I'd go straight from there to hand the package of jewelry over to Kevin.

I was still anxious after my restless night, so I spent a half-hour doing yoga stretches, trying to still my mind. I decided to call Nick to take me to the dive dock to retrieve the jewelry. Then he could go with me to talk to Kevin. He could explain what was going on from his perspective. It was almost eight. I'd wait a while longer to call him. I didn't want to wake him too early. He needed all the rest he could get.

Restless, I went back to the window and stood sipping coffee, watching people scurry out to the parking lot to head to their jobs. I heard Shelley moving around in her bedroom. Even though Shelley didn't have to be at work until late afternoon, she was usually up before eight so she could get to the gym.

I hadn't been looking for the red convertible, but when I spotted it at the edge of the parking lot, I realized I had half expected to see it. Only one man was in it, sitting behind the wheel with sunglasses on. As I watched, the other man returned bearing coffee and a paper bag. He climbed into the car and asked the driver something. The driver shook his head.

I had to assume it was the same men who had shot Nick last night. How many red convertibles with two guys in them were likely to be hanging out near me? I ran to my room to get my binoculars out of my duffle to get a closer look at them, but then remembered the duffle was in my car. And my car was across the island.

With a sigh, I went back to the window. Was it Diego Boland and a friend? Maybe not. It could still be that Didier had found where I was and sent someone to watch me. Were they planning to shoot me when I left for work? When they realized I wasn't coming out, would they come inside to get me? I thought of calling Kevin back but instead phoned Nick.

He answered the phone sounding groggy.

'Hold on,' he said.

I kept my eye on the convertible while I waited.

'Christ! What did they put in that shot they gave me?' He sounded more alert, anyway.

'Did you take any of the pills I got you last night?'

'I didn't have to. I passed out as soon as I got into my room and just woke up.'

'How do you feel?'

'Sore, but I'll live if I can find some coffee.'

'Whatever you do, hurry. The two guys who shot you are outside my apartment building in that red convertible.'

'Stay inside. I'll be right there. Wait. Fuck! My car. Did you bring it back last night?'

'It's in the parking lot at your hotel. I left the keys with the front desk.' I described where I'd left the SUV.

'Hang tight. I'm coming over now. Shit! I have to get some clothes on.' He didn't need to say that putting something on with his injured shoulder would be a problem.

When I hung up, I went back to my room and changed into a pair of cargo pants with pockets, retrieved the Sig Sauer I'd taken from the boat from my dresser, and put it in my pocket, pulling a loose shirt over it.

Shelley was in the kitchen pouring a cup of the coffee I'd made hours earlier. 'Why aren't you at work?' She took a sip of the brew and made a face. She always said I made the coffee too strong. 'And why are you dressed like that? You look like you're going on a safari.'

I glanced back out the window and froze. The two men were out of the convertible and walking toward the building. I whirled back. 'Shelley, don't ask me any questions. You have to get out of here right now.'

'Jessie, what is wrong with you? Have you lost your mind?'

Shelley was dressed only in a skimpy nightgown, so I ran into her room, rummaged in her closet and grabbed a robe. Back in the kitchen, I thrust the robe at her. 'Here. Put this on. There's no time. You have to leave now! I'm not kidding.' I ran to the door and opened it. I heard the elevator making its lumbering way down to the ground floor.

'I'm not going anywhere until you tell me what's going on.'

'No time.' I ran back and grabbed Shelley's arm and pulled her toward the door. At least she had put the robe on. I steered her into the hallway and shoved her to the right. 'Go to the stairs at the end of the hall here. Go either up or down, but you can't stay here.'

'You know, Jessie . . .'

'Go!' I put my hand on the gun in my pocket, ready to draw it out the second Shelley was gone.

Shelley looked like she was going to say something snarky when suddenly her eyes widened and she gasped. She turned and fled down the hallway just as I was grabbed from either side by strong hands.

'Inside. And don't make a fuss or we'll shoot your friend.' The man's matter-of-fact inflection made his words more menacing.

'No, wait!' I glanced frantically up and down the hallway, but Nick was nowhere in sight. He hadn't had time to get here. I tried to pull away, but they forced me back into the apartment, slamming the door behind them.

'What do you want?' I yelled.

One of them yanked me around to face him and slammed me up against the wall, banging my head so hard that I saw stars. The man was tall and dark-skinned, a good-looking guy with deep brown eyes that reflected no light. He was also prison buff, with tattooed arms bulging out of an incongruous island-style shirt with hula girls on it. He gave me a thin-lipped smile. 'You're a hard woman to pin down,' he said.

Up close, I recognized him. Rodney Grant. When my sister first started hanging out with Diego, I had looked him up. I'd found not only his rap sheet but a list of his tight coterie of friends he'd met in prison. Rodney was high on the list. He had done time for dealing drugs, but the file on him said he was a brutal man, probably responsible for more than one murder. Prosecutors had not yet been able to make a case against him, but indications were that it was only a matter of time.

'Anybody else in here?' the other guy asked. If he was with Rodney, this had to be Diego Boland's brother, Paco. I knew less about him. His rap sheet wasn't as long or as violent. But that didn't mean we were going to be friends. Paco was a man with revenge on his mind.

'No,' I said.

'I'll check, in case you're lying,' he said. 'Keep her quiet,' he said to Rodney.

'Who are you?' I asked. I didn't want them to know I recognized them. I hoped to get them talking to buy time for Nick to arrive.

'Paco will tell you all you need to know.'

My heart slammed in my chest. I heard him walking around the apartment. When he came back, I tried stalling longer. 'Your name is Paco? Are you Diego Boland's brother?'

He ignored me and said to his buddy, 'We can't stay here. That blond that ran out of here will probably call the cops.'

Somehow, I had to get them to stay. Where was Nick?

'No, she won't call the police. She's not that bright.'

'Who asked you?' he snarled. 'Let's get her out of here,' he said to Rodney.

'What do you want? And where are you taking me?' I asked.

'Taking you to your sister,' the black man said.

'My sister! Kayla? She's not here.'

Suddenly, Paco stepped close and slapped me across the cheek. Not hard, just enough to sting. 'No more questions. I'll tell you what you need to know when you need to know it.'

Even if the slap had been minimal, I yelped for effect and touched my face. 'You didn't need to do that.'

Rodney smiled. 'It'll go easier if you do what Paco says. He's an impatient guy.'

'What's your name?' I asked, still stalling.

'What difference does it make?' Paco snarled. He grabbed my arm in a tight grip. He was smaller than Rodney but strong. 'Bitch, what don't you understand about "let's get going?"'

He yanked me toward the door.

'Wait, can I get my bag?' If Rodney let me go, I could make a move for the gun in my pocket.

'You're not going to need it, sugar,' the black man said. 'We'll have you back here before long.' If I hadn't known who these guys were, I would have been reassured by his smooth, friendly voice. But they had no intention of bringing me back here. At least not alive. The thought made me want to howl. After all I'd been through, to be killed by these stupid thugs. I had to get to my gun. As if reading my mind, Rodney looked me up and down and said, 'You know, I'm afraid we're going to have to search you for a weapon.'

'Don't touch me,' I snapped.

'Paco,' Rodney said. Before I could react, Rodney grabbed me and held me tightly while Paco ran his hands up and down my body. There was no sexual component to it, merely a job being done. Of course, he found the gun. He took it out of my pocket and held it for his companion to see.

'Good thinking, man.' He pocketed the gun.

TWENTY-SIX

Paco shoved me into the front seat of the convertible, keeping the revolver pushed into my back. Rodney climbed into the backseat on the driver's side but moved over behind

me and sat forward so that I could feel his breath on my neck.
At least we were outside. I'd been afraid Shelley would find my
body when she came back to the apartment.

'Nice car,' I said. 'Red really stands out.'

'Shut up,' Paco said. He handed the gun to Rodney and went
around to climb into the driver's seat.

'I wouldn't provoke him if I were you,' Rodney said into my
ear with his deep, calm voice. 'Paco wouldn't have a bit of a
problem telling me to use this gun.' His voice hardened. 'And I
wouldn't have a problem doing what he said.' I didn't doubt his
words for a second.

Paco wheeled out of the parking lot. I glanced around but
didn't see Nick. It looked like I was on my own, again.

Once we were on the road, I turned sideways in my seat so I
could look back at Rodney. I was surprised that neither of them
protested. 'Is that the gun you shot at me with last night?'

He shrugged.

I needed to get them talking, if for no other reason than to
have something to keep my mind off my grim prospects. What
kind of karma had I been piling up to have two different groups
of men gunning for me? 'How did you guys find me? You were
clever. I thought I was pretty well hidden.'

'Weren't no big thang,' Rodney said, but Paco turned and shot
him a look. He shrugged and winked at me. As if we were big
buddies.

'You said you were taking me to my sister. Where is she? Is
she OK?' I seriously doubted that Kayla was with them. Was
she?

Paco stayed quiet, but he started drumming the wheel with
the fingers of one hand. Rodney said, 'She's fine. Now, why
don't you settle back.'

The two guys were showing off by having the top down in
the convertible, but it could give me an advantage. The traffic
was packed in tight on all sides. If Paco hit me, as I was pretty
sure he was itching to do, someone would see. But would anyone
react?

I looked full-on at Rodney. 'Why won't you tell me your
name?' I made my mouth smile.

'Well, sugar, my name is Rodney. Now, why don't you tell

me what good you think that does you?' For the first time, he sounded annoyed with me.

My mind was churning. Even though I doubted that they really did have Kayla, was I willing to take that chance? If I knew they didn't have my sister, I would take a risk – maybe jump out of the car when it slowed down. Even if Rodney grabbed me and tried to drag me back, I could create a scene and hope that people would come to my rescue. But what if I was wrong and they did have Kayla?

'How can I be sure you have my sister?' I asked.

I thought they were going to stonewall me again, but then Paco threw me a sideways smirk and said, 'She was at Hayworth, in Pennsylvania. We found her there and brought her down here with us. Does that tell you what you need to know?'

Anger slammed through me. How the hell had they found out where Kayla was being rehabbed? John had promised that she would be under an assumed name in a facility where no one could get to her. That was one of the terms under which I had resigned without protest. The fucking FBI! They'd let me down.

But I cooled down quickly. There was another possibility that made more sense. Kayla was a master at manipulation. She wasn't supposed to be able to contact anyone, but she might have persuaded an employee at the facility to let her call our mother. When I set up the rehab, I knew our mother was a weak link in the plan. Because of that, I refused to tell her where Kayla was being kept. She had been furious when I wouldn't tell her the location of the facility. She begged that she needed to know where her 'baby' was. Her histrionics didn't mean much to me. If she had shown more interest in her 'baby' when she needed it, Kayla might not have become a drug addict.

If my sister had managed to call Mother and whined enough, Mother would have done whatever she asked, including checking her out of rehab. I remembered during the phone call I had made to my mother the night I brought *Island Ice* back to Nassau, she had made a cryptic comment that I wasn't as smart as I thought I was. Of course, she would be gloating if she took Kayla out of the rehab facility.

After our dad died, our mother basically gave up on being a parent. The only way she had even managed to maintain a job to put food on the table was because of her relationship with the man my dad had worked for. He overlooked the times Annie couldn't make it in to work because she was 'not well' – meaning too hungover.

Fear butted up against my anger. From what Paco said, it was entirely possible that they had Kayla. 'What have you done with my sister? Where is she?'

'Hey, relax, sugar,' Rodney said. 'You're gettin' all uptight for nothing. You'll find out soon enough. We've got one stop to make, and then we have a plan for the two of you girls.'

Plan. A man with a plan. God, I'd never hear that word the same way again. I'd never wipe out of my memory Didier's voice, saying that Jaggo 'had a little plan.' Or the memory of Jaggo's laughter as Johnny and I hit the water. I sank back against my seat and closed my eyes against the sudden wash of desolation that gripped me. One way or another, somebody was going to be successful in killing me. I took deep breaths to quell my panic and forced myself to come back to the here and now. I wasn't dead yet.

There had to be some way out of this situation. I had to stay focused until these guys either took me to Kayla or I determined that they were lying.

I heard a squeal of brakes and horns honking and looked back over my shoulder. A white SUV had disrupted traffic, forcing its way into line a few cars back from us. An SUV that looked very familiar. I should know; I'd driven it back across the island last night. Or at least one like it. Maybe it wasn't Nick, but it was possible that he had gotten to the parking lot at my apartment in time to see the guys shoving me into their convertible. I couldn't see if it was him because he was behind a big, black SUV. Annoyed, I looked up at the SUV driver. And my heart almost stopped. Didier was driving, and in the passenger seat was the man he'd been with in the café, talking to the Turpins.

I whirled back around and shrank down into my seat, wishing I could disappear. How the hell had they found me? Had they recognized me in the café yesterday after all? That made no sense. They wouldn't have waited to grab me. I bit my knuckle to keep from screaming.

Rodney lunged forward and grabbed my shoulder. 'What's

going on, baby girl? You see somebody you know? You better not try to signal them. Go down bad for everybody.'

I shook my head without looking at him. Not bloody likely I'd be signaling those men!

I wondered if Nick realized Didier was in the SUV. It was a regular parade – the car I was in, followed by Didier, and Nick bringing up the rear. If the Turpins joined them, the whole gang would be here.

I kept waiting for something to happen, but the nose-to-tail traffic continued for a half-hour, with no odd moves. Suddenly, Paco turned off the main road, and I realized we were headed for the Coast Guard dock where I'd been last night. What were we doing here? Even if Paco and Rodney had followed me last night when I came here to plant the backpack on *Island Ice*, they wouldn't have known what I was up to.

Deserted last night, now, at ten in the morning, the warehouse area bustled with activity. Forklifts beeped their way from warehouses to trucks lined up along the sides of roads. Drivers of the trucks, mostly islanders, lounged in the nearest shade they could find, waiting for the loading to be finished.

Paco drove slowly as if looking for something.

'I thought you were taking me to my sister,' I said.

Rodney touched my arm with his gun. 'Like I told you, this is a side trip.'

I risked a glance back to see if Didier's and Nick's vehicles were following. The SUV was several car lengths behind us, but Nick's white vehicle was nowhere to be seen. If it had been him at all.

This time, Rodney had seen me glance back, and he swiveled to look at the SUV. 'Sugar, I hope you're not expecting those guys to rescue you. Because that would be a bad thing for your sister.'

I wondered what Rodney and Paco would say if I told them I'd much rather take my chances with the two of them than with the guys in the black SUV. Not that there was a whole lot of difference.

I almost didn't recognize the Coast Guard station in the daytime. The lot was jammed with cars, and there were several people hanging around in front of the office. The warehouses that had loomed so forbidding last night were, in the light of day, simply ordinary buildings.

'What are we doing here?' I asked.

Paco pulled over in front of the dock, but away from the Coast Guard office, and stopped the car. 'That's what we want you to tell us. And don't get any bright ideas about yelling, or you'll never see your sister again.'

I looked back at Rodney in time to see Didier's SUV continue past us on the road without pulling in. I doubted I'd seen the last of Didier, but at least there wasn't going to be a shootout here and now.

Rodney glanced back, too. He grinned at me. 'Looks like your buddies have had second thoughts.'

'I don't understand what you want me to tell you.'

'We want to know what you were doing here last night,' Paco said.

Rodney chimed in. 'We saw you take a backpack with you when you left your car. You got inside the gate and walked down the dock and when you came back you didn't have the backpack. So, what happened to it? And what's in it that was so important?'

'Where were you? I can't believe I didn't see you.'

'We did good, Paco,' Rodney said, poking his friend on the shoulder. 'She gave us a compliment.'

'Stop stalling,' Paco said. 'What were you doing here?'

'What will you do for me if I tell you?'

Rodney let out a chuckle. 'Sugar, if you make it worth enough to us, things might go a lot better for you and your baby sister.'

I almost laughed. A lovely fantasy blossomed in my mind. I pictured these guys boarding a plane back to the United States with a pouch full of millions of dollars' worth of jewelry. At the top of the ramp, they'd turn and wave goodbye to me and Kayla. Didier and his gang would be left empty-handed. And Nick would have nothing to take back to the jewelry consortium. It would make a cute movie, if Paco and Rodney and Didier's gang weren't vicious killers.

'OK. I'll tell you. But you'll have to get the backpack for yourself. I'm not going back in there.'

'Fair enough. What's in the backpack?'

I described the jewelry with its obscenely big stones and elegant settings. It didn't matter that the jewelry wasn't actually in the backpack. I was playing for time, hoping for a miracle rescue.

'Where did it come from?' Paco asked.

'A jewelry heist in France.'

'How come you have it?'

'It's a long story.'

'How do we know you ain't just jivin'?' Rodney asked.

'I can't prove it unless you get the backpack,' I said. 'You'll see it for yourself then.'

Hearing a description of the jewelry, Paco was practically dancing in his seat, and Rodney was nodding at me, smiling. 'That's real good, sugar. Sounds like you're going to make a good bargain for you and your baby sister. You're a smart girl. Now, where do we find this stash?'

I pointed to the dock. 'There's a boat down there to the left, a catamaran. Do you know what that is?'

They shook their heads. I described the boat, and where I had stashed the backpack. The men squabbled over which one of them would have the job of convincing the Coast Guard to let them inside. Finally, Paco laid down the law. 'Rodney, you're my wingman. I need you to do this. You know you're better at sweet talk than I am.'

'Look, I have an idea,' I said. 'Tell them the owner wanted you to come and look at the boat and give them an estimate for dings that need repairing when they get her back.'

'Her? Her who?' Paco said.

'You dipwad – don't you know anything?' Rodney said. 'People describe boats like they're girls. They call 'em "she" and "her."'

Paco's eyes narrowed as he considered whether Rodney was playing with him. 'Whatever,' he grumbled.

'Anyway,' I said, 'if they think you're here to paint the name, they'll let you go look at the boat, no questions asked. When you get onto the boat, you can go inside and get the backpack.'

'I have a better idea,' Rodney said. 'I'll take you with me and you can get the backpack since you know where it is.'

'Then the story wouldn't make any sense. They'd want to know why I was with you.'

'I could say I was the boss and I hired you to do the work.'

'Rodney, stop fucking around,' Paco said. 'Just do it.'

Rodney got out of the car, and Paco and I watched him approach the guard at the gate. The guard nodded several times while Rodney gestured, and then swung the gate open. He didn't follow Rodney. Rodney was gone for only a few minutes, and when he came back he was scowling. He said a few words to the guard. The guard said something back and pointed to the Coast Guard building. Rodney trudged over there. He was gone for at least fifteen minutes. Paco grew more and more agitated, rocking in his seat and tapping the wheel of the car. I had to pee so bad I was squirming, but when I asked Paco if I could go use the toilet, he said, 'You're kidding, right?'

'No. You could take me. I promise I won't try to get away.'

'I'm not stupid. You can just hold it.'

Finally, Rodney came back, scowling.

'What?' Paco said, as Rodney wrenched the door open.

Rodney's eyes were dead. 'Guard says the owner came and got the boat an hour ago.'

TWENTY-SEVEN

'Do you know who owns the boat and where they took it?' Paco's expression was hard as he zeroed in on me. 'They probably went back to her home dock. It's on the other side of the island, not far from where I live.'

'Goddammit,' Paco said. 'We can't catch a break.' He sprayed gravel as he floored it out of the parking area. At the end of the row of warehouses, I saw the black SUV waiting. It swung onto the road behind us.

'Looks like our tail is back,' Rodney said. 'You want to tell me who those guys are? Are they watching out for you?'

'Ha!' I said, figuring I might as well tell them who they were. 'That's the last thing they would do. They're following me because they're also after the jewelry. They think I have it. I have to warn you, they're dangerous.'

'Ooh, I'm scared,' Paco said with a sneer.

'Honey, don't you worry your precious head,' Rodney said. 'We'll be fine.'

If they only knew.

By now, the sun was hot and I wished I had a hat. Sweat was standing out on Paco's forehead, and whatever aftershave Rodney used was growing more pungent by the minute, mingled with his sweat. Even in the open air of the convertible, it was overwhelming.

'Guys, it's really hot. Could we put the top up?'

'Yeah,' Rodney said to Paco. 'Pull over. I want to see what the SUV will do.'

Paco swung into the parking lot at a gas station convenience store. 'I need to take a leak anyway.'

I could have wept with relief. Maybe he had a heart after all. Or maybe he just was attending to his own needs. Either way, I'd try to find a chance to escape.

I watched as the SUV drove past us. I glanced at the cars following to see if I could spot Nick but didn't see him. I didn't look again, because I didn't want Paco and Rodney to notice that I was searching for another car.

Paco let me use the facilities, too, with Rodney hanging around outside to make sure I didn't have a chance to talk to anyone else. So much for escaping.

'You need to relax,' Rodney said to Paco as we eased back into traffic with no sign of the SUV. 'We lost them back there.'

It wasn't as hot with the top up, but I couldn't see my surroundings as well, either, so I didn't know if we really had lost the SUV, or if Nick had managed to find us again.

I gave directions to Paco to the marina where *Island Ice* had been docked before, and we were there within forty-five minutes. I spotted the boat toward the end of the finger dock. But the security gate to the dock was locked up. When I'd been here before, it had been propped open.

'How're we gonna get in there?' Rodney asked.

'We wait for someone to come out,' I said.

'They gonna just let us walk in?'

'We'll tell them we're visiting *Island Ice*. No one will ask questions. But we may have another problem.'

'What's that?' Paco snapped. Since I had told them the guys in the SUV were after the jewelry, Paco had gotten more and more jittery. The last twenty minutes of the drive, he had repeatedly looked in the rearview mirror watching for our tail.

'The owners are probably on board,' I said. 'So they may already have the backpack.'

'I'm going to drive on past and park somewhere else,' Paco said.

'Why? There's plenty of places to park right in front of the dock,' Rodney asked.

'I want the car out of sight in case those guys in the SUV come around.'

'Man, you're being paranoid,' Rodney said.

I was curious where the SUV had gone, but I had no illusions that Didier had given up on following me – and the jewelry. The question was, how had he found me? He thought I was dead.

The Turpins had probably notified Didier as soon as they got word that the Coast Guard had possession of their boat. And when they found that the backpack didn't contain the package, they must have called him again, blaming him and his men for confiscating it. When they assured her they didn't have the package, attention then turned to the 'mysterious woman' who stole the boat – me. The lieutenant who took my information must have told them my name, and maybe even my address. I could imagine Betty Turpin saying she wanted to know how she could locate me to thank me, and the Coast Guard thinking that was a completely legitimate request.

Betty would have passed that information along to Didier. So it's quite possible that Didier knew my name and how to find me. But he probably didn't know I was the same person they'd thrown overboard.

Paco parked in the lot of a motel a couple of blocks away. 'We're all going to the boat,' he said.

'Do we have a plan?' Rodney asked. That word again. But apparently, Paco hadn't gotten far enough along in his thinking to actually have a strategy.

While they argued over the best way to approach *Island Ice*, I scoped out the surroundings to see if there was anybody around I could appeal to for help, or any way to escape. But on the other side of the street from the marina, there were only narrow side streets with no one in sight, and no place to run.

I had a sinking moment. I had been counting on Nick to save me, but maybe his whole story was bullshit. I had no proof that he was working for the people he had told me he was working for. I hadn't had a chance to call John Farrell. Maybe all his sweet talk last night had simply been to lull me into believing him.

Paco swung his door open. 'I'm done talking. I want this to be over with. I want that jewelry and I want to get out of here. The whole setup makes me nervous.'

'So your plan is to walk onto the boat and ask for the jewelry?' I asked, sneering. 'You think they'll just hand it over?'

'We'll find out, won't we?' He sounded confident. 'Rodney, you with me?'

'We'll be fine. Let's take it slow and be ready if they're stubborn,' Rodney said.

Paco came around to my side of the car and opened the door, and Rodney prodded my neck with the gun. 'Get out. We're going to find out if you're telling the truth.'

'I think you're making a mistake, and I'd rather stay here, out of danger. If the owners are on the boat, they'll put up a fight. The guys who were following us might even be on the boat with them, watching for us.'

'You let me worry about that part,' Rodney said. He brandished his gun like a gunfighter in an old movie.

We walked to the dock, me dragging my heels, and Rodney poking me in the back with his gun every time I slowed down. Now that I was again suspicious of Nick's intentions, I was looking for him in a different way. I was looking to avoid him. He might shoot all three of us once he saw that *Island Ice* was back at the dock. And even if he spared me, I needed Rodney and Paco to stay alive long enough to find out where they had my sister – if they had her.

As we neared the finger dock where the catamaran was tied up, I was relieved to see the Turpins getting off the boat. I had been wondering how Paco would play this with the owners. 'Look, that's the owners. They're leaving,' I said. 'Let's wait for them to go past us and then we can go to the boat.'

'Now you're thinking,' Rodney said.

Carl Turpin said something to his wife, and the two of them glanced around. They were both stone-faced. Who were they expecting? There was only one answer for that: Didier.

'The lady's carrying a purse,' Rodney said. 'You know, Paco, she might have the jewelry with her.'

I didn't plan to tell them that I knew the Turpins didn't have the jewelry. 'Maybe one of you can stay back here and watch where they go, and if we don't find the jewelry on the boat, then we can follow them,' I said.

'No.' Paco stopped at the locked gate that led to the dock. He was now holding a gun, too. The Turpins were almost at the gate. 'We're going to take them now. We don't have time to search the whole boat. If they don't have the jewels with them, we'll make them go with us back to the boat to get them.'

'But . . .' I was trying to think of an argument that would work.

'Shut up,' Paco said. 'We're doing it my way.'

Intent on whatever they were off to do, Betty and Carl Turpin didn't even glance at the three of us standing at the gate. They opened it and started to step through the entry. Rodney confronted them, holding the gun where they could see it. 'We're going back to your boat.'

Carl Turpin looked at the gun, but Betty looked at Rodney. 'Who do you think you are?' she said.

I had to hand it to her; she was gutsy.

'I'm the guy who's going to get you to hand over that bag of jewelry you've got aboard.'

'I don't know what you're talking about,' Betty said. She glanced at me, and her eyes narrowed. 'I bet I know who you are,' she said.

'Get a move on,' Paco said, waving them back toward the dock they had come from.

'You've got the wrong people,' Carl Turpin said. His voice was tight, his expression frightened.

Paco shot a nervous glance at me, as though he wondered if I had lied to them. That brought Betty Turpin's attention to me. She smirked at me. 'How convenient. You're just the person we wanted to see.'

'Do I know you?' I said.

'Don't play cute with me,' Betty shot back.

'We can't stand here,' Paco said. He was glancing around him nervously. 'It's too public.' He prodded Betty Turpin. 'Let's get back to your boat.'

'You're making a bad mistake,' she said. 'We don't have the jewelry. She does.' She nodded toward me.

Suddenly, a shot rang out, and Paco yelled and dropped like a stone.

'Paco!' Rodney cried out and stared at his friend as a red stain bloomed in the middle of his back. Betty Turpin gasped and sprang back from Paco's body, her mouth wide open in a silent scream. Rodney grabbed me and yanked me to him as a shield. He shoved the gun into Carl Turpin's back and pushed him through the open gate, dragging me with him. He pulled the gate shut behind them, leaving Betty Turpin with Paco's body.

'We've got to get to your boat,' Rodney ordered. Carl Turpin started to say something, and Rodney hit him across the side of the head with the gun. Turpin staggered and grabbed the side of his head. It would have been a perfect opportunity for me to take Rodney, but if Paco was dead, Rodney was my only chance to find my sister. Whoever had shot Paco, I didn't want to give him a chance to kill Rodney as well.

Another shot rang out, and Rodney kicked at Turpin. 'Get to the boat!' he yelled. Stunned by the blow to his head, Carl Turpin staggered a few feet away from the gate, not even glancing back at his wife, who was screaming hysterically.

Another shot, and this time Rodney cursed, grabbed his arm, and dropped his gun. He bent to snatch it back up, and I kicked it, sending it spiraling out of reach.

Someone shouted and I heard footsteps running up on the dock. Betty Turpin had disappeared, but I saw her crouched between two cars in the parking lot. Someone in a boat in front of us poked his head up from the interior. 'Get down! Gun!' I yelled, and the head pulled back.

I dropped to my stomach on the dock, peering around. Rodney lunged toward his gun, and another shot rang out. Rodney fell to the dock, holding his side. 'Oh, shit, man,' he said.

Carl Turpin took the opportunity to scuttle down the dock to his boat.

Now there were other shots, but none seemed to be coming our way. I grabbed Rodney's gun and fired off a couple of random shots as I tried to figure out where the other shots were coming from. I had to keep Rodney alive. 'Can you make it to the boat?' I said.

His eyes were glazed, as if he was in shock. I'd have to abandon the idea of going for *Island Ice* and instead get him to the closest boat for cover. I held the gun ready to shoot and tried to drag him backwards.

But then I heard a car squeal to a stop in front of the gate. Nick was at the wheel, with the window rolled down. 'Get in,' he yelled. A shot rang out and glanced off the car. Whatever suspicion I still had regarding Nick, he was a welcome sight.

'I have to bring him,' I yelled, pointing at Rodney.

'Leave him,' Nick shouted.

'Can you get up that ramp?' I said to Rodney.

'I can make it,' Rodney said. He was panting, and blood was leaking freely down his side and onto his pants. But his jaw was set in determination. Reaching the car was his only chance.

'I'll cover you,' I said. 'Go.'

Rodney half staggered, half crawled up the ramp toward the gate, with me crouching behind him, covering his movements with my gun. The tide was low, and the ramp was at a sharp angle, which made us less of a target, but made Rodney's crawl up to the gate harder.

Sirens wailed in the distance. I saw a young Bahamian security guard poke his head up from between two cars, his eyes wide. When he spotted my gun, he ducked back down.

Paco's body was lying so that it blocked the gate. Without a key to the gate, Nick couldn't open it from the outside, so I would have to push the door open from the inside. I didn't know if I could do it without standing up.

Nick saw the problem. He slipped out of the car and, crouching low to the ground to use the car as cover, scrambled over to the body. He only had the use of his left arm, but he managed to drag Paco's body several inches away from the gate. While Nick was vulnerable, I watched the surroundings for movement, holding Rodney's revolver ready to shoot. I could hear Betty Turpin sobbing.

'Stay where you are!' I yelled to her.

'Where is my husband?' Betty wailed.

'He's OK. He's on the boat. Stay down, you'll be OK.'

As soon as Nick had Paco's body pulled away, he scrambled back toward the car, crouching next to it and tracking the area with his gun. Rodney grabbed Paco's arm and tried to pull him toward the car.

'You have to leave him,' Nick said. The sirens were getting closer, and I heard men's voices yelling near one of the buildings on the other side of the street from the dock. There had been no shots for several seconds, and I hoped that meant whoever had been shooting at us had retreated. But it also might mean the shooters were closing in on us.

'I can't! I need him!' I risked standing up enough to force the gate open. But now Rodney was lying still. I tugged at his arm. 'Rodney, move! We have to get to the car!' He lay motionless.

'You have to help me,' I called to Nick. 'I can't carry him alone.'

'He'll be OK. We'll call an ambulance.'

'You don't understand,' I yelled.

The security guard peeked out again. 'Can you help me?' I said.

'Put your gun down,' he said. His voice was shaking.

'You're in no danger,' I said. 'I'm putting the gun away.' I shoved the gun into the waistband of my pants.

The guard sprinted to the gate and crouched at my side. 'Miss, what is going on here?'

'This man is shot and we have to get him to a hospital,' I said. 'Help me.'

He hesitated, peering around for signs of the shooters. He looked down at Paco's body. 'Who is he?'

'No time to explain. We have to get to a hospital now!'

'I can call for an ambulance.' He thumbed his walkie-talkie.

'No. We'll take him.' I wanted Rodney to myself for a few minutes. I had to find out where he was keeping my sister.

I began pulling at Rodney, and the security guard gave in and helped. The two of us dragged Rodney toward the car while Nick fumed. Compared to my scrawny sister, whom I had been able to carry alone, Rodney took a lot of muscle to move. When we reached the car, Rodney moaned and came back to consciousness.

'Get in,' I yelled. He crawled up into the back seat. I pushed his legs inside, slammed the door, ran around to the passenger side, and jumped in.

Before I slammed the door, the security guard said, 'What should I tell the police?'

'Ask her.' I pointed to Betty Turpin, who was sitting huddled against a car. 'She knows the details.' Betty threw me a vicious look as the guard moved toward her.

As soon as I closed the car door, Nick careened away. We met two police cars rounding the corner. 'Go that way,' I said to Nick, pointing east. I had never been inside the hospital, but I remembered that it was a few blocks away.

Rodney was keeping up a continual moaning in the back seat.

'Why the hell did you insist on bringing him?' Nick said. 'You could have gotten yourself killed.'

'He has my sister,' I said.

His head whipped toward me. 'What do you mean? Has her where?'

Ignoring Nick, I levered my seat back as far as it would go and maneuvered around so I could crouch on my knees looking over the back seat, near Rodney. I shook him. 'Rodney! Tell me where Kayla is.'

Rodney groaned louder and said something I couldn't understand.

'Rodney, please. Is she here in Nassau?'

Rodney was whimpering and clutching at his stomach. His face was losing color. Blood from his wound was continuing to bubble out. I didn't think he had lost enough blood that he would die from the wound, but the wound was in his abdomen, and that could be bad.

'Don't die on me,' I said to Rodney. It was obvious I wasn't going to get anything out of him now – if ever. I turned around and pulled the seat back up.

I took Rodney's gun out of my waistband where I had tucked it. It was an old single-action revolver, and I realized I didn't even know if it was loaded. I snapped it open and saw that there were only four bullets in it. It hadn't been cleaned in a long time. No doubt Rodney had bought it on the street after he got here.

Nick flicked his eyes to me, then to the gun. 'Where did you get that?'

'It's his.' I nodded in Rodney's direction. 'Turn right at the next corner. We're almost there.'

We pulled up into the ambulance lane, which, of course, brought people swarming out to tell us we couldn't be there. But it also meant they got Rodney out of the car fast. I went inside with him and explained to the skeptical desk nurse that the only thing I knew about Rodney was his name. 'We were down at the Harbor Club Marina. Someone started shooting and killed his friend, and wounded him. The police showed up just as we left.'

The large, imposing nurse gave me a stern look. 'You must wait here for the police. Anyone brought in with a gunshot wound must be investigated.'

'Believe me, I'll be happy to talk to the police. In fact, let me call someone I know with the police department.' I dialed Kevin's number.

'Where are you?' Kevin demanded when he came to the phone. 'I thought you were going to be here an hour ago.'

'I ran into trouble. There's been a shooting. I'm at Princess Margaret Hospital in the emergency waiting room. Can you come?'

'I heard about the shooting. Why were you involved?'

'I'll tell you when you get here.'

Kevin said he'd leave for the hospital right away. Nick walked in as I was putting away my cell phone. 'I've talked to the police,' I said. 'They'll be here soon.'

'We have to talk.' His face was grim.

'Miss, you need to sign some papers,' the nurse said, glaring at Nick.

'Why do I need to sign? I don't even know the man.'

'You brought him here, so you must sign. The paper signifies no liability. But someone has to sign.' That was the islands. There was always a paper to sign.

I started to look over the papers, and Nick said to the nurse, 'I need to talk to her. She'll sign in a minute.'

'But, sir . . .'

Nick took me firmly by the arm and led me several feet away. 'We have to get out of here. We can't involve the police.'

I was trying to trust Nick, but he kept upping the ante. 'Someone is out there shooting at people. Someone killed a man who was standing right next to me and critically injured another one. These men say they have my sister. I need to talk to the police, so they can find out if that's true, and get my sister.'

'I told you, the Bahamian police can't be relied on.'

'Don't tell me that! Kevin is a friend of mine. I trust him more than I trust you!'

Nick glared at me. 'Didn't I save your life?'

'I don't know what happened. I don't know who was shooting. It might have been you for all I know. You told me your story last night, but how do I even know if it's true?'

'Jessie, for Christ's sake . . .'

A tall, hawk-faced uniformed cop came striding into the emergency room. He looked like a take-charge kind of guy. He stepped to the front desk. 'I'm looking for Jessie Madison.'

'That's me,' I said, relief coursing through me.

The guy badged me. 'I'm Detective Greg Callen.' He glanced at Nick. 'And you are?'

'Leonard Crow,' Nick said.

Callen hesitated, eyes narrowed. 'Mr Crow, I need to speak to Miss Madison.'

'It's all right,' I said. 'This is the man who rescued me from the shooters.' *Leonard Crow?*

The cop frowned at Nick. 'Kevin Riley radioed for help. I was close by, and I said I'd get over here. Let's get you two to police headquarters so we can hear your story.'

'Kevin told me he'd be here. Shouldn't we wait for him?'

'I told him I'd bring you to headquarters.'

For the first time in hours, I felt safe. Kevin and this cop were taking control of the situation.

'I'd prefer not to get involved,' Nick said. I couldn't believe it. He was trying to weasel out of going with us.

'It would be best if you cooperate,' the cop said. 'We won't keep you long. But you do need to come down to the station with me.'

The nurse called out to the cop. 'She must sign these papers before she goes.'

I went to the desk, signed the damn papers and turned back to Detective Callen. 'Someone needs to be here to question Rodney Grant when he wakes up.'

The cop looked at his watch and frowned. 'Who is Rodney Grant?'

'He's the man who was wounded in the shootout. He said he's holding my sister. I need to find out where she is.'

'What do you mean, holding your sister?'

'It's a long story. He told me he and his friend have her captive on the island. I need to know if he's telling the truth. The last I knew, she was in a rehab facility in Pennsylvania.'

'Jesus,' Nick said. 'You seem to attract trouble.'

Callen huffed impatiently. 'Never mind. We can sort this out at police headquarters.'

Nick said, 'I'm telling you, there's no reason for me to go with you. I didn't have anything to do with this shooting. I didn't see anything. She's your best witness.' He nodded toward me.

'You're coming, too,' Callen said coldly. 'If necessary, I can arrest you. Now let's go.'

I put up my hand to stop him. 'Not before I know someone will be here to question Rodney Grant. For all I know, my sister may be in danger.'

He glared at me. 'Look, Kevin is expecting us. As soon as we get to the station I'll send someone back here to question the man. With this shooting at the dock, everything is in an uproar. We have to take care of that first.' He turned back to the nurse. 'What's the condition of the man who was brought in with the gunshot?'

'Let me find out.'

Callen grimaced. 'Make it quick.'

The nurse narrowed her eyes at him 'Of course.' She picked up the phone.

Callen glanced toward the front door of the waiting room and back at the nurse. He chewed the inside of his lip while he waited for her to make her call.

'You in a hurry?' Nick asked the cop.

'Yeah, as a matter of fact, I am. There's been a lot of action today.' He seemed ready to say more, but the nurse broke in.

'The patient is being prepared for surgery, so it will be some time before he is available to talk to anyone.'

'Satisfied?' Callen asked. 'I'll have plenty of time to send someone to question him. Let's go.'

I saw beads of sweat standing out on Nick's forehead. 'Do you have pain medication with you?' I asked him.

He shook his head.

'We'll stop for something,' I said.

The cop was holding the door for us, looking annoyed. As we got to his car, his cell phone rang. He excused himself and walked a few feet away.

'Why did you give him a false name?' I whispered to Nick.

'I told you, I don't trust the Bahamian cops,' he whispered. He eyed Detective Callen, who had turned his back to us. 'You're sure this friend of yours is reliable?'

I was relying on Kevin Riley, but I really didn't know him well at all. Before I could decide what to tell Nick, Callen turned and walked toward us. He was saying into the phone, 'OK, we'll be there soon.'

He switched off his phone and slipped it into his front pocket. 'That was Kevin. He's been called to the scene of the shooting down at the marina. I told him you knew the guy who was killed, and he'd like you to make an identification. I'll take you back over there.'

As we climbed into the back seat of the car, Nick grunted and closed his eyes, gritting his teeth with pain.

'We need to stop by a pharmacy,' I told Callen.

Callen slammed his door and looked back at me, his eyes steely. 'What for?'

I was afraid if I said it was for Nick, this guy would do some kind of macho thing telling Nick to man up. 'It's been a rough morning. I've got a headache. I want to get something for it.'

The cop sighed and started the car. A couple of blocks away, he almost passed up a large pharmacy, but I yelled for him to stop. He roared into the parking lot and into a handicapped space. 'Make it quick,' he said.

'I don't have any money,' I said to Nick.

He handed me several bills in Bahamian currency. In the pharmacy, I picked up some Advil and Tylenol and two bottles of water. And at the last minute, I grabbed a packet of M&M's.

I hadn't eaten anything since the piece of toast early this morning. While I was paying at the check-out counter, my cell phone rang. It was Kevin.

'Hey,' I said. 'We'll be there soon.'

'What are you talking about?'

'Your partner, Callen, picked us up at the hospital. He said you radioed for help.'

Silence for a few beats. 'No, that's not right. Are you sure that's what he said?'

'Yes. Otherwise, we would have waited for you.'

I walked toward the entrance. Callen was coming in. He strode toward me. 'Put away the phone.'

'Where are you now?' Kevin asked.

Before I could tell him, Callen grabbed the phone and switched it off. 'You're coming with me.'

'No, I'm not. Not until you tell me what's going on.'

The greeter at the front of the CVS was eyeing us. Could I count on his help?

'I told you. I'm taking you to headquarters.' He grabbed my arm.

I yanked it away. 'Kevin said he didn't radio you for help.'

The greeter was sidling towards us, frowning. 'What's going . . .'

Callen whipped out his badge. 'Police business. I'm taking this woman in.'

'No! This man is lying.' I stepped back, but he grabbed me, tighter this time.

He drew his weapon. 'Miss, please come quietly,' he said loud enough for others in the store to hear.

The greeter stepped away.

I knew I had no choice but to go. Even if people didn't completely trust cops, they'd see no reason to believe that I was being abducted.

As we approached the car, Nick looked out and saw us. He grabbed for the door, but Callen had locked it. Callen took me to the other side of the car, unlocked the door and shoved me in, brandishing the weapon. 'Don't try anything,' he said to Nick.

'Wouldn't think of it,' Nick said. He gave me a wry smile.

Callen got in and shut the barrier between the front and the back.

'Well, well,' Nick said. 'Looks like your friend Kevin can't be trusted after all.'

'It's not him,' I said. I told him about the phone call. 'He didn't know Callen had come to get us.'

'Maybe,' Nick said. 'Whether Kevin is involved or not, it looks like we've got trouble.'

'Shit!' I fell back in the seat and covered my face with my hands. 'I screwed up.' I felt like a complete fool. I had been so relieved to have the cops involved that it hadn't occurred to me that Kevin hadn't sent this guy. 'I feel so stupid.'

'You couldn't have known.'

I opened one of the bottles of water and the Tylenol and fed Nick twice the regular dose. I tore open the M&M's and offered Nick some. He rolled his eyes. 'Candy?'

'Sugar is good for you.' I shook some into his open hand. 'We'll need the energy.'

TWENTY-EIGHT

Detective Callen drove fast into an area of the island I'd never been to before. After a while, we were on a rough road full of potholes, with weeds sticking up through cracks in the broken tarmac. We crossed a rusted iron bridge into a deserted area surrounded by derelict wooden buildings.

The whole time, my mind was reeling and I was kicking myself. I'd been so focused on Rodney that I hadn't paid attention to the signs that Callen wasn't what he seemed.

'We've got to get out of this car,' I muttered to Nick.

'How do you figure that will happen?' he asked.

I sighed. He was right. We were trapped and on our way to nothing good.

After another quarter-mile, Callen pulled into a weed-infested gravel lot and parked in front of an old, rundown dock. Only a few boats were tied up there, all rusted, filthy hulks. We were next to a big, dark SUV, which I recognized. My heart sank and I glanced over at Nick. He was cradling his arm. Sweat shone on his forehead.

The doors of the SUV opened, and Didier and the other man

got out and strode toward the patrol car. Callen got out to meet them. Like yesterday, Didier was dressed in rumpled jeans and a wrinkled T-shirt that outlined his big muscles, while the other man wore crisp khaki pants and a light blue, linen shirt. They shook hands with the cop, who said something I couldn't hear and gestured toward the patrol car, smiling eagerly.

Seeing the three of them together, one thing fell into place. I had been wondering how the smugglers had known I was still alive. First, I suspected Nick of telling them, then I blamed myself for being recognized, and finally I thought maybe the Turpins had gotten the information from the Coast Guard.

Now I knew how they had found out. Kevin Riley must have told Callen my story, not knowing that Callen was dirty and that he would pass the information along to the smugglers. At least, I *hoped* Kevin didn't know.

Didier walked to my side of the car, yanked open the door and poked his head inside. His lips were trembling with rage under his bristling mustache, his eyes dark with hatred. 'You have caused me a lot of trouble.'

'Why am I not sorry?' I said, bracing myself for a blow.

He gave a low growl, but his eyes flicked to where the other man was still standing with Callen. 'If it was up to me, I would kill you now.'

'It *was* up to you, and you failed.' I put all the contempt I had into my voice. I didn't give good odds to my chance of survival, but I was determined to fight back any way I could.

'Not again, I won't,' Didier snarled. He pulled back and straightened.

The other man had come to Nick's side of the car and opened the door. 'Both of you, please get out of the vehicle.' His voice was courteous but full of authority.

I hesitated, and Didier reached in and yanked me out, slamming me against the car.

'That's not necessary,' Nick snapped loudly. Favoring his injured shoulder, he got out on his side. The well-dressed man said, 'Nick Garnier. What a pleasure to meet you. I'm happy to find that your employers sent their finest agent.'

'Henri Perrault. The pleasure is all mine.' Nick's eyes were glittering. He spoke rapidly to the man in French.

'Move,' Didier snapped. He pushed me, and I stumbled to a halt next to Nick and Perrault.

Perrault nodded to Callen. 'Please relieve them of their weapons and their mobile phones.'

'I already took her phone,' Callen said. He searched Nick first, taking two handguns and a knife. Then he moved to me, patting me down. He grabbed Rodney's pistol that I had stuck in my waistband. 'What have we here? You know handguns aren't allowed in Nassau. I could arrest you for that.' He snickered. 'Nice gun,' he said.

'It's a piece of shit,' I said. 'Like you.'

His mouth hardened. He took out his cell phone and punched a couple of buttons.

'Who are you calling?' Perrault said sharply.

'I need to square things with my partner. She told him I had her, and I don't want him to come looking for her.'

'Leave it,' Perrault said. 'He won't know where we are.'

Callen snapped his phone off and sneered at me.

'Well, at least I know you're the snake, not Kevin,' I said.

Nick's mouth was set in a grim line, and he flicked a glance in my direction. I hadn't seen him look this bleak. At that moment, I knew that he didn't hold out much hope for our survival. He was probably right. I closed my eyes and swallowed against the regret that made my stomach flip over. I could have been out of here by now if I hadn't been so intent on revenge.

Perrault said, 'Now we have you, and I'm happy to tell you that if you cooperate, you may be allowed to live.'

I didn't believe him.

'Cooperate how?' Nick said.

Perrault stepped close to me. 'This young woman has stolen property that belongs to us. We want it back.'

'It isn't your property,' Nick said.

Perrault cocked an eyebrow. 'I don't believe that's an argument you can win.'

He turned to Detective Callen. 'It would be best if you leave us now. And take the weapons with you. I will contact you when your money is available.'

'Wait, I thought we—'

Henri Perrault interrupted him. 'One more thing. Do you have handcuffs?'

Callen nodded, frowning.

'I need two pairs.'

Callen went to his car and came back with the handcuffs, which he handed to Perrault. He took out a key ring. 'Do you need the key?'

Perrault's smile was wolfish. 'That won't be necessary. Now, be on your way.' He handed the cuffs to Didier, turning his back on Callen. The cop bit his bottom lip and glared at Perrault's back before he reluctantly headed for his car.

'Good riddance,' I snapped, as Callen passed close to me. He threw me a poisonous glance.

I still held out hope that Kevin might think something was fishy. If he went to the hospital, it's possible the nurse might tell him that Nick and I went with Callen. If he asked. And if the nurse remembered. And if we could stay alive long enough for it to matter.

After Callen drove away, Perrault walked over to the dock and looked toward the mouth of the inlet, then came back. He took out a pack of cigarettes and offered them around. Nick eyed the pack like an ex-smoker, but he refused. Then Perrault took out a gold lighter and lit a cigarette for himself and one for Didier.

'Now what?' I said.

Perrault glanced at his heavy designer watch. I wondered where he had stolen it from. 'Now we wait.'

'You don't mind if I sit down,' I said. I dropped to the ground near the car, leaning back against the car door.

'Make yourself comfortable.' Perrault reached into the SUV and came out with a Glock. 'Don't get any ideas of running away.'

TWENTY-NINE

It was one o'clock, and the sun was brutal. There was no shade anywhere in the area, and I was drenched with sweat. Perrault was leaning against the SUV, smoking. He seemed not to be affected by the heat, but, of course, he could afford to be cool.

He was the one with the weapon. Nick was standing a few feet away with his back to me, looking toward the dock. I hoped he was coming up with a plan to get us out of this, because I was all out of ideas. Nick had said sooner or later I was going to run out of luck. Maybe later had arrived.

I had always had the idea that you made your own luck, and in that sense, I had walked right into this situation. Was it because I was stubborn, like John Farrell said? Or because I was brave, which was the version I preferred. Either way, this time it was going to take some serious luck to get out alive. A lot more luck than Paco and Rodney had managed.

It hardly seemed possible that Paco Boland was dead. It had happened so fast. I wondered how badly Rodney was injured. Even though I had a hard time believing he and Paco had Kayla stashed somewhere on the island, I worried that I was wrong. I had to get out of this situation, go back to the hospital and make Rodney tell me the truth. I kept getting shivers of panic, thinking of my sister locked up somewhere waiting to be rescued, slowly dying of thirst and starvation.

But I had to admit part of me was angry. I was tired of always being responsible for my sister. If it hadn't been for her drug habit, I wouldn't have been in the situation I was in now. I would have been a newly minted FBI agent, with an assignment, and a life, the way I had planned it. I would never have heard of Didier, or Louis, or Jaggo. And I wouldn't be sitting in this filthy, weedy vacant lot waiting to be murdered. Or would I? What did I think going into the FBI meant? That I would have free rein to investigate my dad's death? That I would get to walk around looking like one of the cool kids, in a black skirt and blazer? What, exactly, had I thought it entailed? I would surely encounter such dangerous situations working for the FBI. If I couldn't handle what was happening to me now, it was just as well I had left before I was an agent.

I was so hot that I thought I would faint. Even the oily, sludge-filled water in the inlet off the dock looked inviting. Maybe I should take my chances that Perrault wouldn't actually shoot me, and run for the water and dive in.

My fantasy was interrupted when Didier walked over to the dock. He was smoking and eying the open water beyond the estuary. We had to be waiting for a boat.

Didier straightened and threw his cigarette into the trash-filled water. I looked in the direction he was watching and saw a boat coming from out in the open bay. I was surprised they would take a chance coming into a derelict harbor like this, where there was a better than even chance that a sunken boat lay hidden under the surface of the water. As it neared, I saw that it was a catamaran. It had to be *Island Ice*. I wondered if the Turpins were aboard or if someone from Didier's gang had commandeered her. Everyone turned their attention to the boat as she moved slowly toward the dock.

'Good, here they are,' Perrault said, flicking aside his cigarette. 'Now we can take care of our business.'

I got to my feet, momentarily dizzy from the heat, and glanced over at Nick. Sweat was beading his face and his jaw was tight. The Tylenol wasn't taking care of the pain.

Didier walked out onto the dock to meet the boat. The unstable structure swayed and groaned with his weight. As the boat neared, I saw that Louis was on the boat. He threw a line to Didier, who grabbed it and tied it onto a cleat on the dock that looked so rusted out that I wasn't sure it would hold. The dock creaked ominously as the big boat moved alongside. I noticed that they were towing a dingy that hadn't been there the night I brought the boat back to Nassau.

'After you,' Perrault said to Nick and me, pointing toward the dock with the Glock. 'I believe we'll all be more comfortable if we board the boat and sit down inside.'

'Glad to know you're interested in our comfort,' Nick said.

Perrault's smile was thin. 'I'm sure you know what my main interest is. Now, if you would be so kind.'

I eyed the rotting boards on the precarious dock, wondering what would happen if one of the four of us crashed through into the water. But although the boards trembled with our weight, the dock held.

As I boarded the boat, Carl and Betty Turpin came down the steps from the flying bridge. Apparently, they had recovered from the trauma of the shootout. Or maybe they had no choice in the matter. 'Thought you were pretty clever, didn't you?' Betty said. So much for trauma.

'Clever?' I said.

'Leaving me with that body and the security guard. Now we'll see who's clever.'

'It was your husband who left you high and dry, not me,' I snapped.

Carl Turpin shot an anxious look at his wife. I could imagine the verbal abuse he'd taken from her for abandoning her at the marina. He looked worse than his wife, his face gray, his temple red and bruised from where Rodney had hit him.

'No need for bickering. Let's move on,' Perrault said, prodding Nick and me past the Turpins and into the saloon.

The boat had been cleaned up, but I noticed some tools on the navigation station. A hammer and chisel and a pair of pliers. Unusual tools for a boat. Unless you planned to use them on someone. My heart skittered.

Perrault ordered Nick and me to sit on the banquette up against the wall, with the Turpins facing us across the table, and Perrault himself in the captain's chair in front of the navigation station. Louis and Didier stood in the doorway leading to the outside cockpit.

'Where's the crazy guy?' I said. 'Jaggo. What happened to him?' I knew, of course, that Jaggo was dead. But one of the psychology courses I had taken in FBI training had emphasized that it was important to use every psychological advantage if you were in a tight spot. It wouldn't hurt to remind Didier and Louis that their colleague was dead.

'Jaggo won't be joining us,' Perrault said. 'He had other matters to attend to.'

'Like dying?' I prodded.

Annoyance flashed in Perrault's eyes, but he squelched it. 'So, you are aware of what happened?' he said.

'Not really. I know he was in a shootout at a casino. I saw his picture in the newspaper. And I also know he was a nutcase. What was he up to that got him killed? And, of course, got that poor tourist killed. You people don't care much if innocent bystanders get hurt, do you?'

I was rewarded with the tiniest twitch of Perrault's left eye.

'Who shot him?' I persisted. 'Was it you?'

Beside me, Nick pressed my knee ever so slightly with his. I wished I could see his face. Was he telling me I was doing the right thing to goad them, or was he warning me to back off?

Perrault crossed his leg at the knee, adjusting the perfect crease in his trousers. 'We don't need to concern ourselves with Jaggo. As you say, he is no longer with us.'

'I don't know your feelings in the matter,' I said, 'but I think we're all better off without him.'

I heard Didier huff, but I didn't look at him. Did he mourn Jaggo? Were they related? Like me and my drug-addled sister?

'I thought we might start our conversation with a bit of entertainment,' Perrault said. He addressed me, but he glanced at Didier and Louis, his mouth twitching in a smile. I would not have wanted that smile turned in my direction, but I had a feeling it would be before the day was over.

'Entertainment?' I asked.

'You used the term "innocent bystander," and I've been given to believe that the term describes you as well. But if you're innocent, I'm sure Didier and Louis are as curious as I am to know how you managed to escape when they threw you overboard. They told me it was impossible.'

'You want me to tell you how I got out of the rope and the chains? And how my friend Johnny didn't make it?' I snapped the words.

'I am sorry you were unable to save the young captain, but we need not concern ourselves with him. Pretend you are Scheherazade, keeping yourself alive by telling an interesting story.'

I shuddered. Having him put the blame on me for not saving Johnny was gut-wrenching. But I had to put that aside if I was going to save myself. How would it be best to tell the story of how I managed to escape? One of a woman's best weapons was to appear weak. I needed these men to think I was weak. Maybe one of them would underestimate me and make a mistake I could take advantage of. I had to emphasize an element of luck. But I also wanted Perrault to think Didier and his crew had been incompetent. I wanted him to be annoyed with them. I wanted the focus to be on their mistakes.

Beside me, Nick said, 'I hope you don't mind if I take a nap. I've already heard this story.' He slid down and rested his head against the back of his seat, closing his eyes. Was he trying to be funny?

I told a revised version of my escape, telling them that the chain had not been properly secured and that it slipped off, and that the rope had become slack in the water.

'You didn't secure the chain?' Perrault asked Didier.

For a big man, Didier looked like a child when he sulked. When he replied, his accent was more pronounced. 'I don't believe this girl. We draped forty feet of chain and more around her and the man.'

I shrugged. 'I don't care what you believe, that's what happened.'

Didier's voice was louder. 'It is impossible that the chain simply slipped off. I'm telling you, this woman had a friend there – maybe this Nick – who helped her get away.'

'Leave me out of it,' Nick said, his eyes still closed. 'I don't know a damned thing. The story sounds as far-fetched to me as it does to you.'

Perrault said to me, 'Are you sure no one was in the harbor and saw you going overboard and came to your rescue?'

'Ask your men. It was dark and there were no other boats around. I was just lucky the chain wasn't secured.'

'Why was your friend Johnny not so lucky?'

'These men had hit him repeatedly. I think he died from head wounds.' It wasn't true, but I didn't want to let them know how sharp my skills were in the water. The less they knew about me, the better.

I glanced at the Turpins. Despite Betty Turpin's bravado, she looked the worse for wear. Her hair was frizzing out and her lipstick had worn off, leaving her looking frazzled. Carl Turpin was watching me intently. His expression was hard to read. But he, too, looked tired and worried. I suspected that they had failed to appreciate the brutality of the men they had conspired with.

'But you were also able to get out of the rope. You say it went slack. I don't understand how that could've happened.'

'To tell you the truth, I'm not sure how it happened either. Maybe the sharp coral frayed it.' I wasn't going to reveal that I had had the presence of mind to slip my arm between me and Johnny, giving the rope play. 'Or maybe a shark swam by and nicked it. Who knows?'

'No!' Didier shouted. 'A shark would never get that close.'

Perrault ignored him and inclined his head toward me. 'Your good luck, then. Tell me, after that bit of luck, how did you manage to get off the island?'

'I found a surfboard washed up on the east coast of the island. It must have broken loose from a sailing vessel out on the Atlantic side and washed up on the shore. I paddled it back to Trophy Cay.' No need for him to know the work I'd had to put into making the surfboard buoyant enough to make the trip.

Perrault raised his eyebrows and looked at his two henchmen. 'And you two did not bother to go back to the island to make sure you had done a thorough job of taking care of this woman and the captain.' He stated it as a fact, and neither man replied. I noticed that although Didier's glances at me were full of fury, Louis's held an element of admiration. I remembered that he was the only one of the three who had seemed reluctant in his role as executioner.

'So, you were lucky once again. And stealing this boat that we are on now. How did that happen? More luck?' His tone was sarcastic.

Betty Turpin suddenly interjected, 'The only luck was that the three men you sent to take care of your business were obviously incompetent.'

'Exactly!' I laughed. Didier growled and stepped toward me, hands clenched.

'Stay back!' Perrault said sharply. 'I'm sure hearing the truth is difficult, but Miss Madison is merely trying to bait you. Don't be a fool by letting her get to you.' His voice became silky again with me. 'Please continue.'

I told Perrault that I had seen Louis and Jaggo drinking in the bar, and when I saw Didier get off the boat to join them, I realized that it might be possible to steal *Island Ice*. 'I couldn't believe my luck when I saw the boat had been left unattended,' I said. 'But don't be too hard on them. Remember, they thought they had murdered me.'

'Indeed. Once again, I remind you of your claim that you are an innocent bystander,' Perrault said. 'If that's so, how did you know how to drive the boat? It is not easy to operate an unfamiliar vessel. And a catamaran is hard to maneuver.'

Carl Turpin sat forward, hands on his knees. 'There's no way

she could have navigated those waters at night. She's lying.
Someone helped her.'

Nick pressed his leg up against mine again. I almost laughed.
He was teasing me for gaining Perrault's respect!

'Oh, please! I didn't need luck. I work on dive boats every
day and I frequently drive them to and from our dive sites. Plus,
I was with Johnny when he drove this boat from Trophy Cay to
Minor Cay where your men boarded her. I saw as much as I
needed to know about how the boat works. It isn't rocket science.'

'But I am told the waters between the Exuma Islands and
Nassau are treacherous. How did you manage to stay off the
shoals? And in the night, at that. You strain my ability to believe
you.'

'I've learned the waters where we take people to dive. I know
where the depths tend to be shallow, and I steered clear of them.
But I do have to admit I was scared. I took the long way around.'

Perrault raised an eyebrow. 'Miss Madison, I'm sure my adver-
sary Mr Garnier will agree with me that most people make their
own luck.' Funny, he was echoing my thoughts on the subject.

Nick didn't budge, but he said, 'I told you. Leave me out of
this. Her luck has nothing to do with me.'

Perrault got up and paced from one side of the saloon to the
other. 'Your story was entertaining. But now it is time for business.' His voice sharpened. 'You managed to bring this boat back
to Nassau. And you stole a package when you left the boat.'

'What? No. I didn't steal anything. I couldn't wait to get the
hell off this boat.'

Perrault stopped in front of me. I could feel Nick tense beside
me. 'I have been willing to give you the benefit of the doubt in
the wild stories you have told me.' He held up his hand as I
started to protest. 'Please, we are done with the stories now. Last
night, my men watched you bring a backpack to the dock where
this boat was being held.'

'Yes. Of course I did. I admit it. If you'll let me explain, you'll
understand.'

'I can't wait to hear this.' Betty Turpin said.

Perrault ignored her. 'Please. Let's hear one more story from
you.'

'When I left the catamaran with the Coast Guard, I took the

backpack with me because it belonged to Johnny. I wanted to see if his address was in the pack so I could return it to his family. The family who would be mourning him after your men killed him. But when I opened it – surprise, surprise – I found a pouch full of jewelry. I knew then what everyone was after, and I wanted no part of it.'

Carl Turpin had been squirming, getting more and more agitated. He jumped to his feet and said to Didier. 'You idiot! You left the jewelry on the boat unattended?'

Didier stood erect, his face fiery red. 'The boat was a safe place to keep it. No one would suspect where it was.'

'Obviously, it wasn't as safe as you thought,' Betty said. She was practically spitting.

'Stop quarreling like children,' Perrault snapped. 'And where is the jewelry now?'

'I'm trying to tell you. When I saw the jewelry – what had almost gotten me killed,' I added, sweetly, 'I knew having it in my possession was a bad idea. I put it back in the backpack, and thought if I put it back on the boat, everyone would be satisfied and you'd leave me alone.'

Perrault threw his head back and laughed. 'You do know how to tell a good story.' He paced back and forth, shaking his head. 'A good story.' Suddenly, he pounced, yanking me up from my seat by my shoulders and shoving his face close to mine. I was surprised at his strength. 'But we saw you with Nick Garnier last night in the restaurant. And then everything made sense. I knew then that you must be one of his agents.'

'No way! I work on dive boats. I only met Nick when I got to Trophy Cay.'

Nick opened his eyes and sat up. 'So now we get to the heart of the problem, Perrault. You've lost the jewelry and you're trying to figure out who to blame.'

Perrault let go of my shoulders, glancing at his hands as if touching me had left them dirty. 'We're going to find out who has the jewelry, I can guarantee.'

I did my best imitation of innocence. 'What do you mean? Isn't it in the backpack? It was when I put it back on the boat last night. Someone else must have taken it.' I took a long look at the Turpins to emphasize who I thought he should blame.

'I have had people watching, and the only people who have been on the boat are the Turpins. They have no reason to have stolen the jewelry and every reason to want it delivered to me.'

'Oh, come on,' I said. 'They might have planned to bypass you.'

'Never!' Betty Turpin yelled.

Perrault smirked. 'No one bypasses me. Mr and Mrs Turpin know that.'

'She has the jewelry,' Betty Turpin said. 'No one else has had a chance to get their hands on it.'

I opened my hands out in appeal. 'It was easy for me to get onto the boat, so anyone else could have, too. Maybe one of these two.' I waved toward Didier and Louis. They were already on the carpet for stupidity. They could take the rap for greed as well.

'We will get the answer to this problem soon enough,' Perrault said. 'But now there is one more thing I want to know. Who were the two men you were with this morning? Why did they follow you after you left the Coast Guard dock last night?'

'They're friends of my sister. It's a long story.'

Perrault chuckled, but it was an unpleasant sound. 'You seem to have many stories to tell.'

I shrugged. 'They have nothing to do with this. Are you the ones who shot them?'

'Sadly, there was no choice. They seemed to have ill intentions toward you,' Perrault said. 'We couldn't let them kill you, because we needed to find out where the jewelry was.'

'Nice of you to save me,' I said.

He walked over to the navigation station and picked up a pair of pliers and a hammer. He weighed them as if thinking. Then he took them over to Didier, who snatched them as if eager to get his hands on them. Both men turned to look at me. 'I'm going to give you another chance to tell me what you've done with the jewelry. I guarantee that Didier will find out in the end, so you may as well make it easier.'

'I told you . . .'

'Cool it, Jessie,' Nick said. His voice was steel. 'Tell them what you did with the jewelry.'

I met his eyes. Was he serious? It was our only bargaining chip. He nodded slightly, as if he knew I wanted to hold out.

'You see, Mr Garnier understands the difficult situation you are in.'

I sighed, trying to think of some way to stall.

'Now, please. Tell us where it is.' Perrault's voice was steel.

'I'll tell you, but . . .'

Perrault laughed. 'There are no "buts." You should listen to Mr Garnier. He knows me well, or at least he knows something of my methods.'

So I told him where the jewelry was. And said goodbye to our chances of coming out of this alive.

'Not a particularly clever hiding place,' Perrault said. 'Suppose someone finds the jewelry?'

I plopped down wearily next to Nick. 'Then I guess we're all out of luck.'

Perrault stroked his chin. 'I need to confer with Mr and Mrs Turpin for a moment. Didier, please watch our two guests – carefully, this time.'

THIRTY

As soon as Perrault and the Turpins were out of earshot, I turned on Nick. 'Why the hell did you want me to tell them where the jewelry was?'

'I know these guys. There was no sense in putting yourself through torture. We'll most likely be killed, but at least we don't have to be miserable before that.'

'Oh, great. I'm stuck with a philosopher. How's your shoulder?'

'On fire.'

I stood up. 'I need to use the bathroom,' I said to Didier.

'Sit,' Didier said.

'Look, I'm going down to use the head. You know there's no way I can escape from there. Shoot me if you want to.'

'Go with her,' Didier said to Louis.

I took the steps down into the owner's cabin, with Louis hanging back as if reluctant to carry out Didier's order. I shut the door in his face. Inside, once I had obeyed the call of nature,

I rummaged around in the cabinet to see if there was anything I could use as a weapon. Lots of face cream, shampoo, and make-up. The only hardware was a pair of tweezers and nail scissors, too small to be of apparent use. Nevertheless, I slipped them into my pocket. I still had the ibuprofen and acetaminophen with me. I shook some out into my hand.

Louis banged on the door. I waited another minute, flushed the toilet and came out.

Back in the saloon, I ambled over to the refrigerator and took out a bottle of water. I handed it to Nick, along with the pills. He gulped them down.

Didier was at my side in two steps. 'What is that?'

'It's ibuprofen,' I said. 'What did you think it was? Heroin?' I smirked. I liked needling him.

Didier's face had become beet-red. He grabbed my arm and shoved me down next to Nick. 'Don't move again,' he said.

'No problem,' I said. I settled back and crossed my arms across my chest.

Nick shook his head. 'Even if you get us killed, with your attitude at least we're going down in style.'

It was pure bravado. If he'd known how scared I was, he wouldn't have been so cheery.

Perrault appeared back at the door of the saloon, and I didn't like the satisfied look on his face. He conferred quietly with Didier and Louis, who kept looking over at Nick and me.

'Here we go,' I whispered.

'It can't be good,' Nick said. 'Are you ready?'

'I doubt it.' I looked into his eyes, and we smiled at each other.

He reached his good arm out and touched my cheek. I covered his hand with mine. Might as well give in to my attraction to him.

Perrault stepped away from his henchmen and lifted an eyebrow. 'How sweet. Now if you'll both stand up, Didier will escort you to your quarters.'

I took Nick's bad arm, to prevent it from being grabbed by Didier.

Didier pushed us down the port-side steps and into the aft cabin. Louis followed, keeping a gun trained on us. As if we could go anywhere or make a false move. Didier produced the two pairs of handcuffs Perrault had gotten from Detective Callen and proceeded to cuff our hands behind our backs. Nick winced when his arm was wrenched behind him, but he didn't make a sound.

Didier stepped away, and Perrault stood in the doorway of the cabin. 'I'm sure you're wondering what the plan is, so let me lay it out for you. Mr and Mrs Turpin will be taking the boat outside the harbor. Didier, Louis and I will go to the dive dock and wait for the return of the boat where Miss Madison said she hid the pouch that belongs to us. If we find it, the Turpins will let you go. If not, we will radio them to bring you back here. And believe me, at that time, you will wish you had told me the truth.'

'What do you mean, "let us go"?' I asked. 'You don't have the keys to these cuffs.'

Perrault sighed. 'Oh dear, I guess I misspoke. I meant, let you go *in a manner of speaking*.'

I understood what he meant. We would be heaved into the water, again, but this time in deep water. Even if the Turpins didn't shoot us, which they likely would, the only way we could hope to survive was if we could stay afloat with our hands cuffed behind our backs. And once we were out of the harbor, we would be at the mercy of the currents. The best we could hope for was that a passing boat would see us before we drowned. I clenched my teeth to keep from shuddering. I'd been through a near-drowning too recently, and I wasn't looking forward to going through it again.

When Perrault closed the cabin door, there were clicking sounds and thumps on the door. I cocked my head. 'They must have some kind of mechanism for locking us in.'

'At least they didn't put us in separate cabins.'

I nodded. Already I was trying to think of a way to get us out of there.

THIRTY-ONE

The boat rocked, and I presumed that meant Perrault and the other two men were getting off. It actually had a nice symmetry. My misadventure had started with three men stepping onto the boat. It could end with them stepping off. Luck had been with me the first time. But now I was pretty sure my luck had run out.

I perched at the edge of the bed, and Nick propped himself against the door. He said, 'Looks like we have some time. Do you want to explain who those guys were that you were with this morning? I presume they're the ones who shot me last night.'

I blew out a breath. 'God, that seems like a long time ago. They did shoot you, but I don't think they intended to. They were after me.'

'What did you do to get on their bad side?'

'The short version? I was involved in the death of Paco's brother. He was a drug dealer, and my sister was living with him. One night, he attacked her, and I went to her rescue. I paid a big price for it.' I couldn't keep the bitterness out of my voice. 'I've been rescuing her my whole life, but this cost me big. You said you talked to John Ferrell, my FBI trainer. Maybe he told you that's why I was kicked out of training. They don't like it when somebody has problem relatives.'

He shook his head. 'He told me you made an impulsive decision. Why didn't you notify them your sister had a problem earlier?'

I shrugged. 'I thought it was under control.' Not entirely true.

'So, that guy Paco was after you for revenge?'

We both became alert as the motor started up with a dull rumble. Here I was, on *Island Ice* again. At least whatever happened, I'd never have to see the damn boat again.

'Paco?' he prodded.

'Yeah, he wanted revenge. He brought along his sidekick, Rodney Grant. Paco is a nasty guy, but Rodney is a psychopath. The kind of guy who seems to be able to slither out from under any blame.'

'He's the one we took to the hospital? Why did you bother?'

'When they grabbed me, they told me they have my sister somewhere on the island. I doubt it's true, but I need him alive in case it is. I'm sure as hell glad you showed up when you did. Paco was going to kill me.'

'Sorry I didn't get there earlier. I got to your place in time to see them force you into their car. Why did they take you to the Coast Guard dock?'

'Last night, they followed me when I went to stash the jewelry on the dive boat. Apparently, they were in the parking lot, but I didn't notice them because I was too scared that Didier and his men would find me.'

'They must have followed me. I didn't see them.'

'Anyway, they saw me return the backpack to *Island Ice*.'

'How did they find out you were here in the Bahamas?'

'Good question.' I had a suspicion, but I didn't want to focus on that now. The way things were going, it hardly mattered.

'Well, at least we don't have them to contend with now.'

'Ha! Those two were amateurs compared to your friend Perrault and his men.'

'Really? They shot me! And they were using you to get to the jewelry, and then they would have killed you, too.'

'But they didn't.'

He laughed. 'You're right, they didn't. The FBI made a big mistake,' he said.

'What do you mean?'

'They let you go. You're too smart, or maybe lucky, to waste.'

'Yeah, so smart that I'm on the verge of being killed. Again. You were right I should have dealt with my sister's problems before they got out of hand. Especially as soon as I found out she was living with a drug dealer. I knew that Diego, Paco, and Rodney had all done prison time. I should have gone to John Farrell as soon as I knew she was with them. If I had, by now I'd be an FBI agent and I'd never have set eyes on Didier and that murderous crew.' I wouldn't have met Nick either, but that was a price I would have been willing to pay, no matter how attracted I was to him.

'Why didn't you go to Farrell?'

'I thought I could handle the situation myself.' I stood up and looked out the porthole as the boat began to move away from the dock. 'I have to get out of here and find out if Rodney actually has my sister.'

'Get out of here?' He snorted. 'Good luck with that. See anything out there?'

I shook my head. 'I wish we were on the starboard side, so I could make sure all three of those men got off the boat.'

'You mean we're more likely to be able to overpower the Turpins if they're alone?' His grin was mocking.

I shrugged. 'Who are the Turpins, anyway? How are they involved with these guys?'

'Turpin is a prominent diamond dealer in New York. Good reputation. But it turns out he's the middleman between Perrault's gang and a fence who deals with stolen jewelry. For some time, we've suspected Perrault of the thefts, but we couldn't figure out how his people were getting the stolen jewelry into the United States. Then, recently, we got a break from an informer who said Turpin had shown up with some jewelry he shouldn't have had. It gave us the answer to several loose ends.'

'Why would a successful jeweler get involved with someone like Perrault?'

He shrugged. 'Greed – what else?'

'So your jewelry group came after Perrault.'

He sighed. 'Twice. I wasn't here the first time. It was a bust, and we lost two good agents. They were working with the Nassau cops, and I figured we had a leak. That's why I didn't want to involve the cops this time.'

'I still don't think Kevin is the problem.'

'I realized that when Callen called him.'

'So what was your plan? How was Johnny involved?'

'We planted Johnny on this boat.'

'He was one of your agents?'

'No, but we'd worked with him before, and he seemed to know how to take care of himself. All we wanted him to do was transport the goods. He wasn't supposed to stray off the plan.'

'You're blaming him? You used a civilian and you think it's his fault that he got killed?'

His face was grim. 'He should have stuck to the plan. I tried to tell him.'

I felt sick with regret. If I hadn't given in to my impulse for one last fling, none of this would have happened. John Farrell had told me I had poor impulse control and needed to work on it. 'Even if he had met you in Nassau as planned, he would have been in danger when you sprang the trap.'

'We had told Johnny to get off the boat as soon as it landed in Nassau. Remember, Didier's gang wasn't supposed to be on the boat. They were supposed to meet it. We thought the Turpins were going to be on it. Instead they called Johnny and said they would meet him in Nassau. Another agent was coming in, and we were going to be at the dock when it arrived in Nassau. We figured Perrault and the Turpins would meet the boat. Then Perrault would turn over the jewelry, and the Turpins would pay him for it. We planned to catch them in the act.'

'Why were you in Trophy Cay?'

'Johnny said he was going to stop there overnight before he went on to Nassau. The trip from Georgetown was hard, and he needed rest. I went to Trophy Cay to check in with him and make sure everything was going according to plan. And if we hadn't met you . . .'

'That's right. Blame the woman.'

'You held out the apple.'

'Right.' One last fling.

While Nick talked, I had been mulling over our predicament. If we were going to get out of this, I had to figure something out, now. I backed up to the closet and opened it from behind, then turned around and looked inside. There were a few jackets hanging there and a couple of bags on the floor. I pulled the bags out with my feet, then sat on the floor with my back to them so I could feel for the zippers and get them open.

'What are you doing?' Nick said.

'Trying to find something to help us get out of here.'

I glanced at him. He raised an eyebrow.

I got the zippers pulled open and turned around onto my knees to peer inside the bags. One of them was full of shoes, but the other contained tools.

The boat was picking up speed, which meant we had cleared the deserted marina and were out in the estuary. Soon we would be in the harbor, headed for open ocean. Then we were truly screwed.

'You looking for anything in particular?' Nick asked.

'Duh. Something to get these handcuffs off with. I don't know if you noticed, but these are not exactly state-of-the-art cuffs.' We were lucky that the Bahamian police weren't equipped with zip ties.

'Could we use pliers or that wrench?' He nodded toward the tools.

'No, something thin that I can pick the lock with.' I remembered the nail scissors and tweezers in my pocket, but they were both too big for the job.

Nick laughed. 'You've got to be kidding.'

'No, I'm not kidding. A few years ago, one of the agents got in a situation where he was handcuffed, and someone lost their life because he couldn't do anything. So they brought in this ex-safecracker to teach us how to pick the lock on handcuffs.'

'It's worth a try.' He sat down with his back to the bag and began taking things out one at a time while I watched. He grunted with pain a couple of times. There were screwdrivers and wrenches, a few aerosol cans and a whole bunch of other useless items. And there was a boat knife, the kind with all manner of implements on it, but most prominent a sharp blade. Usually, the most important thing a boat knife was used for was if a sail line got snarled in a gale and had to be cut to release the sail. But they were good for all kinds of odd jobs, like repairing a dinghy engine or loosening screws. I set it aside.

There was nothing thin enough to use as a pick. I sighed. 'Let me see if there's anything in the jacket pockets.' My back to the jackets, I fumbled through the pockets with my cuffed hands, going by feel. There was nothing in any of them except a couple of tissues. Nick continued to sit on the floor, watching me. His face was pale. The effort to remove the tools with his hands twisted behind his back had tweaked his shoulder.

There were storage cabinets across from the closet. I backed up to the bottom one and clicked it open, then turned around to peer inside. It was full of towels. I kicked off my flip-flops, and using my toes dragged them all out onto the floor. As one dropped, I heard a tiny ping. I flipped each towel aside with my foot, looking for the source of the sound. 'Bingo!'

I was looking at a stray paperclip that lay on the floor. I crouched down and picked it up from behind and began to straighten it out by feel.

'You really think you can open the handcuffs with that?' Nick said. His voice held a whole load of skepticism.

'Normally, yes. But I've never tried opening the lock without being able to see what I'm doing.'

'Let me try using the wrench.' Nick picked it up. 'If I can pry yours off first, then you could do mine.'

'In training, they told us that people had tried all kinds of tools for getting the things open, without success. The only thing that might work is a hacksaw, which takes forever. That's why they taught us to pick the locks.'

'If you say so. Give it a try.'

I was annoyed at the skepticism in Nick's voice. I was determined to prove myself. It was hot in the cabin, and my hands were soon slick with perspiration. Now nerves were added to the equation. I was wasting precious time. Even though it was a calm, clear day with little wind, once the boat got out of the harbor, the water would be more turbulent – which meant it would be harder for me to accomplish the delicate operation of picking the lock.

I used one of the towels to wipe my hands. Then I tried moving the clip around to insert it into the lock. But I found that my hands were in such an awkward position that I couldn't reach the lock. Then I had an idea. 'I'm going to have to undo yours instead of mine,' I said. 'And then I'll have to tell you how to do mine.'

We moved back to back, but he was taller, and I had trouble reaching the cuffs. 'Wait. Let's move over here.' A couple of steps were built in on each side of the bed, to make getting onto it easier. I stepped up one step, which put my hands on a level with Nick's.

I felt the lock and was able to insert the clip into it. But then my hand cramped. 'Ouch!' I yanked out the paper clip and shook her hand to ease the cramp.

'What? Did you poke yourself?'

'No. I have a cramp in my hand. It's nerves.' I flexed my fingers to relax them. 'Let me try it again.'

The clip went back into the lock, and I concentrated on remembering how the mechanism worked. There were more intricate handcuffs but, thank God, these were older standard issue. Still, not being able to see it meant I had to go by feel, and everything was backwards. Suddenly, I felt a shift as the clip tucked into one of the lock mechanisms. I took a deep breath, holding my hands steady. 'Don't move,' I said. My voice was shaking.

Nick grunted, and I could hear him swallow. I pictured the

mechanism again, and then flipped the image. There. Another give. And there was a chink of sound, and the lock gave.

'Oh, shit!' I breathed. My hands were trembling so hard that I dropped the paper clip. 'OK, OK, one down.'

I turned around and watched as Nick flexed his hands and the cuffs fell away. 'Brilliant!' He grabbed each of his wrists in turn, rubbing away the feel of the cuffs. Then he turned to face me. 'You are truly amazing.' I was still standing on the step, which put me at equal height with him.

He took my face in his hands and kissed me gently, his tongue finding mine and lingering. My knees went weak. Having my hands tied behind me was a bigger turn-on than I would have thought. I made a mental note to remember that for future reference. If I had a future.

He pulled away. 'I shouldn't have done that.'

My throat was tight. 'I'm glad you did. Even if was sort of a waste of time.'

'Maybe. But I figured it may be the last chance I'd have if we don't get out of here.'

I turned around and brandished my handcuffs. 'You think you could . . .'

'Right. Tell me what to do.' He picked up his cuffs from where they had fallen to the floor. I told him to close them, and then took him through the process of how to open them. He was a fast learner, which didn't surprise me.

'OK, let's get those things off you.'

When the cuffs slipped off, I shook my hands to loosen them. Without the handcuffs to focus on, I felt more claustrophobic in the cabin. My heart was tripping as I tried opening the cabin door, hoping we weren't really locked in. The door didn't budge. 'I don't know how we're going to get out of here.' I could hear the fear in my voice.

'I have an idea,' Nick said. 'We can lure one of the Turpins down here to the cabin. They won't be expecting us to have our cuffs off. We'll overpower them.'

'Lure them how?'

'Yell. Bang on the walls and the ceiling.'

'Whichever one of them comes will surely have a gun. And we have no weapons.'

'We have those tools. When we get them inside, one of us will hit them with the wrench.' He bent down and took it out of the duffle and hefted it. Doubt clouded his face. 'It's not really heavy enough.'

'I wonder if we could force the door open,' I said. I grabbed the handle and, using my foot to brace against the frame, put my whole weight into pulling. The door didn't give at all.

We both stared at it, and then I sprang to action, frantically searching through all the closets, and even the side compartments next to the bed for anything we might use as a weapon, or even something to break through the door. I realized that I was acting crazed, but I couldn't seem to slow down. Finally, I stopped looking and stood chewing a knuckle.

I was used to being strong and brave. I'd had to be since my father died and my mother fell apart. I'd been the one to buoy my mother's spirits, I'd been my sister's cheerleader; I'd been the rock that both my mother and sister had turned to when things went wrong. Now, I'd give anything for someone else to be the brave one.

All the things that had happened in the past week rushed at me, overwhelming me to the point of paralysis. I was scared and discouraged. I gritted my teeth and sat back against the bed, telling myself that I couldn't fold now. There was no one but me to rescue us.

'What's wrong?' Nick touched me gently on my arm.

I shook my head. Suddenly, my eyes filled with tears. 'Just having a stupid moment,' I said, my voice quivering.

'Well, get over it,' Nick said. His voice was suddenly cold. 'We can't afford for you to go all soft.'

I spun away from him to keep from slapping him. How dare he talk to me that way! With my back to him, I closed my eyes and fought for control. It didn't take a genius to figure out that Nick's words had been meant not to hurt me but to spur me to action.

'Jessie, look, I'm sorry.'

I opened my eyes and started to reply, but then my gaze fell on something I had noticed before but hadn't given much thought to. Now it was like a bright light, shining at me. Positioned right above floor level on the inside wall of the cabin was a rectangular porthole, down low near the water's edge, big enough for someone to crawl through. It had handles like any porthole. The boat's designer had clearly included it as a way for someone in a cabin to escape if the boat was sinking. It was plastered with a couple of stickers warning people not to open it while the boat was underway.

'Found our escape route.' I pointed to the hatch.

Nick stared at the hatch, hesitation clouding his expression. 'OK, so we get into the water. But what happens then?' He pointed to his shoulder. 'I'm pretty sure I can't swim back to shore.'

I knew I could swim to shore and get help – eventually. But not before the Turpins discovered I was gone and took out their fury on Nick. 'Let me think how this can work.' I sat down on the step next to the porthole.

Once I was out the hatch and into the water, I would be under the belly of the boat, between the pontoons. But at the rate of speed we were traveling, the boat would leave me behind in no time. Or I could be swept dangerously close to the engine propellers, depending on the current. For my escape to work, the second I dove out the window, I would have to lunge for the back platform of the boat. If I did manage to grab it – a big if – then I'd have to climb up onto the boat's platform, race up to the bridge and somehow overpower the Turpins. All this without them seeing me.

How I wished I hadn't taken the gun that Johnny had hidden in the nav station. It would have come in handy. I didn't see how I could gain control over the Turpins without a weapon. Then another idea came to me.

'The dinghy,' I said. I closed my eyes, trying to remember exactly what the dinghy looked like. I had barely noticed it when we boarded earlier, but I remembered that the Turpins hadn't bothered to put it up on the davits, so it was trailing behind the catamaran. And it had a motor; it was cocked back out of the water. 'We can use it to get away.'

'How do you think we're going to get to it?'

'Let me think.' The line tethering the dinghy to the boat would be at least fifty feet long, and would be high off the water, stretched tight by the force of the catamaran's forward progress.

I tried to remember if the dinghy had handholds low enough to grab onto. But it didn't matter, because I'd be swept past it too fast to grab them, even if they were placed where I could reach them. But there was another way.

I opened my eyes. 'I think I've got it.'

'What?'

'When I get into the water, I have to grab hold of the back platform, shinny along the line holding the dinghy and then jump into it. That is, if the Turpins don't spy me and shoot me first.'

Nick laughed. 'Even if they don't see you, it sounds impossible. We're going too fast.'

'Do you have a better idea?'

'No, but do you realize how fast this boat is going? How do you think you'll be able to hold onto that line?'

'I have to.'

'And if you manage to do that, what's the plan? You'll go for help?'

I shook my head. 'I'm not leaving you behind. When they find out I'm gone, and they *will* find out, they'll kill you.'

'How am I going to get into the dinghy?' He pointed to his shoulder.

'We'll make it work.' I was thinking fast, planning on the fly. We had to act soon, or we'd be in open water. 'OK, once I get into the dinghy, I'll cut the line. You'll be watching out the porthole, and as soon as you see me cut it, you'll go out the window into the water. I'll grab you as you float by.' Or get swept by, but no need to tell him that.

'You can't possibly haul me into the boat.'

'Oh, please. I've dealt with hauling much heavier loads than you into dive boats.' I put all my bravado into my words. Yes, I had hauled big people into dive boats. But it was always people who had two good arms for helping themselves, and it was when the boat was stationary. Plus, getting into the dinghy wasn't the only problem. First, Nick had to avoid the propellers in the rear engines, and with only one arm.

'You looked worried.'

'A little.' A lot, but I wasn't going to say it out loud. 'There's an engine on the back of each of the catamaran's pontoons. You'll only be fifteen feet from the back of the boat when you jump out the window, but we're going fast, and the props will create a pull.' I pointed out the window. 'When you hit the water, you've got to keep to the center under the boat until you get past the propellers.'

He nodded, his expression grim. 'How far down do the props go? Maybe I could swim underwater.'

'No. You can't count on the turbulence not to sweep you up. But I've got an idea.' I flung the bedcovers back and stripped off the top sheet. 'I'll attach this to one of the handles on the window. When you go out, you hang onto it. That way you can get your bearings and kick your legs to get out into the middle between the pontoons. Then, when you're ready, you let go. If you're in the center, you'll get swept back so fast that you won't get near the propellers.' At least I hoped so.

'You really think you can make this work?'

I shrugged. 'I have to. I don't know what else we can do.'

We stared at each other, neither wanting to admit the consequences if it didn't work. Time was racing by, but I wanted to give Nick time to accept the plan. I glanced at Johnny's watch, thankful that at least they hadn't taken that from me. It was after two o'clock. The dive boats would be coming in by four.

Nick looked through the outside porthole. He pointed out to me that the land was receding quickly. We may already be out of the harbor. 'What if the dinghy doesn't start?' he said. 'Then we're sitting ducks.'

'No more so than we are now.'

'I don't like it.'

'There is another possibility. The Turpins likely have more than one weapon aboard. I could search for it, or for something else I could use as a weapon.'

Nick shook his head. 'I like that option even less.' He gritted his teeth. 'This goddamn shoulder.'

I grabbed his good arm and squeezed it. 'I can do this.'

'If one of the Turpins comes down to the saloon while you're trying to get into the dinghy, they'll see you,' Nick said.

'It's our only chance.'

'I still think we could overpower them.' His expression was desperate, something I hadn't seen before. With one arm out of commission, he felt powerless.

'We can't wait,' I said. 'It will only be a couple of hours before Perrault retrieves the jewels and notifies the Turpins. By then, we'll be too far out to sea to survive.' And that was assuming they didn't kill us before they threw us overboard.

Besides, although I wasn't going to tell Nick, I wanted to get back to land for another reason. I was desperate to find a way to stop the three men before Jeremy came back from the dive today. When they went after the jewelry on the boat, they wouldn't hesitate to kill Jeremy if he put up a fight. He wouldn't even know what they were after.

I was done negotiating. 'I'm ready. We're going for it.'

I was afraid the cargo pants I was wearing would get in my way, so I stripped them off. My T-shirt should be fine. I grabbed the boat knife and stuck it into my bra, hoping it would stay put. I'd need it to cut the line holding the dinghy to the boat. 'Let's do this.' I grabbed the handles of the escape hatch and yanked. They wouldn't budge.

THIRTY-TWO

The locks on the escape hatch were so tight that I suspected they had never been opened. So much for escaping if the boat was sinking! I found a can of WD-40 in the duffle bag and sprayed the lock hinges, then took the wrench and a screwdriver and went to work to loosen it. I had to bang on the handle, which made so much noise that I was afraid the Turpins would hear it, even over the noise of the engine.

Sure enough, just as I managed to get the second handle open, the engine speed decreased and I heard footsteps in the saloon. Whoever it was then tried to move silently down the steps to the cabin, except that one of the steps creaked. The listener stopped at the door. I could imagine Betty Turpin with her ear to the door.

'What's going on in there?' Betty Turpin said. 'We heard banging.'

'We're trying to get these cuffs off,' I yelled back.

Betty gave a nasty laugh. 'Good luck with that.'

I held my breath, half hoping she'd open the door, but afraid she'd have a gun if she did. We stood there with our hands behind our backs. I was ready to spring at her if I had the chance. After a few more interminable minutes, Betty retreated and soon the engine came back up to speed. We waited several minutes longer to give the Turpins a chance to settle down.

I could hardly stand the wait, knowing that every second took us farther out. The boat was beginning to bounce more on the waves, which meant we had left the harbor and were in open water. If I was going to manage to climb onto the dinghy, it had to be now, before the waves made it impossible. My heart was banging so hard that I felt like it was trying to leap out of my mouth. So much could go wrong. My nerve almost failed. But it was better to go down fighting.

'We can't wait any longer,' I said.

Nick shrugged. I wrapped the end of the sheet around his good hand a few times and attached it to one of the handle slots.

Even with the locks opened, the hatch itself was stuck. It opened inward, so we couldn't kick it out. I grabbed one handle with both hands, bracing my body with my foot on one side for leverage, and Nick used his good hand, and we tugged it hard. Finally, it creaked open. The boat was going so fast that water immediately began sloshing into the cabin. I leaned out and peered at the dinghy. It was bouncing like crazy. If only they'd slow down! How was I going to hang onto that line between the catamaran and the dinghy? It looked impossible. I mentally slammed the door shut on my doubts. It had to work.

At the last second, I remembered seeing a pair of gloves in a closet. If I did manage to get to the rope, I'd have a better chance of clinging to it with gloves on. I grabbed the gloves, put them on, took a deep breath and, with one last thumbs-up from Nick, launched myself out the porthole.

I was immediately snatched up by the current. It was even stronger than I had imagined it would be. I had to swim with desperate strokes to stay in the middle of the current under the bridge deck between the pontoons. I was glad I had thought of tethering Nick. Using only his legs and one arm, he might not have been strong enough to avoid being swept into the props.

Within seconds, I hurtled to the back of the boat. I would have only one chance to grab hold of the platform. I kicked my legs hard and lunged for it. It took all my strength to grip the platform hard enough for it not to be torn out of my hands. I felt like my shoulder was being wrenched out of its socket. I grabbed the slippery back end with my other hand and knew I couldn't hold on for long. There was a handrail along the side of the steps leading from the platform up into the cockpit. I grabbed for it, emitting an involuntary grunt as my ribs banged against the platform. Kicking hard once more and pulling myself up at the same time, I managed to hoist myself up onto the edge of the platform. I paused to catch my breath and steady myself, and then risked a quick glance up to the bridge where the Turpins were driving the boat. I couldn't see them over the cockpit cover – which meant they couldn't see me, either. A small win.

Then I focused on the dinghy and almost lost heart. It was bouncing crazily behind the boat, practically airborne each time it hit a wave. Most boaters didn't lug the dinghy between their boat because it took such a beating, but the Turpins were likely in a hurry and didn't take the time to secure it. In one way, it would help us. It meant we had a chance to get away. But that depended on whether I could hold onto the rope and manage to get into the dinghy.

I quickly took stock of my situation. The tug on the line holding the dinghy to the back of the catamaran was exerting tremendous force, holding it taut, even though it was seesawing violently up and down with the movement of the dinghy. Theoretically, I should be able to pull my way along the line, hanging under it. Thank goodness I had thought to bring the gloves. I crawled up onto the edge of the deck where the line was secured. I didn't give myself time to change my mind or get any more scared than I already was. Taking a deep breath, I pushed off the ledge, hooking my hands and feet around the line. Although the rope had looked taut, it flailed violently every time the dinghy bounced. It was all I could do to hold on. I let myself hang for a few seconds until I got the rhythm of the way it bucked against the waves. The drag on my arms was tremendous.

Sliding along the rope toward the dinghy was easier than I thought it might be, because the line sloped downward. Quickly, my feet bumped into the rubber deck of the dinghy. If the Turpins saw me, I was completely vulnerable, but there was nothing to be done about it. Now for the real challenge. I had to figure out how to get myself into the dinghy. If I let go with my legs, they would dangle into the water and the force would pull my hands off.

Scooting closer to the bow, I was able to get my feet onto it. Gradually, I inched farther toward the cockpit, taking punishing blows to my body. Then came the moment when I had to let go of the towline and fling myself into the dinghy. I waited, knowing I had to get the timing right so that the dinghy was on a downward plunge. One last surge upward and I dove.

For a horrifying second, I thought the dinghy was going to pitch me off while I had nothing to hold onto. But I drew my legs up and thrust them hard and I shot forward, landing in the bottom of the dinghy and cracking my forehead on the center bench. I lay in the bottom for a few seconds, stunned and gasping. But I couldn't take time to assess the damage. Every second counted. Every second meant a worse situation for Nick. I shook my head to clear it and pulled myself upright, still on the bottom of the dinghy. I peeked over the bow up to the bridge and was relieved to see the Turpins still sitting with their backs to me.

I looked toward the porthole I had escaped from, and Nick had his head out, watching. I gave him a thumbs-up, and he returned the gesture.

I pulled out the knife I'd stashed in my bra, opened it and tested the edge. Even though the tool was rusted, the knife felt sharp enough to cut the line.

Grabbing hold of the handhold on the side of the dingy, I crawled onto the bow on my stomach and began frantically sawing at the rope. Every part of me was alert, in case one of the Turpins happened to turn around and spot me. I was completely exposed out here in the open. If they saw me, I'd be an easy target. What would I do if that happened? No clue.

When the line was almost parted, I signaled for Nick to go out the window. He didn't hesitate but pitched right out into the water and I saw him frantically kicking and hanging onto the sheet with his good arm, sweeping past the propellers. But before I had time to be relieved that he'd made it, I saw the sheet slip off his good arm, and he was swept past the dinghy. He threw up his arm in surrender.

Seeing him swept away, my stomach did a flip. It was truly up to me. First, I had to get the dinghy separated from the boat and pray that the motor would start. And then hope that I could spot Nick. Finding someone in the water was harder than it seemed. But I knew he'd be watching for me, too. He'd be able to see me coming a lot more easily than I could see his small head bobbing in a big body of water.

When the rope finally parted, the dinghy surged so hard that it threw me off balance and I fell into the bottom again. I looked forward and saw that the catamaran was speeding away from me. The Turpins had apparently not noticed anything when the dinghy came free.

I scrambled to the rear, to the dinghy's engine. It was cocked up and tied off so that it wouldn't accidentally tip into the water while they were underway. I slashed the line that held it cocked. My heart was in my throat. What if the damn engine didn't start? It was an electric motor, which meant at least I didn't have to yank on a cord to try to start it. It started right away, emitting a lovely purr. I revved it a couple of times.

I was ready to take off when I looked up at *Island Ice*'s bridge and saw a very peculiar scene. The Turpins were both standing up at the wheel, looking at the instrument panel. Betty Turpin had her hands on her hips and Carl was pushing buttons. But the important thing was that the boat was dead in the water. There was a puff of smoke lingering over the starboard engine. And then I realized what had happened. When I cut the dinghy line, with the momentum of being suddenly released, the line had whipped forward. And it had snaked under the catamaran's engine and fouled the propellers on one side. The boat had two engines, so – theoretically – it should still have been able to run on one engine. But either both of them had been fouled, or when one went off, the other had stalled.

Betty Turpin turned and looked at the back of the boat. It took a few seconds for her to register what she was seeing. Her mouth gaped as she realized that the dinghy was moving away – and that I was sitting in it. I saw her contort her face in a scream, although I couldn't hear it over the noise of the dinghy motor. Her husband wheeled around in his seat and then stood up.

With a disabled boat, the Turpins couldn't catch me, but I was still close enough so they could shoot a bullet into the dinghy, deflating it. I revved the dinghy engine again and took off.

Once I was out of gunshot range, I slowed down to search for Nick. I couldn't begin to estimate how far he'd gone since he drifted away. I observed the direction of the current and adjusted for it as I slowly traversed the area.

The sea was fairly calm, but even with minimal wave action, I couldn't spot Nick. I saw what looked like a log in the water, a curious pelican circling over it. 'Got to be him,' I said. I slowed down and steered closer. It was Nick. When he heard the engine, he brought his good arm up out of the water and signaled to me.

I brought the dinghy close, put the engine in neutral, and drifted to him. 'I'm awfully glad to see you,' he said. The wound in his shoulder had begun to seep blood onto the bandages.

'You're bleeding again.'

'No shit. I was afraid sharks would come after me. Now can you get me into the boat?' He looked around him uneasily. I didn't have the heart to laugh at him. I could have told him the likelihood that a shark would go after him in any serious way was practically nil. People frequently got coral scrapes when they dove or snorkeled. If sharks in the Bahamas routinely went after blood, there would be hundreds more shark bite victims every year, and a lot fewer tourists.

'This is going to be tricky,' I yelled. I spotted a filthy towel in the bottom of the boat and brandished it. 'Grab hold of the towel, and when I tell you, kick as hard you can to get some propulsion, and I'll pull.'

Nick wrapped the towel around his good hand. 'Ready.'

'One. Two. Three.'

Nick kicked and surged upward and I yanked hard. Nick belly-flopped onto the side of the boat, teetering. I grabbed him and steadied him so he wouldn't fall back into the water, but also wouldn't flop into the boat onto his shoulder. He managed to get his legs into the boat and sank onto the bottom.

We locked eyes. 'I was terrified that I wouldn't find you,' I said.

'Yeah.' He closed his eyes. He lay in the bottom for a few minutes, lips set in a grim line against the pain in his shoulder. 'I don't suppose there's any water aboard?' he said.

I rummaged in the forward compartment and came up with a warm but unopened bottle of water. I opened it and handed it to him. He drank and then looked back at the stranded catamaran. 'What's happening? Why aren't they moving?'

I told him what had happened.

He laughed. 'It was time we caught a break.' He sobered quickly. 'You realize they'll call Perrault and tell him we've escaped.'

'Nothing to be done about that. We have to get out of here, though. If they manage to get one of the engines started, they'll catch us in no time. Brace yourself; it's going to be a rough ride.'

'Do it.'

I revved the engine up out of neutral and drove forward fast, coming into a plane, which minimized the bounce of the boat, but I could see that the trip was still punishing for Nick.

Once we neared the mouth of the harbor, a speedboat raced by, almost swamping us. The engine sputtered, and I cursed them soundly. But the engine held, and soon we were cruising into the narrow harbor passage toward the marina where Jeremy docked his dive boats.

I cut the engine speed way back and said, 'We have to dock somewhere other than where the dive boats are kept. When we get to land, I'm going to call Kevin. Now that we know Callen is the dirty cop, we can ask Kevin for help.'

During the trip, Nick had pulled himself up to sit on the forward seat. He shook his head. 'I've been thinking. We don't know for sure that the two of them weren't involved. We can't risk it.'

I ran my hands through my hair. 'I don't know what kind of fantasy you have about how we're supposed to catch these guys. They've got guns. We don't. And you're injured.'

Nick scanned the passing docks. 'What time will the dive boats be back?'

'I don't know if the one I hid the pouch in was on a full-day or half-day dive today. If it was a half-day, they'll already be back.' It was almost three. 'The full dives don't get back until after four o'clock, usually closer to four thirty. I'm taking us close enough to see which boats are back.'

'We can't risk having Perrault see us.'

'We're on the other side of the harbor, so they won't spot us.'

Nick winced. 'How far are we from the hotel where I'm staying?'

'I can get us there in ten minutes. Why?'

'I have a spare gun there. Do we have time?'

'Yes,' I said, 'but that won't be necessary. Jeremy keeps a thirty-eight in the shop.'

Nick groaned. 'A thirty-eight? Not much of a gun. Do you know if Jeremy even takes care of his weapon? He might not have maintained it, and for all we know, it's not even loaded.'

'I can guarantee he takes care of the gun and keeps it loaded.'

Jeremy had shown the gun to me not long after I started to work for him. He kept it under the counter in a plain wooden box.

'I'm showing it to you, so you won't be surprised if you run across it,' he said. 'But don't try to be a hero if anyone robs you. This is for me, not anyone else. If someone robs you, hand over the money.'

I didn't tell him that I was likely a lot more familiar with guns than he was.

A lot of business owners and big yachts kept shotguns, but Jeremy said he preferred a smaller gun. 'Something to scare a burglar away. I don't want to kill anybody.'

I had asked Jeremy if he maintained the weapon. If he had said no, I planned to tell him I would clean it and make sure it was in good shape. But Jeremy said he had made it his business to learn how to shoot it and take care of it. And knowing Jeremy, I trusted that he meant it.

I slowed the dinghy even further, eyes trained on the docks on the other side. 'OK. There's the parking lot, and there are the docks.' I pointed. 'One of the boats is there. But not all of them go out every day.'

'How many are there?'

'Jeremy has four. But sometimes he keeps one in another marina. We have to find out what the situation is. I'd like to get in touch with him to warn him, which means I need to get to a phone fast.'

'How do you plan to do that?'

'I have to get to my apartment. I'll use Shelley's phone. Plus, it might have escaped your notice, but I don't have any clothes on.'

He looked me up and down. 'I'm injured, but I'm not dead.'

'Very funny.' I turned the boat around and headed around to the dock near my apartment.

'Wait,' Nick yelled over the noise of the engine. 'Why don't you take me to my hotel, let me out, and I can go get my gun. After you go to your apartment, you can come back and get me.'

I didn't waste time arguing. He was right. Having another gun would be better.

When I pulled the dinghy into the docking area of Nick's hotel, I realized that Didier or one of his men might be there. 'You have your room key?' I asked.

'No. I left it at the desk. I'll have to go in and get it.'

'You know, you could run into those guys.'

'I doubt it. They're going to be focused on getting the jewelry.' He climbed out of the boat and walked swiftly toward the front entrance.

'I'll be right back.' I roared away and tied up as close to my apartment as I could get, leaped out and ran.

It was after three and I was hoping Shelley would be in so I didn't have to go to the manager again. She was there. She opened the door and stared at me. 'Thanks for letting me know you weren't dead.' She whirled and stomped back into the apartment.

I didn't have time to make nice. 'Sorry, I can't talk now,' I said over my shoulder as I raced for my room. I threw on a pair of shorts and a dry T-shirt.

Shelley was standing in the doorway to my room. 'You know, Jessie, you've gone too far. You owe me an explanation. Who were those guys this morning? What did they want? Do you have any idea how embarrassed I was in my robe and no make-up?'

I didn't have time for this. But something did occur to me. 'Shelley, do you happen to have a gun?'

Her eyes got wide. 'Are you crazy? Of course I don't have a gun.'

'OK. Well, I need to use your cell phone.' I shoved past her and ran into the living room. I spotted her clutch on the kitchen counter. I opened it and grabbed her phone.

'No. You can't use my phone. Give it back.'

'I have to take it with me. I'll bring it back to you soon.' I raced for the door.

'Wait! I want you to move out. I'm tired of . . .' The rest of it was swallowed up as I slammed the door.

Not waiting for the elevator, I sprinted down the stairs and ran back to the dinghy. I hopped in and roared away, toward the far end of the dock area where Nick's hotel was. I took my eyes off the water long enough to punch in Jeremey's number. Thank goodness Shelley didn't use a password.

'Dammit,' I yelled as Jeremey's phone went to voicemail. I left a message. 'Jeremy, don't go back to the dock. Stay out. Call me back on this number.'

Nick wasn't waiting outside, which made me uneasy. I'd give him two minutes and then I was going in after him.

I phoned the dive shop. Molly, one of the assistant instructors answered. 'Molly, I need your help. Is Jeremy's boat out?'

'Yes. Where are you? Everybody's mad because you keep screwing up.'

I ignored her complaint. 'Is Jeremy the divemaster on his boat?'

'Yes, why?'

'I don't have time to explain. Molly, there's big trouble, and I need Jeremy's gun.' I was afraid if I went to the shop that Didier and his group would show up. I'd be dead meat – and so would Jeremy.

'Jeremy has a gun?' Her voice had gone up an octave. 'I hate guns.'

'He keeps one under the counter in a box. I need you to get it and bring it to me.'

'No way.'

'Molly, everybody on the dock, including you, is in danger. I have to have that gun.'

'I'm not touching it. You'll have to come and get it.'

'Look. Remember that cute top that came into the shop last week? You said you couldn't afford it? It's yours if you do this.'

Molly groaned. 'All right, but if Jeremy finds out . . .'

'I'll take the blame.' I told her where to meet me.

'And Molly, if you see some men on the docks who look like they don't belong there, don't stop to talk to them. Tell them you've got an emergency and run away from them fast.'

I ended the call and then dialed Jeremy again. Still no answer.

I was a wreck while I waited for Nick, afraid something would happen to him or that we'd get back to the dive dock too late. We were cutting it too close.

THIRTY-THREE

The five minutes that Nick was gone seemed like an hour. He had changed out of his wet clothing, and when he climbed into the dinghy, he told me he had decided to take one of the pills I'd picked up last night. He gave me the evil eye. 'Don't say "I told you so."'

'Wouldn't think of it.' I spun the boat away from the dock and headed back to the dive dock.

Guiding the dinghy down one of the many finger waterways that wound off the main estuary, I tied it up at a small dock near a grocery store, where I had arranged to meet Molly to pick up Jeremy's gun. Growing increasingly nervous, I waited outside the Quickie Mart for several minutes before I saw Molly practically running toward me carrying a ditty bag that had a bulge in it. She kept glancing around as if someone would be able to tell that she was carrying a weapon in the bag.

I hadn't realized how tense I had been, worrying that Molly would decide at the last minute not to go through with bringing the gun, or that she would run into trouble. I ran toward her, grabbed the bag, and gave her a quick hug. 'You go, girl!'

She backed away. 'I hope you aren't going to get me fired, Jessie.'

'I promise that won't happen. Now, you should get back. And if Jeremy comes in early, tell him to get everybody off the boats and off the docks.'

Molly bit her lip. 'You're really serious.'

'Totally.'

She started to walk away but turned back. 'Oh, I wanted to tell you. There was an extra box of bullets in with the gun, so I brought that, too.'

'Genius! Now go.'

'That didn't take long,' Nick said when I jumped back into the dinghy. 'Let me see that gun.' He held his hand out for the bag.

I handed it over and watched as he took the .38 out of the bag. His look was incredulous. 'Jessie, this is barely a gun.'

I glared at him. 'Come on! It's a thirty-eight special. That's a perfectly good weapon. If we catch them by surprise, it's all we need.'

'All I can say is it's a damn good thing we've got my Beretta.'

I drove back and pulled up at a small dock near the back door of Jeremy's shop. I flipped the line onto a cleat, leaped out, and put my hand out to help Nick out of the boat. 'I hope we aren't too late.'

If Jeremy's boat hadn't arrived yet, Nick and I planned to hide on the dive boat that was already at the dock and ambush Perrault and the other two men when they showed up. If they had arrived, we'd have to wing it.

'I don't think we're going to be able to ambush them,' Nick said. 'They'll be looking for us. The Turpins probably phoned Perrault to let them know we got away.'

'Maybe,' I said, as we hurried toward where the dive boats docked. 'But it's possible the Turpins were scared to tell him. They've screwed up way too much.'

I led the way down an alley used for garbage cans behind the row of businesses near the dive shop. We came up behind the dive shop and crept along the side of the building. I peered around the side.

'Oh, shit!' I jerked back into the shadow of the building. 'The boat just arrived and Perraut and Didier are already here. Perrault is talking to Jeremy. I don't see Louis.' I peeked again.

Jeremy had his hands on his hips and was shaking his head.

People were slowly making their way off the boat, lugging their gear over to the dive instructors, who were spraying down the equipment. I figured that while there were so many people around, Perrault and Didier wouldn't make a move. But I was wrong.

I gasped. 'Oh, shit! Didier pulled a gun.'

We heard a woman squeal and someone shouted, 'Gun!'

Abandoning their totes and equipment, people started running for cover, making for the buildings, or scampering down the docks toward the parking lot. A woman with two pre-teen kids shielded them with her body, pushing them in front of her as they fled.

Didier waved to Jeremy and Perrault to get onto the dive boat. Jeremy looked calm, despite the gun being trained on him. With his height and physique, he was used to being the most commanding presence in the room. He said something to Perrault, and Perrault shrugged. Jeremy turned his attention to the dive boat and shouted, 'This is an emergency. Everyone off the boat now. Leave the area immediately.'

A woman holding her dive vest and her tank stood frozen on the stern of the dive boat, staring at Didier's gun.

'Drop the gear,' Jeremy yelled at her. 'Come back and get it later.'

Suddenly, I saw Mike Boyle, one of the young guys I worked with, circle behind the three gangsters and ease toward the building Nick and I were hiding behind. I could see that he was planning to rush at Perrault and Didier from behind. It was a suicide mission.

'Mike, no!' I yelled. 'Get down!' Stepping from behind the building and aiming high, I shot off a round from the .38 to cover him. Mike leaped back and, with a wild-eyed look, took off running toward me. A bullet from Didier's gun caught him before he could reach us. Another shot bounced off the corner of the building as I ducked back.

I turned to tell Nick to cover me while I tried to get to Mike, but he wasn't behind me. I ran to the back of the building and found him opening the back door of the dive shop. He disappeared inside.

I darted back to see if I could help Mike. He was groaning, but it was too risky to try to reach him. 'Stay down,' I called out to him. He started crawling toward me, grunting. Louis was running from the parking lot toward the dive boat, holding a gun, creating further panic as the stragglers scrambled to get away.

Another shot rang out, this time from inside the dive shop.

Didier went down on one knee, holding his arm. Louis turned and shot in Nick's direction, then sent off another round at me, but it was a wild shot that went wide. Perrault pulled Jeremy in front of him and used him as a shield as he backed toward the dive boat. They stepped onto the boat. I hoped that Jeremy didn't try to get away from Perrault. It would be suicidal. But I saw that he had sense enough not to struggle.

Louis hauled Didier to his feet, and the two men leaped aboard the boat, waving the guns back and forth to keep everyone at bay. When they were all four aboard, Louis hauled the lines off the cleats, pausing to take random shots at Nick and me. Nick got off another couple of shots, but he had to be careful not to hit Jeremy.

The dive boat was almost all cockpit, wide open to the outside, so to get out of range, the four men moved up near the boat's control panel, which was shaded by a canvas cover so it was impossible to see them well enough to get off a good shot without endangering Jeremy. I heard the boat's powerful engine turn on and rev a few times. Then it took off so fast that the back slewed from side to side, barely missing a second dive boat that was arriving.

THIRTY-FOUR

As soon as the boat left the dock, Nick and I ran out of hiding toward the dive boat that was maneuvering into the dock.

We passed a couple of men hovering over Mike. A woman alongside them had her phone to her ear, calling 911.

People on the boat screamed when they saw our guns.

I ran to the guy on the dock, who was securing a line. He leaped back, hands in the air as I approached with my gun. 'Don't tie up! We have to take this boat.'

Janelle Bryant was at the helm of the boat.

'Janelle!' I yelled. 'Don't kill the motor. We have to take the boat. Get these people off!'

'What do you mean?' a guy hollered from the deck of the boat.

'Emergency,' Nick yelled back. 'Everybody off the boat. Now! Leave your things!'

'What's going on?' Peter, the other dive master called from the cockpit. 'Why do you have guns?'

'Law enforcement,' Nick yelled, showing a badge he had produced from somewhere. 'We have to take this boat. Everybody, off!'

Janelle wasted no time asking questions. 'Off, off, off!' she started yelling. 'Leave your stuff! Get off the boat. It's an emergency.'

People scrambled over each other to jump onto the dock, but the boat was unsteady and some people hesitated. One of the tourists, a big guy with an air of authority positioned himself on the dock next to the boat and helped them. As the last few people made it off, he said to Nick, 'I'm a cop from St. Louis. Can I help?'

'We're OK,' Nick said.

Janelle was last off. She looked shaken and stared at me as if she'd never seen me before. 'What the hell?' she said. 'Why do you have a gun?'

'No time to explain. We've got to go.'

Nick and I scrambled aboard.

'Jessie, I hope to hell you know what you're doing,' she yelled. Hands on her hips, she watched as Nick and I ran forward to the controls.

I grabbed the wheel and pushed the throttle forward. 'Hang on!'

Nick grabbed a bar. The boat took off, fishtailing away in the direction Jeremy's dive boat had gone.

I still had Shelley's phone and I took it out of my pocket and handed it to Nick. 'Call the Nassau police and talk to Kevin. There's no password.' I was having to yell over the noise of the engine. Dive boats were not designed for peace and quiet.

He shook his head. 'No cops. Not after that mess with Callen.'

'We have to trust Kevin. He'll know who to notify at the Bahamian Coast Guard. They can send a boat to intercept those guys.' *If we find them*, I added under my breath.

He hesitated and then dialed. 'I hope you're right.'

While he made the call, I kept the boat throttled as high as I dared, focused on threading through the boat traffic in the harbor while maintaining a sharp eye out for a sign of Jeremy's dive boat. I couldn't figure out why Jeremy had taken off to the west, where the narrow channel was full of vessels of all sizes and shapes, instead of the open water to the east. Maybe Perrault was giving the orders and he had a destination in mind.

Paradise Island, off the coast of Nassau, was in this direction. There was a marina at the Atlantis Resort. Maybe Perrault had planned to rendezvous with *Island Ice* there after they retrieved the jewelry. But getting to the marina from here was dicey. Jeremy would have to head east at some point and give the island a wide berth to avoid the shoals directly to the north of the island.

'I reached Kevin's voicemail,' Nick said. 'I told him it was urgent and to call you back at this number.'

'Damn! We don't have time to wait for him to call back. We have to call the Coast Guard ourselves.'

Nick did a search for the number and started to punch it in but paused when I yelled and pointed. 'There they are!' Jeremy's boat was to starboard at approximately two o'clock, a quarter-mile away. What I saw was crazy. They were moving toward the end of Paradise Island, headed directly toward the shoals. I had no choice but to move in behind them, even though I knew it was a disaster waiting to happen.

Nick went back to the phone. When he reached someone, it was clear that they didn't want to take him seriously. I waved to get his attention. 'Tell him there are drugs involved. That'll get their interest.'

That did the trick. 'They want to know where we are,' he said.

'Tell them we're rounding the end of Paradise Island.'

That confused them again. They knew as well as I did that this was treacherous territory, threaded with shallow coral reefs. Nick had to assure them that we were serious. I told them to mention Jeremy's name and that convinced them.

'They're sending a cutter out,' he said. 'They also said we should be careful of the shoals off the island.'

'No shit.' What could Jeremy be thinking? He was heading right into the shallow area.

'Why do you suppose they're going this way?' Nick said. 'The guy I talked to said it was dangerous.'

'Remember that one of their men, Jaggo, was killed?'

'Yes. No great loss to mankind. He did a lot of Perrault's ugly work.'

'The shooting took place at the Atlantis. It's on Paradise Island right over there.' I pointed toward the massive resort. 'Maybe Perrault has a boat docked there, probably the same boat Didier and his crew were on when they boarded Johnny and me that night. Or maybe they had planned to meet *Island Ice* there. The problem is the guy you talked to was right. It's really shallow through here.'

'Didier knows these waters.'

'If he knows, why would he be going into shallow water?'

'Maybe he was injured worse than we thought and he's having to rely on Perrault. But wouldn't your captain friend tell him?'

Maybe, maybe not. I didn't like what I was thinking; that Jeremy was deliberately sending them into an area where they'd get stuck. He was trying to be a hero.

We were gaining steadily on the other boat, and I cut the engine speed. I didn't want to get into firing range; just keep them in sight. Nick had moved close to me and was watching the boat. His color looked better. The drugs he had taken must have kicked in.

'Nick, look around in the cabinets below and see if you can find a chart of New Providence.'

He rummaged around, one-handed, in the two big cabinets below the instrument panel where I was standing. He pitched out cleaning equipment and extra gear, finally pulling out a stained and torn chart that had been folded up in the bottom of one of the cabinets. I slowed way down and told Nick to take the wheel. 'Steer a course directly behind them, but not too close. Something's not right.'

I smoothed the chart out on the deck, growing more alarmed the more oriented I got. 'Holy shit!' I yelled. 'Jeremy is going to deliberately run aground!' I leaped up, carrying the chart with me, and grabbed the wheel. 'Jeremy, you idiot!' I knew now that I was right about what he was up to, and it was likely to get him killed.

'What's going on?' Nick said. He was peering forward as if he should be able to see an obstruction.

'You see those dark spots all around us? They're only a couple of feet deep. Jeremy is threading us through a swamp, basically. He's going to ground the boat so that Perrault is trapped.'

'No! When Perrault realizes what Jeremy has done, he'll kill him.'

My heart was skittering. I had to figure out a way to keep Jeremy alive. And then I knew. 'Fuck! There's only one thing we can do.'

'What's that?'

'Ram them.'

Nick stared at me. 'You're kidding, right?'

'Nope. If we ram them, then they won't suspect what he's up to.'

'And after we ram their boat?'

'We'll have to take them.'

Nick shook his. head. 'I can't figure out if you're really smart, really brave, or really reckless.'

I glared at him. 'If you have a better idea, I'm happy to hear it.'

'Wait for the Coast Guard?'

'Even if they get here soon, they won't risk running their boat aground. By the time they figure out what to do, Jeremy will probably be dead.'

'If you ram the other boat, won't they sink?'

'Of course not. The water isn't deep enough.'

Nick looked out at the surrounding water and the island that was coming up on their right. 'Jesus! We could wade over there.'

'Duh. OK, here goes.' My breath coming in short gasps, I slowly pushed the throttle forward. I had to thread my way through the shoals exactly following Jeremy's path. Even the slightest deviation could have us snagged on a reef. There was no room for error.

Jeremy had managed to keep the boat moving forward, but eventually he'd be hemmed in by reefs. How did he intend to get away from his captors? He probably didn't have a plan. I had to create chaos to give him a chance.

I wiped perspiration from my forehead with the back of my hand and squinted at the water ahead. I was going too fast, but that was the only way we were going to catch them.

'I wonder why they named the boat *Island Ice*,' I said.

'What kind of question is that?'

'I wonder what the name means.'

'Are you nuts? You're thinking about that while you're maneu-vering us through a . . . a maze?'

'Keeps my mind off how nervous I am.'

The boat lurched and there was a horrible crunch, but then we surged forward. 'Oh my God,' I muttered. Another lurch on the other side. I knew Jeremy was familiar with every inch of the waters around here, but this was too much.

'Why are we hitting the reef and they're not?' Nick shouted.

'I don't know, maybe they have a shallower draft. It only takes a few inches to make a difference.' I was closing the gap between the two boats, and it seemed to me that the other boat had slowed.

Suddenly, the windshield shattered. 'They're shooting at us,' I yelled.

Nick grabbed me and pulled me down.

THIRTY-FIVE

I raised myself far up enough to sneak a look over the naviga-tion counter and flinched. The other boat was dead ahead of us in the water. We were heading slowly but inevitably for a crash. I reached up and grabbed the wheel and steered a few inches to starboard, so our boat would ram their stern at an angle, minimizing the damage.

The men were crouched low in the open cockpit. I heard one of them shout, 'They're going to hit us!'

I ducked back down as another flurry of shots rang out, but reached up and pulled the throttle back to neutral. 'We're on them,' I yelled to Nick. 'Hold tight.'

Even at our slow rate, the collision was tremendous. I tumbled forward, hitting the cabinets beneath the navigation station. Nick managed to hang onto one of the side benches.

'You all right?' he said.

'I'm good.' I retrieved the .38 from where I had stowed it in one of the cabinets.

I could hear yelling from the other boat. I risked a quick look and fired off a couple of shots. I didn't aim; I just wanted to let them know that Nick and I were armed.

'Perrault,' Nick yelled. 'You don't have a chance. The Coast Guard will be here soon. Let the hostage go.'

There was no reply.

'Now what?' Nick said. He looked around at the deck as if some solution would present itself. I explained my desperate plan. He didn't like it, but I persuaded him that it was our only alternative.

'All right, but you have to take the Sig.'

Although I preferred the lighter weight .38, Nick said he knew the Sig would shoot well even when it got wet. I knew something of the weapon from the FBI training, so it wasn't a completely unknown quantity, but it was heavy.

A minute later, while Nick kept up sporadic shots to keep Didier and Louis from coming out into the open, I slipped off the back of the dive boat into the water. I ducked under the surface, but it was so shallow that I could barely stay under. I pulled myself along the starboard side of our boat, so the men on the other boat couldn't spot me.

I made my way past the junction where the two boats had collided and then went under their boat, tucking up under the keel, my stomach scraping the reef. I pushed myself along on the rocks directly below me until I reached the bow of their boat. I came up under the corner of the port bow, opposite from where we had collided, hugging the side of the boat to remain hidden. The only way anyone could see me was if they stood directly on the bow and looked over the side.

I lifted my head out of the water straining to hear talking or movement so I could determine where people were positioned on the boat. I heard more gunshots. Nick was keeping them focused on him. Thank goodness Molly had brought the extra rounds with the .38.

I had hoped to find a way to board their dive boat to catch them by surprise, but the bow was too high out of the water for me to reach and there were no handholds. If the boat had been at anchor, I could have shinnied up the anchor line, but it wasn't.

If I couldn't board the boat, I had to find a way to fire into it without being an open target for return fire – and without hitting Jeremy. I painstakingly duck-walked my way back along the starboard side through the shallows to the stern, until I was at a point where if I stood, I would be able to see over the side of the boat. But that meant they would be able to see me. Whatever I did had to be fast.

I glanced up and back at Nick, but couldn't see him, which meant he was ducked down. But as I watched, I saw him peek around the starboard side panels in the back of the boat. He was lying on the floor. He saw me, and I pointed to the gun. He nodded and scrambled back to be ready to cover me.

If I could get any sightline, there was a good chance I could shoot at least one of the guys before they could fire at me. I knew I could count on Nick to do his part. I held the Sig Sauer close to my body to muffle the sound when I racked the slide back. I doubted anyone would notice anyway, but I waited a few seconds to hear if anyone reacted to the sound.

Nick shouted at Perrault again. 'We need to talk. You're not going to get out of this alive.' Again, no answer. I had been hoping Perrault would begin an exchange with Nick, giving me an edge in surprising them.

Nick must have been thinking the same thing. He tried again. 'We can work out a deal. You hand over the jewels, and I'll give you a head start.'

Very clearly, I heard Perrault say in French, 'Where's the girl? She hasn't made a sound.'

'Maybe I shot her,' Didier said. His voice sounded ragged. He had been shot back at the dock, and although he'd been able to make it onto the boat, the wound was probably slowing him down. That was good. Anything to give Nick and me an advantage.

'Go and look in the water,' Perrault ordered. There were footsteps out on the deck. Nick had been waiting. There was a gunshot and the sound of a body falling to the deck.

'Merde!' It was Didier's voice.

Now was the time. I leaped up, shooting in the direction where I had heard the body fall. Hearing my shots, Nick fired several times. With a scream, Louis fell. Before I slipped back into the water, I saw Perrault huddled far inside the cockpit, next to the navigation station brandishing his gun, using Jeremy as a shield.

'I will shoot this man,' he yelled. 'Miss, you need to come out of the water now and we can negotiate.' Perrault sounded calm. He knew he had the upper hand.

'Perrault, that won't work,' Nick called. 'Let the man go. Then we'll talk.'

I considered how I could maneuver into position to get a shot off at Perrault without hitting Jeremy. Farther along the side of the boat, the water got deeper again, which meant I wouldn't be able to leap up and hit him from the side. At the bow, it was worse. Even if I could clamber up, he would hear me and be able to quickly shoot me down.

Still crouched, I called out, 'All right, we'll trade you the man you're holding for our boat. Our boat is not badly damaged. You'll have time to get away.' I lay flat in the water in anticipation of the shot that zinged past me.

I sprang out of the water and yelled, 'Hey!' and then threw myself sideways. Perrault's bullet ricocheted off the boat.

Nick realized what I had hoped he would – that when Perrault's gun swung in my direction, it was momentarily not focused on Jeremy. Nick fired. Jeremy gave a shout, and someone fell to the deck. Christ! What if Jeremy had been hit? Nick fired again, and I came surging up out of the water and clambered up onto the back of the boat, the Sig Sauer ready.

But there was no one to shoot.

Didier and Louis lay closest to me. They were both still alive, but both incapacitated. Didier had been shot in the chest, and the way blood was bubbling out of his mouth, it looked as if a lung was involved. He wasn't moving around, but he kept up a steady string of whispered growls that I assumed were curses. Louis had been shot in the leg and one arm. He was curled on his side and lay very quiet.

As I passed by them, I kicked away their weapons and collected them. Farther inside, Perrault lay sprawled out, face forward. He wasn't moving, and a dark stain ran out from under his head. Jeremy lay next to him. I rushed to Jeremey's side and knelt down, feeling like my heart had stopped. 'Jeremy!'

He lifted his head, scowling. 'Has everyone stopped shooting now?'

I threw himself on him, hugging him fiercely. 'God, I thought we had shot you!'

He sat up, taking a couple of ragged breaths. He was the calmest person I knew, but not now. 'What the hell is going on here?'

'I'm coming over,' Nick shouted. He slipped off the back and waded on the shallow side. I went over to help him climb up onto the stern of the boat, since he was working with one arm. He checked on the two injured men and then crouched next to Perrault. 'Pity. I was hoping to see him stand trial.' He stood up. 'Now what?'

Jeremy stood up, looking dazed. 'Jessie, what's going on here? Why were you chasing these men? What did they want?'

'It's complicated,' Nick said. His theme song.

I introduced the two men.

'Complicated? Please tell me anything,' Jeremy said. 'I was afraid I was going to be killed. I at least deserve to know why I was at risk.'

I had never seen Jeremy so ruffled. If I had to guess, I'd say this was what he looked like when he was angry.

'The short version?' I said. 'There are millions of dollars' worth of jewelry on this boat. We were trying to get to it before these men could get away with it.'

'How did it get onto my boat?'

I sighed. 'I put it here. I thought it would be safe.'

'What were you doing with it?' He looked at me as if he'd never seen me before.

'It's a long story.' My theme song.

'Where did you put it?' Jeremy asked.

'I'll show you.' I picked up a towel one of the tourists had abandoned and laid it over Perrault's body, so we wouldn't have to look at it. Then I retrieved the jewelry pouch from where I had hidden it with the defib unit. I laid another towel on the deck and opened the pouch, pulling out a few of the cloth bags that held the jewelry. 'Take a look at this,' I said to Jeremy. 'This is what they were after.' I brought out one of the necklaces and a couple of bracelets.

Jeremy whistled. 'No wonder they were willing to risk their lives for this. Where did it come from?'

'A jewelry store in Paris,' Nick said.

Didier snarled and lifted himself up enough on one elbow to curse us soundly.

Jeremy stared at me. 'Jessie, how did you get hold of this jewelry? Did you steal it?'

I laughed, feeling slightly hysterical. 'Not intentionally. But we'll have to tell you the rest of the story later. Now we have company.' I pointed off to our rear, where a Royal Bahamian Defense Force cutter had approached and was maneuvering into position off the shallow area several yards behind us. A large dinghy was pulling up beside it. We could see people conferring and pointing to the shallow waters.

Jeremy walked to the stern of the boat and looked down at where the two boats had collided. He shook his head with dismay. 'My poor boats. How are we going to get them out of here?'

'Please tell me you have insurance,' I said.

'Of course I do, but how are we going to get them out of this trap? And I don't know if the insurance will cover that.'

'I wouldn't worry,' Nick said. 'There's a significant reward for the recovery of that jewelry. As a citizen who helped in the recovery, you'll get enough money to cover expenses.'

'If I can get them off these reefs,' Jeremy said gloomily.

We watched as the Coast Guard dinghy headed toward us, moving slowly. Two men were looking over the side to guide the pilot.

When they arrived, Nick was standing over Didier, who was still grumbling.

'What language is that?' I asked Nick.

'It's the dialect of French that they speak in Marseilles.' He shrugged. 'There's a little Catalan too. I didn't know he had any Catalan background.'

Louis was in obvious pain, but he wasn't putting up as much of a fuss. When he saw me watching him, he said, 'It was you. If we had taken better care to make sure you couldn't escape, we would have been rich men.'

'Sorry,' I said. 'Life can be tough.'

Nick rolled his eyes at me.

The dinghy came alongside. It was carrying two officers in their crisp white-and-green uniforms. I was surprised to see that Kevin Riley was with them. He looked grim and barely glanced my way. He knew by now that Callen had conspired with Perrault. Was he feeling guilty because he had been responsible for Callen finding out I had survived the attempt to murder me?

After securing the dinghy to the side of the dive boat, the three men boarded. One of the officers, older than the others and with more green braid on his sleeve, introduced himself as Lieutenant Commander Howell. He demanded to know who we were and what had happened.

Nick stepped forward. 'Nick Garnier. International Security Group.' He pointed toward Perrault's body. 'These men have been responsible for a number of jewelry thefts in Europe.'

'And what were they doing here?' Howell asked.

Nick was like a different person, completely in charge. 'The French police have been after these men for some time. They asked our group to step in. We weren't sure where they were taking the contraband. We had a man infiltrate the organization. He discovered they were using the Bahamas as a transfer point to get their goods into the United States.'

'Why didn't you notify us that you were working in our country?' the officer asked.

'I apologize. We would have involved the Bahamian authorities, but the situation evolved too fast.'

'And who is this woman?' He nodded in my direction.

'I'm . . .' I started to speak, but Nick cut me off. 'She's an innocent civilian who got caught in the situation. When we get back to land, I'll give you a full report.'

'There are two other people involved,' I said. I intended to tell the officers about the Turpins, but he turned his back on me.

'Nick,' I said, annoyed at being cast in the role of the 'innocent civilian.' 'Tell them about the Turpins.'

'Oh yes,' he said. The officer who ignored me came to attention when Nick spoke. 'There's a disabled catamaran outside the mouth of the harbor over to the south. Carl and Betty Turpin. They're in on the scam. Someone should be sent out to take them into custody.' He described *Island Ice*. 'You shouldn't have any trouble finding them, unless they managed to repair their engine.'

I could tell that Howell was by no means satisfied, but there was nothing more to be accomplished by hanging out here. It was six o'clock, with only a couple of hours' more daylight.

After conferring about whether to call for paramedics to be brought out, Howell and his men decided the injured men would be seen to more quickly if they were transported to shore. The officer told Jeremy he was welcome to go back with them, to arrange for someone to come out and haul the boats back.

Jeremey shrugged. 'No, man, I can't leave these boats. You know that. That would make them fair game for anyone to take them.' There were murky maritime laws to do with abandoned boats being declared salvage and subject to takeover. Although it might not stand up in court, it could mean an expensive legal fight if someone decided to board the dive boats and make an issue of it.

Howell nodded toward Perrault's body. 'We'll be sending people out to take charge of the body.' He turned to Jeremy. 'We can also have someone come out and help you get the boats back to the dock.'

Jeremy thanked him politely, but I knew he didn't have much faith that they would actually send someone tonight. He would probably have to sleep out here. I decided that when I got back, I'd find a dinghy to bring provisions out to him to make his overnight ordeal more palatable.

'I assume you'll be staying here,' Howell said to Kevin.

Kevin nodded gravely. He still hadn't met my eye.

After the two Bahamian officers left, Jeremy announced that he was going into the water to assess the damage to the boats.

Once he was off the boat, Nick introduced himself to Kevin. 'Thank you for coming out with the Defense Force.'

'Not a problem,' Kevin said. 'But it wasn't benevolence that brought me here. I have the same question the commander asked. Why didn't you let the police know you were operating in the area?'

'Good question. The answer is that a member of your police force was cooperating with these criminals,' Nick said.

Kevin frowned. 'You mean Callen.'

Nick nodded. 'We knew somebody was tipping them off. We

had a failed operation to catch them a few months ago, and two men got killed.'

Kevin stared past Nick, considering. 'I remember that. It was hushed up when those guys were killed. Nobody could figure out who the men were or why they'd been murdered.'

'We told your chief what happened. They should have told you. I'm worried that someone higher up than Callen is involved.'

Kevin looked from Nick to me and back to Nick. 'If he is, they'll get the information out of Callen.'

'If they can find him,' Nick said.

Kevin glanced at me, his face a mask. He hadn't reacted much to the news of Callen, which surprised me. Something wasn't right, and it was making me nervous. Nick had been reluctant to involve Kevin because he didn't know exactly who the informant was, or was it informants? Had Nick been right not to trust Kevin?

'Kevin, I need to ask you something. I told you Callen had picked us up. When he called you, didn't you at least wonder what he was up to?'

'I did. But his answer seemed plausible. The whole thing was confusing. We were trying to figure out what happened with the men who got shot at the marina.'

'You didn't think Callan might intend us harm?'

His expression was bleak. 'You don't want to believe it of your partner . . .' His voice trailed away. 'Anyway, I'm glad they didn't kill you immediately. How did you manage to get away from them?'

Nick said, 'Jessie was clever. She hid the contraband they were after on this dive boat, and they needed to keep her alive to make sure she told the truth about where she had hidden it.'

Kevin looked at me with outright hostility. He said, 'Well, she's pretty clever, isn't she?'

I flushed at the sarcasm in his tone.

Nick stepped closer to Kevin. 'You didn't answer the question she asked. Did you suspect your partner was corrupt?'

Kevin glared at him. 'No, and I resent the insinuation.'

Jeremy popped up out of the water and swung up onto the back deck. 'Jessie, I think we can get these boats back under their own steam. You could drive one and I could take the other one.'

'How are we going to get them turned around?'

'We don't have to. The tide's coming in, and when it's high

enough, I think they'll float off. I'm sure I can find a way out
of here. You can follow close behind.'

'That's not going to work,' Kevin said.

'Oh, yeah, man . . .'

'No. I don't mean you can't get the boats off. I mean she can't
help. She's coming back with me.'

'Why?' I asked.

'I have to take you in for questioning. You're under suspicion
for killing a man in Virginia by the name of Diego Boland.'

Nick stared at me, his expression hardening. I'd never
explained to him exactly what happened, and now I regretted
keeping quiet.

THIRTY-SIX

Kevin wouldn't listen to my protest that his information was
wrong, and he insisted that I come back to police headquarters with him. Nick said he was coming, too.

When we got back to the dive dock, there were still people
hanging around, worried about Jeremy. Kevin let me stop long
enough to tell people I worked with where Jeremy was and ask
them to go out to help him bring the boats in. They seemed
relieved to have a mission.

Kevin refused to explain anything or listen to me until we got
back to police headquarters. Nick disappeared as soon as we arrived.

In a freezing interrogation room, in the presence of another
officer, Kevin told me that when Rodney Grant woke up from
surgery, he claimed to the police that I had murdered Paco
Boland's brother, Diego.

'He said he and Paco came here to find you and take you back
to the United States to stand trial,' Kevin said.

I shivered and hugged my arms to myself. I couldn't believe
I was having to go through this interrogation after all I'd been
through today. 'He's lying. They were here to kill me.'

'Why would they do that?'

I gritted my teeth. What a nightmare! 'Five months ago, my

sister killed Diego in self-defense. After it happened, she called me to come and help her.' No need to tell him what it had cost me personally. 'When I got there, I found Diego dead and Kayla barely conscious.'

'How did she kill him?'

'Stabbed him.'

'What was her motive?'

I sighed. 'This is all public record. You can call the police in Newport News.'

'I'll get to that after you've answered my questions.'

I wanted the interrogation over with. 'I don't know what the fight was about. She's a drug addict, and he was a dealer. Diego was dead when I arrived. My sister was bruised and had a broken arm, but she was too out of it to remember what happened.'

'Did you call the police?'

'Not immediately. I knew if I didn't get her out of there and Diego's friends found her in the house, they'd kill her.' And I had hoped somehow to avoid involving the FBI.

'So you helped her get away with it?'

'Not get away with the crime, just get out of the house. She was arrested, but eventually the case was dismissed because she acted in self-defense.'

'And you had nothing to do with the murder?'

'No. The evidence was clear.'

'Then why did this man Rodney think you killed Diego?'

I let my head drop forward. Where the hell was Nick? I was tired and sore and angry and could have used his support. I sat up straight and looked Kevin in the eye. 'He didn't think that. I'm sure he knows that Kayla's case was dismissed. It doesn't matter to them that it was self-defense. All that counts is that she killed Diego. They wanted to find me because I helped her get away from them. He's lying to try to get himself exonerated. Like I said, the court records and police evidence are all available.'

'I'll need confirmation of this from the US, but I won't be able to get court records until tomorrow.'

'You can call the police department in Newport News, Virginia. They'll confirm it.' He could also call John Farrell, but I didn't want to involve Farrell if I didn't have to. I told Kevin who the lead detective had been on the case and he went off to make the call. He was gone a long time. After a while, I put my head down on my arms and nodded off.

It seemed like minutes later I was awakened by someone touching my shoulder. 'Jessie?'

It was Nick.

'Where were you?' I asked.

'I had to call my boss and arrange some things. Louis and Didier have to be extradited back to France, and I had to arrange to transport Perrault's body. I'm back now. Jesus, you're freezing. Get her a jacket!'

I realized that Kevin was back in the room.

'And something to drink,' I called out, as he left.

He came back with a windbreaker, a cup of coffee and a packet of cheese crackers. Nick put the windbreaker over my shoulders and sat down next to me, with Kevin facing us. I broke open the crackers and stuffed one into my mouth. I offered one to Nick, but he curled his lip as if I'd offered him wood shavings. 'I suppose you're used to French cuisine,' I muttered.

'Real food,' he said.

Kevin cleared his throat. 'I'm waiting for a call back from Newport News,' he said. 'But there are a few things I want to clear up with you, Mr Garnier.' He said he understood who Nick was and why he was involved in hunting down the smugglers. 'But I don't understand how you got involved in the shootout this morning between Jessie and those two men.'

Nick explained that the two men had wounded him in a drive-by shooting the previous evening. 'I think they meant to shoot Jessie and hit me instead. Neither of us knew who had shot at us, though. All we knew was that they were driving a red convertible. I was on my way to her place this morning when I saw the two men force her into their car. I followed them.' He was doing his best to summarize, but as we had been saying all along, it was complicated.

Kevin still looked skeptical. 'So how did those two get tangled up with this jewelry gang? What were they doing on the dock where they were shot? According to a witness . . . hold on' – he opened a file folder in front of him and glanced over it – 'Betty Turpin. She said the two men were coming in through the gate when people started shooting. What were they doing there? Did you bring them?'

I groaned. 'Can we back up? It's better if I tell it from the beginning.'

'Be my guest.'

Nick sat back in his chair, cradling his injured arm.

'We have to go back a bit. I told you I was abducted from the catamaran, and the man I was with died? And that later I stole the catamaran and brought it back to Nassau?'

He nodded, but I could tell from his expression that he was ready to discount the story.

'When I got back here, I had Johnny Durand's backpack with me. I looked inside and discovered the jewelry. I realized that's what our abductors had been after. I wasn't sure what to do with it. I wanted to turn it over to you, Kevin. That's why I called you, but you were so wrapped up in the shooting at Atlantis that I couldn't get you to pay attention. I decided to hide it until I could get it to you.'

'It's probably a good thing you weren't able to talk to him,' Nick said to me. 'If Callen had found out, he probably would have done anything to get the jewelry. Including kill you.'

'I'll grant that,' Kevin said. 'But it still doesn't explain how those two men, Paco Boland and Rodney Grant, are involved.'

'I'm getting to that,' I said. 'I decided to hide the jewelry on the dive boat where I worked, but to take the backpack back to the catamaran and put it where I had found it. And here's where your so-called witness, Betty Turpin, comes in. Betty and her husband own *Island Ice*, the catamaran. They were part of the jewelry theft gang. I figured that when they found the backpack on the boat without the jewelry, they'd think one of the gang members had stolen it. That's why I took the backpack back to the catamaran.'

'Are we getting to the part that involves Boland and Grant?' Kevin snapped.

'Paco and Rodney saw me when I hid the jewelry and the backpack.'

'What do you mean, they saw you?'

'Apparently, they were following me. I didn't know they were here in the islands, so I didn't know they had found me.'

'Wait. Back up. You said they were here to avenge the death of Paco Boland's brother? How did they know you were here?'

'I have no idea. Maybe they got the information from my mother.'

He looked horrified. 'Your mother would tell them where you were?'

'I don't think she would intentionally tell them, but it's possible she'd let it slip.' I grimaced. 'She drinks.'

Kevin was starting to thaw. He nodded. 'I see. Continue.'

I told him that they followed me when I stowed the jewelry and then followed me when I took the backpack back to *Island Ice*. 'I did it to fool the jewelry thieves, but I fooled Paco and Rodney, too. They wondered what I was up to. These guys are greedy, and they couldn't let go of the idea that I had something of value. Before they killed me, they wanted to know what it was. This morning – God, was it only this morning? – they kidnapped me and forced me to tell them about the jewelry.'

'And you told them?'

'Look, Kevin, the jewelry was the only bargaining chip I had. But I lied and told them it was in the backpack on *Island Ice*. They drove me to the Coast Guard dock where the boat was being held, but it turned out the Turpins had already picked her up. So we drove back to its home dock, and that's where the shootout happened.'

'Weren't you taking a big risk giving them the runaround?'

Nick snorted. 'Risk is her middle name.'

I glared at him. 'Not really. I saw that Nick was following us, and I figured between the two of us, we'd be able to do something.' I sighed. 'Unfortunately, the jewelry theft gang were following me, too. When we got to the dock, Perrault and his men opened fire on Paco and Rodney.'

Kevin insisted that I tell the story again with his captain.

'Wait. Are you sure he wasn't involved with Callen?'

'Yes. He only came on six months ago. He couldn't have been part of the previous sting operation that went wrong.'

Nick agreed, so the captain came in to hear the story. I was pretty sure the night would never end.

Eventually, they got word from Newport News that my story checked out, and around two a.m. I was free to go.

'What's going to happen to Callen?' I asked.

'We'll take care of him,' the captain said, and then he grimaced. 'When we find him, that is.'

Nick laughed. 'He's around here somewhere. He'll be waiting to get his payoff from Perrault.'

I wasn't so sure. Once Callen found out that Perrault was dead and the gang rounded up, he'd find a way to get out. A lot of boats came and went from these islands, with no way to keep tabs on who was on them.

When I expressed that, the captain said, 'There's a chance he's holed up with the man who had my job before I was hired. Turns out the reason he was "retired" was because there was a suspicion that he was involved in some shenanigans.'

I still had my doubts, but at this point, I didn't care what happened to Callen. It was out of my hands.

Once we were outside police headquarters, I said to Nick, 'I want to go to the hospital and talk to Rodney in person.'

'Can it wait until tomorrow?' Nick said. 'I'm beat.'

'No, I have to talk to him tonight. They said they had my sister and I want to be sure they were bluffing. I'm scared they were holding her somewhere and with both of them out of commission, if no one comes to get her, she'll die.'

Nick nodded. 'All right, let's go.'

'You don't have to go.'

He shook his head, a grin playing at the corners of his mouth. 'Yes, I do. I need to keep an eye on you.'

There was another reason I wanted to talk to Rodney. I wanted to know how they had found out where I was.

Getting into Rodney's hospital room took some fast talking, but Nick had credentials that worked. Rodney was asleep and hooked up to all manner of tubes and wires. When I called his name, his eyes fluttered open. 'I'm not talking to you,' he said. 'I already told that cop everything. You're going to jail. You killed my best friend.'

'No, Rodney, I didn't kill Paco. You were there. You know I didn't.'

Rodney opened his eyes wider and glared at me. 'I told you, I'm not talking to you. Diego is dead, and now so is Paco. He was my main man. He's dead because of you.'

'Not because of me,' I said. 'It's because you guys got greedy.'

'Yeah, but you killed Diego.'

'No, Rodney, you know it was my sister who killed Diego. She did it in self-defense because he attacked her. I saw her bruises. He broke her arm. If she hadn't fought back, he would have killed her.'

Rodney shook his head back and forth violently and slammed his fist on the bed next to him. 'That's what you say. And that's what you tricked the cops into believing. But that's not what your sister said.'

I froze, my head buzzing. For a few seconds, I couldn't process what he had said. Kayla had told them I killed Diego? When I realized that's what he meant, I thought I might faint, maybe from horror, but more likely because fury was coursing through me. They must have tortured her to get her to point a finger at me. 'What do you mean? Did you hurt my sister? How did you find her?'

'I didn't do nothing to her. Nobody had to find her. She checked herself out of the rehab place and came back to town. To Paco. She said she needed some help – you know what I mean.'

'She was back on drugs.' My voice sounded hollow.

'That girl is never going to get off drugs. She's hooked.'

Humiliation made my cheeks burn. Not public embarrassment, but private anguish. I had taken care of Kayla her whole life, at great cost to myself. To help her, I had lost the only job I ever wanted, had supported her through the trial, had begged for help from John Farrell to get her into rehab. I thought Kayla would turn her life around. Instead, she used me. I'd been a fool in every way.

So it wasn't my mother who had engineered her escape. It was worse than that.

'How did she convince Paco to help her?' I knew the answer, but I needed to hear it.

'Said if Paco would fix her up, she'd tell him a secret. He was all in. Got good stuff for her, and when it was her turn, she told him you were the one who killed his brother. And then she told us where you were.'

Nick slipped his arm around me. I was grateful for his strength because mine was all used up. All the years I had given to supporting Kayla, bailing her out of jams, propping her up mentally and physically. And Kayla had sold me out for a bag of drugs.

THIRTY-SEVEN

I stared into my cup of coffee that had gone cold.

'Hey,' Nick said.

I forced myself to look up. Nick's eyes held mine. 'You don't have to decide now.'

We were sitting in a coffee shop in the airport terminal, waiting for Nick's flight back to New York. He had things to clear up there regarding the Turpins, who were already back in New York in custody. From there, he'd be headed home to Paris.

For two days, we had been together, me trying to make peace with my sister's betrayal, and the two of us properly mourning Johnny Durand.

We spent the time getting drunk and making love as if we were the last two people on earth. I discovered that Nick's intensity spilled over into sex. He made love the way he did everything – with all his attention.

'First I have things I need to do. I wish . . .' I couldn't finish the sentence. But Nick read my mind.

'You can't cling to the idea of helping your sister.'

He laced his fingers in mine. 'Maybe you don't want to hear this, but you've got to stop trying to be Kayla's father.'

I studied him. 'I always thought I was acting as her mother. Our mother was . . .' I shrugged. 'Not exactly capable. She could barely keep herself on track, much less raise Kayla.' But as soon as Nick had said it, I knew he was right. I had been trying to be a father to Kayla. All the times I yearned for our father, it wasn't so much that I wanted him to be alive for myself, but because if he had been alive, I wouldn't have to take his place. 'Whichever parent I was trying to be, I failed,' I said.

'It shouldn't have been your job.'

I shrugged. 'Maybe someday I'll believe that.'

The loudspeaker announced Nick's name. He squeezed my hands. 'I have to go. Give my offer some consideration. You'd be good on the security team. I've seen you in action.' At some point, he had gone into the details of the security force he was part of, the clandestine arm of a group that worked to protect jewelers from international jewel thieves. It turned out that the jewelry that had almost gotten me killed was actually a small heist. 'There are much larger thefts. They try to keep it quiet,' Nick said. 'People have no idea how much jewelry gets stolen each year.'

He told me that the Turpins' involvement was particularly odious because they were well-known diamond brokers in New York. They had used their inside knowledge to work with Perrault's organization.

'*Island Ice*,' I said. 'Ice, as in diamonds. I guess that explains why they named the boat that.'

We rose, and Nick kissed me – a long, lingering kiss that almost undid me. Then he held me at arms' length and took me in with his serious, dark eyes. I fought the urge to beg him to stay longer. He was already a day late.

'I'll be in touch,' he said.

I watched him head toward the TSA line. I smiled as he stepped into the fast lane, showed his identification and was waved through. I wondered when I'd see him again.

I sat there for another hour, watching people come and go. The pale-skinned newly arrived tourists, struggling with luggage, short-tempered and tense; and the browned, relaxed tourists headed for home. I'd be among them soon. I had to get home and sort out my life.

I'd had a call from John Farrell. He didn't go into details but said he had an intriguing proposition. I hadn't told Nick, not wanting to jinx it.

Before I'd heard Rodney's bombshell, I'd hoped that when I got home I could reconnect with my sister and try to help her remake her life. Now, I knew that was a fool's mission.

Nick's advice echoed in my head. I had to stop trying to be her father, and instead just make peace with her and my mother. Could I? I had a feeling that in order to do that, I had to start at the beginning and find out exactly what had happened to my father.

But first, before I left Nassau, I needed to make amends with my roommate and my boss. I got up, threw my cup in the trash and headed back.